Rhythmic,
of the sw
Strip illur
wandered
the soul-s

Satisfied
edge and
it carefull

sheath and strapped them to her back. The rig was custom made and fit her perfectly. It sat against her spine, unobtrusive enough that most people didn't see it as she made her way through the city. If they saw it, it was usually too late for them anyway.

What most people did see was a redhead who stood at just six feet. Wary brown eyes and a hard-set mouth. They definitely saw her body. Tall and battle-hard, her frame attracted many an eye to the voluptuous curves and the long-as-sin legs. She wasn't beautiful. Not by general standards. Her features weren't perfect or symmetrical, and freckles scattered over her cheeks and the bridge of her nose. But there was something magnetic about her just the same. Something that made people look twice and want to know her.

Rowan knew it was the blood in her veins. Blood running not only in her maternal line. Blood descended from the Celtic triple goddess Brigid, whose sacred tree was the inspiration for Rowan's name. The goddess who manifested herself through Rowan's body and soul. But also her father's blood. It made her minor royalty and connected her to the Vampire Nation tracing back thousands of years. Blood that made her intelligent, calculating and cruel when she needed to be. And bent on revenge.

The wristbands she wore stored garrote wire. Her belt had small phials of holy water. Most important, her blade was created on a sacred forge with blessed steel and bore the holy cross along its edge. Her blade was made to kill Vampires. Just as she was.

It was time to hunt.

Also available from Lauren Dane and Carina Press

Second Chances
Believe
Blade to the Keep

LAUREN DANE

GODDESS WITH A BLADE

CARINA PRESS™

ISBN-13: 978-0-373-00208-5

GODDESS WITH A BLADE

This edition published by arrangement with Harlequin Books S.A.

www.CarinaPress.com

Printed in U.S.A.

Dear Reader,

Some years ago, friends and I went to Las Vegas on a writers' retreat. While there we went to a show. The camp was pretty high with the story of a virginal maiden ensorcelled by a vampire king of sorts. Hoops, ropes from the ceiling—you know the drill. But as I waited for my plane home, I asked myself what would happen if, say, those showgirl vampires really were vampires?

That was the seed for *Goddess with a Blade*. Las Vegas is a great setting for just about any book. It's a city with multiple facets. The shine and glitz of the Strip, the miles of suburbs—it's got a seedy underbelly, too. The perfect background for Rowan Summerwaite and the Vampires she polices.

Rowan isn't always nice. She's broken and jagged and she's also the human vessel for a goddess. She's got a lot on her plate, but she knows her job and she approaches it with a burning, soul-deep commitment. Sometimes she has to kill people. She's got to guard her identity and the existence of Vampires from humans. She's got a lot of defenses that tend to keep people away.

That she also ends up in a complicated, not always nice relationship with the Scion Vampire of Las Vegas is oddly fitting in her already complicated life. Also? It's really, really fun to write scenes with Rowan and Clive.

I hope you enjoy *Goddess with a Blade* as much as I enjoyed writing Rowan's story! I love hearing from readers, so you can email me at laurendane@laurendane.com. You can also find me on my website, www.laurendane.com, or on Twitter @laurendane.

Happy reading!

Lauren

This book has been with me since I took my first trip to Las Vegas with some friends and we went to a show with fake vampires with fake other stuff. Big thanks go to my husband for being so supportive and for all the plotting help! You even got me to kill people in this one, LOL.

Margo Lipschultz spent a great deal of time and energy with me on the phone two years ago. Sadly, she couldn't buy the book in the end, but her advice and enthusiasm about the project helped me revive it and gave me some great insight into how to make the book better.

Which brings me to Angela James. We all say books are special to us, and they are. But this one has been with me since 2006 in one guise or another. There are very few people I'd have trusted with it and Angie is one. And for good reason. Her edit notes went way above and beyond the call of duty. All the extra care and butt kicking she did made the book better. This is why I love her to pieces and why she's a fabulous editor. Thank you for that, Angie.

Readers, you all make this possible—
thank you for your continued support and love.

GODDESS WITH A BLADE

The story goes like this: while on pregnancy bed rest, Lauren Dane had plenty of downtime, so her husband took her comments about "giving that writing thing a serious go" to heart and brought home a secondhand laptop. She wrote her first book on it before it gave up the ghost. Even better, she sold that book and never looked back.

Today Lauren is a *New York Times* and *USA TODAY* bestselling author of over forty novels and novellas across several genres. Though she no longer has to deal with Polly Pocket and getting those tiny outfits on and off, she still has trouble blocking out the sound of Taylor Swift so she can write a love scene.

Visit Lauren on the web and view her blog at www.laurendane.com. You can email her at laurendane@laurendane.com or write to her at P.O. Box 45175, Seattle, WA 98145.

ONE

THE SILVER CHALICE was vintage Vegas in deep reds and golds. Whatever it was, the place managed to carry off the Rat Pack feel but made it modern and clean while also seeming luxurious. Hunter Corporation owned the residence tower to the south of the main casino floor and hotel. A nice sideline and a way to have heavy security without being too obvious.

Outside the revolving glass doors, the air was still warm. The streets teemed with tourists. Rowan understood the allure of being lost, of choosing to be someone or something else even for just a few days.

Vegas was a big game of pretend for a lot of people. And why not? Most had a great time and didn't go too far. Some stepped far enough out of line to have secrets to carry for the rest of their lives.

Some didn't go home at all.

In the circular drive just outside the doors, her valet, David, waited next to her Porsche. Even vessels for goddesses had guilty pleasures. Some women liked shoes and Coach bags. Rowan loved fast cars. The sexy sound of the engine always charged her blood. Something about the power that lurked there beneath the hood intoxicated her.

David nodded as he opened the door. She slid inside, the leather smooth and supple against her back and legs.

"The Scion sent a call for you to come to his office, *Déesse*." He called her *goddess* because he knew what she was. "He says he needs to see you tonight. He was informed that should you find it in your schedule, you'd return his call." Efficient and not entirely humorless, David had served the Hunters his whole life as Rowan's father had served the Vampires. She hoped it ended better for David.

"Always so urgent, these Vampires. You'd think with such long lives they'd be more relaxed." *Arrogant bastard.* Not an unusual trait for a Vampire. They did arrogant like no other species she'd ever dealt with. She wondered if this one would be as pompous as the last one.

David hid a smile and stepped back as she made to pull away from the drive. "Be safe, *Déesse.* The policeman was also looking for you."

She smiled at the mention of Jack.

"Thank you, David. Have a lovely evening."

He inclined his head and she pulled away, maneuvering around the knot of drunken people being delivered into cabs and vans in the drive on her way out.

After she'd pulled safely out onto Las Vegas Boulevard without mowing down any civilians, Rowan called Jack.

"'Bout time you called back, Rowan."

"I'm sure all you do all day is lay around and wait to hear from me."

He snorted.

"What's up?"

"What's up? Gone for months and..." He sighed. "Listen, can you meet me for a drink? Come by the station, we can grab a bite or something."

"Can it wait a few hours? I have a prior engagement but it shouldn't take overlong."

"I'm not gonna be here in two hours. I can come to your place or you can come to mine. Only I live in a townhouse a ways from town and you live in a swank apartment on the Strip. Personally I like your place better."

She laughed, despite herself. "Fine. I'll meet you at my apartment in two hours. I'll instruct David to let you in if I'm late."

"Fine. I'll see you then."

"Okay." She hung up and called David to let him know Jack would be coming over. She didn't need to tell him to keep Jack on the first floor. David was relentlessly efficient and she knew he always took care to keep the Hunter Corporation part of her life as secret as possible. Humans didn't know about Hunter Corporation but for a few key people in G8 countries and those serving Hunter Corp. Jack thought she was a private investigator. It kept them both safer that way.

In a handy bit of coincidence, by the time she'd finished arranging things, she'd reached Die Mitte, the casino/hotel run by the Vampire Nation. Oh, if those tourists only knew. Die Mitte meant "The Center" in German. It was the center of Vampire politics and jurisdiction in Las Vegas. The Scion ruled the local Vamps with an iron fist.

Once she'd stopped the Porsche, the valet rushed forward. When he saw who she was, he inclined his head slightly. Not quick enough for Rowan to miss the hatred and distrust in his eyes. Still, the awe tingeing the edges of that hatred was enough for her. The moment she got out, one of the Scion's toadies rushed toward her with a sycophantic smile. Rowan didn't return it.

There were times she wished she could be softer, but soft meant people took advantage or saw it as weak. She couldn't afford to be anything but cold and hard. Even if it left her alone in bed at night.

Mr. Toadie's smile edged into a smirk. "Mr. Stewart is ending a business call, Ms. Summerwaite. Please come with me and I'll escort you up to his quarters. He appreciates your coming to see him this evening."

She looked through him, dismissing any potential threat. "He should. I'm not an employee. He can't just call me when he gets the urge to meet a Hunter face-to-face." She didn't wait to see the flinch the toadie gave when she used the *H* word.

There was a reason they flinched, a reason they all hated and feared not only Rowan but the Hunter Corporation. For centuries, the Vampires had marauded across the world, preying mercilessly on humans. It was, after all, their nature to do so. Until a group of priestesses, mages, holy men and women and other warriors stood together and waged war on the Vampires beneath the veil of secrecy while humans had no idea the paranormal not only existed but threatened to exterminate them.

Everywhere Vampires pushed, Hunters pushed back until there was no ground left. Vampires, however, would not have existed as long as they had without being pragmatic beings, and so they entered into negotiations with those Hunters and from that the treaty was forged and the Vampire Nation was born.

The Vampire Nation didn't like Hunter Corp. and Hunters hated the Vampire Nation but as far as Rowan was concerned, neither could exist without the other. For better or worse.

Mr. Toadie kept his mouth shut as he led her into the private elevator to the top floor. When the doors opened, she had to admit she was impressed. Her penthouse was luxurious. *This* place was a freaking palace.

The last man to hold the position had lived in a mansion just outside the city. Just like him, the place had reeked of trying too hard.

By contrast, the new Scion had damned good taste and a whole lot of money. His quarters took up pretty much the entire top floor of the hotel. Lush white carpets alternated with Italian tile and Persian rugs. Antiques and expensive paintings dotted the place in an unobtrusive fashion. Yes, it was clear wealth ruled the space, but it wasn't the kind of place most powerful Vamps had. It didn't scream new money, it emanated with the surety of class.

Clive Stewart was old money. That much was obvious. She knew he'd had five centuries to amass capital, but money, even five-hundred-years' worth, couldn't buy class.

The Hunter Corporation had given her a dossier on Clive Stewart and she'd read it on the way back to Vegas from London.

She'd had a less-than-personable relationship with the last Scion. Oh, okay, so she staked him. Which made for a huge political problem for nearly eight months as she had to prove it was a defensible kill and that Jacques Martin had broken their laws.

The dossier was full of examples that told her the new Scion was capable of total ruthlessness. Other Vampires feared him and *The Powers That Be* admired his business sense and ability to keep his population in check. So much so that he'd been near the top of the Vampire Nation power structure for the last four-hundred-and-fifty years. Vampires respected and feared one thing—power. If Clive Stewart had held that much for that long, he'd be a force to be reckoned with. She didn't want to be impressed.

She stood, looking out the windows over the Strip, watching the fountains at the Bellagio. In the background she heard him come in.

"Ms. Summerwaite, thank you for coming to see me."

She turned. *Well.* That was unexpected. Holy shit, the man was delicious. No. The *Vampire* was delicious. Tall and substantial, he wore his Armani suit well. His eyes were a brilliant green. A blunt jaw framed lips that looked absolutely lickable. He was a big man. Imposing. The accent was quite nice. Like caramel.

She gave herself a mental slap. Focus! *He's a Vampire and therefore off the menu.*

"If I hadn't come, you'd have pestered me endlessly until I did. Next time, ask instead of commanding me. I'm not one of your minions."

His eyes flared for the briefest of moments but the mask never slipped otherwise. That little dig would have pushed a lesser man into a snit, but he wasn't a lesser anything apparently.

"Would you like something to eat or drink?" He waved at a long bank of couches and she sat, crossing her legs. His control impressed her even as she began to wonder what it might take to make him lose it.

"No, thank you. I'd prefer you get to the point, Scion."

He inclined his head and sat across from her. "Please, call me Clive. Since you're newly returned and I'm here in charge now, I thought an introduction would be of use to us both. And I'd like to get some ground rules laid down. Just for safety's sake."

She raised a brow at his haughty tone. "*You'd* like to lay down ground rules? As far as I know, those are laid out in the treaty. I can retrieve a copy for you if you're unfamiliar with it."

"Ms. Summerwaite, I'm aware of the treaty's tenets. I like to avoid murders on my watch. It costs me money. I don't like that. There's no need to be defensive."

She realized then *he* was pushing her buttons too. She wasn't sure if that irritated her more than it amused her.

"I'm pleased to hear that. I'd like to avoid murders on your watch too. My superiors'll be relieved you plan to keep your people in line."

"We both know what I meant. It's your behavior I'm concerned with."

"I obey the *rules* laid out in the treaty, Clive. Your people don't. And when they don't, I do my job."

"And how does it feel that your job is killing people?" The taunt was delivered in a smooth, almost casual fashion. He watched her carefully, his body language deceptively relaxed. He was every bit the predator and she had no misconceptions about that. He'd be on her in a moment if she posed a real threat.

But he wasn't the only predator in the room and she knew, as well as he did, that this little meeting was a show of dominance. She didn't have a dick to take out to measure against his. But she wasn't going to allow him to out-badass her either. Taking a calming breath, she put her hands on her knees and leaned forward. "As it happens, I like my job just fine. The dental plan is first-rate. My training started very early, I believe you know my first teacher. Let me simply reiterate this so we're clear, because I completely agree that it's important to be straightforward. I'm a Hunter. That means my job is to keep an eye on you all, and, if need be, kill Vampires who kill people. I don't like Vampires who kill people. So when I have to slay them for breaking the treaty, I don't need to go hug a teddy bear or talk to my therapist."

"From where I sit, I come into town and find my people in utter disarray. An associate has been brutally murdered and you're at the center of it. Surely you can understand my need to get things straight between us." He looked so reasonable just then she wanted to smack him. But she wasn't going to blink first.

She sighed, leaning back into the cushions. "Clive, Clive, Clive. Compared to being alive before electricity and all, I know I'm young. But I'm not new to this game. So let's just cut the shit. You rolled into town and saw the mess *Jacques* made. I cleaned house for you people when you were too lazy to do it. Instead of thanks for identifying the Vampire who stole fifty million dollars—a Vampire who I hasten to add also killed multiple human beings—you pretend shock that I slayed him. You're not werebunnies, you're Vampires. You eat humans for pleasure, and not in the good way. I. Culled. The. Herd." She shrugged.

His jaw tightened and a thrill ran through her that she'd affected him. Just as quickly, he forced himself to relax. Jacques would have popped a vein ten minutes ago but this one was made of far sterner stuff.

"I don't need a rule breaker in my territory. My people don't exist for you to make your reputation on. So we're clear, Hunter, keep yourself in line or I'll do it for you. I won't abide any terrorizing of the Vampires here in Las Vegas."

She stood but forced herself to do it slow. "I do my job. I obey the rules. I kill Vampires who don't. Your *associate* Jacques didn't. He violated the law and when he did, he stepped into my world. That's the treaty *your* people worked out with the Hunter Corporation. You don't like it, take it up with them. I didn't make the rules, I simply enforce them. Me? I couldn't possibly care less what you like or don't like." *You uptight British asshole.* "And as for you keeping me in line?" She looked him up and down very slowly. "The heat is making you delusional. I keep hearing what a big, bad tough guy you are, but that statement there is simply stupid."

"You seem to have a problem with control, Ms. Summerwaite. Las Vegas is my town, I am in charge." He held out his hands, oh-so-reasonably. "I want to be sure you don't lose your temper and kill anyone else."

She picked her bag up and turned, giving him her back. The message clear. Rowan Summerwaite didn't fear him or his Nation. The minion who'd stood near the doors pretended he hadn't heard the entire conversation and kept his eyes averted.

"Ms. Summerwaite." His tone said he couldn't quite believe she was walking out on him. She'd told him she wasn't a minion and yet, he certainly liked to think so.

Turning to face him, she stayed where she was. "Yes, Scion?"

Fascinated, she watched as he unclenched his jaw. Apparently he'd never been disobeyed before. Well, she was all about bringing new experiences to those around her. A missionary of sorts even.

Idly, she wondered how much it would take to push him into developing a tic in his neck. With that ironclad control, it would be a huge undertaking but in the end, after she'd broken him, it would be a job well done. She kept her amusement inside, though, since they were playing a game of chicken like two fourteen-year-old boys.

"You have no reply?"

She raised one eyebrow at him. "To what? Your ever-so-manly threat to keep me in line? The accusation that I have *control* issues?"

If I had control problems, you'd be dust and I'd be covered in Vampire blood as I killed every fucking one of you people in this hotel right now. If I had anger management problems I'd have jammed the pointy toe of this lovely boot up your ass for being such a prick.

Instead of saying that, she simply smiled. "I do my job. Sometimes my job is to kill Vampires who break the treaty. That I manage to do so less often than is warranted by the treaty is a *testament* to my control."

He straightened his tie but she caught the tightening of his fist for just a moment. "I'm not interested in sparring with you over this. I want to be clear about the rules here. These are my Vampires. You seem to like killing Vampires. This presents a problem. I don't know if it's your untouchable status that gives you the idea you have carte blanche." He shrugged. "But I do not want to start off our relationship on the wrong foot."

She nodded, so very understanding. "It works like this. Don't kill humans. Don't break the treaty. Be good Vampires and I won't have to deal with you at all. That there is called a win-win situation."

She moved into the hallway and the assistant called the elevator. When Rowan looked back over her shoulder, Clive stood in the doorway, watching her.

"I'm not stupid. You're not stupid. There's nothing more to discuss." She got into the elevator and waved. "And this is *my* town. You can keep the Vampires, but stay away from my humans."

The doors slid closed and she saw her own nearly feral smile reflected back at her.

CLIVE WATCHED HER go. Waited for the place to be empty for several long seconds before moving to the phone. He wanted to throw something but that infuriating woman wasn't worth the cost of losing a vase.

He punched the speed dial and waited as the lines connected halfway across the world.

"It's Stewart. Is He available?"

Clive waited until the other Vampire finally answered.

"Clive. I'm going to wager you've just had a face-to-face with my goddaughter," The First said with a ragged sound, much like a laugh. "I warned you to leave her be."

"It's my assessment that the Nation pursue her removal and replacement with a different Hunter. The woman is impossible. She hates us."

"Useless. All silly and useless and a waste of time better spent on issues important to us. As for Rowan, it may help if you view her as a Vampire in human skin. She's more like us than you give her credit for. In any case, you hate her, too. But none of that matters. We have a treaty. She's the keeper of that treaty where you are. You're too smart to believe Hunter Corp. would ever replace her. She's one of their favored. Do not test my patience on this, Clive. She is protected. You know it. As long as she doesn't violate the law, she has status both because of the treaty and because of who her father was. And who she is to me." The hair on Clive's arms stood at the menace, the warning in The First's tone.

"Now, I suggest you make sure the Vampire citizens of Las Vegas realize she'll kill them should they stray and then continue about your business."

Clive erased all irritation from his voice. He was smooth as glass. "Yes, Sir. Thank you."

The First chuckled again. "I know her better than most ever will. She will ruffle you because it's in her nature to do so. And because she will find pleasure in it. But she's deadly and righteous. She will kill you without blinking. She's quite exceptional that way." The admiration and pride in his voice were unmistakable, and, Clive had to admit, she was an astonishing specimen.

Chastened, and knowing he could only push so far on the issue, Clive thanked him and hung up.

He straightened his tie and went down several floors to his next meeting. Once the sun went down his schedule was unremarkably like a lot of other executives. He attended a great many meetings. Signed a great many documents. Since he'd fallen into a routine in Vegas it hadn't been as bloody as his first days in town.

Five months earlier he'd come to a territory lacking any sense of moderation.

Undisciplined people had been running neighborhoods like fiefdoms. Infighting. Skimming of the books, which he'd ended within minutes of finding out of every incidence. The Nation did not tolerate theft. There were no second chances to steal from The First.

After the first few Vampires simply disappeared, they began to understand and fall in line. He'd learned several centuries earlier just how effective a beheading at a conference table or around a campfire could be at correcting any behavioral issues among his people.

Upon entering, he surveyed the room. All the most powerful Vampires in Las Vegas—the ones left alive and those who'd risen to replace those who were no longer—sat utterly still, eyes lowered in deference.

Momentarily satisfied, he nodded, smoothing his tie down.

"The Hunter has returned to Las Vegas. I've just met with Rowan Summerwaite. China, you need to tell those mongrels at the Vampyre Theatre to keep their activities in check and I want each of you to underline, with all of your people, the importance of avoiding entanglement with her."

"How could they let her come back after what she did to Jacques?"

The room chilled as Clive turned all his focus on the female who'd spoken. "I believe we've had this discussion before, Wendela. To rehash it is a waste of my time. Is there some reason why you'd want to waste my time? Or perhaps you're questioning my leadership?"

Wendela shook her head vehemently, lowering her eyes again. They'd all seen a demonstration of just how their Scion could be if he was angry.

Alice, Clive's personal assistant, sighed and tapped her pen against the tabletop and he repressed a smile at her impertinence.

She looked to him and he nodded slightly, urging her to speak. "We know what Jacques was and what he did. Aside from the messy complication of the human women he killed for sport, he stole from the Nation. Jacques should have been glad the Hunter killed him before The First's lieutenants arrived." A unified shudder ran through the room at the memory of the five who'd arrived, silent and stinking of death, and'd gone by the following moonrise.

Clive looked each one of them in the eyes for a moment as he scanned the room. "Many of you are new to Las Vegas so I understand you may not be that impressed by stories of what the Hunter can do. But I want you to believe me when I tell you she will kill you as easily as she draws a breath. She's a killing machine. *We* trained her and then the Hunter Corporation finished the job.

"The treaty allows her to kill any of our kind who break the law. I will not tolerate any rule breaking. Do you understand me? I want to be exceedingly clear on this point. I will kill you before she can if I hear about any lawbreaking. And I will enjoy every moment of it. I do not care if you fuck humans and take their blood. But if you kill them? You're on your own and you'd best walk into the sun rather than face me. I won't make it fast or easy."

"What is she, anyway?" China asked. "Sure she's a Hunter. But what makes *this* one so special?"

Clive sat a little straighter. "A history lesson? Why not." He shrugged. "Brigid is a Celtic triple goddess. Which means her power is threefold—the forge and martial arts, inspiration, and healing and fertility. It's the first one you should worry about. Rowan carries a blade, a blessed blade forged by warrior shamans and monks of silver and steel. The blade was created to kill Vampires and you shouldn't forget that.

"Rowan Summerwaite is the first true Vessel of Brigid in centuries. There's obviously a dearth of information on just exactly her strengths, but from what I understand, she's able to channel the power of the Goddess in battle. She's also arrogant and unafraid, and willing to kill us if she has to.

"Most important to all of you, however, was that she was raised by The First. He was her foster father after his personal servant, her father, was killed. The Hunter knows us all very well, which makes her all the more effective."

Clive stood, straightened his jacket and went to the door. "Get your quarterly accounting statements to my people by the end of the week."

TWO

ROWAN PULLED THE Porsche into the VIP lot behind the Corsican. The casino was at the far end of the Strip and catered to a younger, edgier clientele. It also housed the Vampyre Theatre.

While the Lucky Seven had the hottest buffet in Vegas, the groupie line-up backstage at the VT was the best Vampire buffet in the entire state. If you liked to snack on skanks who needed to touch up their roots and should not have gotten tattoos from friends working out of their garages.

Annoyed young women in far too little clothing gave Rowan dirty looks as she cruised past them and through the back door. The bouncers didn't stop her but she knew they'd called Marv the minute she had her car parked.

She breezed past the ticket booth and took a seat at a table to the left of the stage and declined the drink but accepted the bottled water. They wouldn't dare attempt to harm her. But she still didn't plan to lower her reaction time with alcohol either.

The Vampyre Theatre put on a live show complete with fire, bare tits, shaking asses and audience participation. The entire audience thought the Vampires were actors with fake teeth and theatrical makeup. Humans were fascinated with many things they should fear. They went to the show to be fed on as a lark. Oh, and to look at the boobs. One really couldn't underestimate the draw of naked breasts in any city, especially Las Vegas.

Rowan knew for a fact the fake feedings from audience members were real. Technically, that broke the treaty. All blood exchange with humans had to be consensual and knowing. But she couldn't stop everything and she didn't hate Marv enough to stake him over it. In fact, though she'd never admit it out loud, she sort of liked him and the banter they'd honed over the years.

She watched the first part of the show and after half an hour, satisfied they'd all seen she was back at work, got up and left side stage.

The big man waited, arms crossed, blocking her way as she entered the backstage area.

"Hunter. What are you doing here?"

"Did you miss me?" She fluttered her lashes at him.

"Like the fuckin' clap."

"I thought you people didn't get social diseases," she said, deadpan. "Which, if you don't mind my saying so, is a good thing given the quality of, um, women you've got lined up out there. Mere humans would be burning and itching and stuff." She shuddered.

"Ha. What are you doing here?"

"Just a hello and friendly reminder that taking blood from humans without their knowledge is a violation of the treaty. It'd be a shame if any of those lovely young women got hurt."

"If we did that—and I'm not saying we do—they consent when they come in the front door. The ticket says they may be called up on stage to be fed to a Vampire."

She shook her head. "Don't try to be a lawyer, Marv. Knowing and consensual. Those are the rules. I'd hate to have to come in here every night and watch you juggle fire sticks. Although you know, I was thinking that what this show needed were Vampire poodles jumping through flaming hoops. I'd so totally dig that."

The glower was back. "Fine. Now go, you're harshing my buzz. Or are you in charge of that now, too?"

She blew him a kiss as she walked past. "Oh, Marv, how I've missed you and your wit! I don't care about your buzz. But if I'm harshing it, that's just a wonderful benefit of my job. I'll be seeing you around. Behave yourself."

Slipping the valet a five, she slid into her unscathed car and headed out to the other end of the Strip. She had an appointment to meet a contact who supposedly had some hot information for her.

JUST MINUTES LATER and yet a million miles away from the hotel she was just in, Rowan walked into a dark bar filled with the seedier and more craptastic members of the Las Vegas tourism contingent. This particular casino bar wasn't going to be featured prominently in the tourism ads.

Smoke hung in the air like a veil, the stink of body odor, desperation and too much alcohol omnipresent.

The carpet had seen better days, along with the cocktail waitresses apparently. But the place sold a real drink. No umbrellas or frothy concoctions. Here in The Reef, two bucks got you plenty of alcohol in a glass and a bowl of pretzels at your table. When you really thought about it, it was more pleasant than fire juggling and fake/real Vampires any day.

Through the haze, Rowan caught sight of Mary Pena waiting at a small table at the back. Ignoring the leers of the leather-skinned men in leisure suits bearing white marks on their fingers where their wedding rings usually sat, she made her way over.

"Hey, Mary." Rowan sat and flicked her gaze to the waitress and nodded for another round. "What do you have for me?"

Mary's normally happy expression tightened, along with her mouth as she pushed a file folder across the table to her. "They found a girl outside the city. It's odd. They don't know what the hell happened to her. It looked like something up your alley."

Rowan opened the folder and slowly looked through the pictures and reports. Odd was a word, she supposed, to describe it. Flashes of gaping wounds, of violence and the face of a woman who'd once been someone's something stayed with her even after she closed the folder.

She pushed a hundred dollar bill across the table. "Thank you, Mary."

Mary's brown eyes lit up. "Of course. You know I want to serve."

As an acolyte to the Goddess, Mary, who worked in the file room of the Las Vegas Police Department, often sent things Rowan's way. The folder in her hand was pretty big stuff.

"I'll remember this one. Excellent job." Rowan

stood. "I need to go now. But thank you again." She touched Mary's forehead, turned and left the bar.

The night outside had deepened, cooled. Being two miles off the Strip meant the parking lot wasn't quite as bright or shiny. Quiet was still hours away though.

She'd have to seek out the Scion again and warn him to get his people in check. He'd take it the wrong way and be defensive. Tedious, this whole business.

But for now, she needed to talk to Jack to get his take. Problem was, she'd have to find a way to do it without letting on just how much she knew or how she knew it. Her old friend wasn't prone to missing many details and she'd have to handle this very carefully.

THREE

After returning home, she got rid of her blade and other weapons and left them, along with the file, well out of sight.

She'd gone out to find Jack in her living room, long legs stretched out, feet on her coffee table as he watched television. A beer sat near his right hand. He'd looked entirely at home there and she had to admit, she liked the way he looked drinking her beer and watching her television.

He fit in her place. They'd been friends a long time and she trusted his opinion, but she knew they had to have it out about her very long absence from Vegas before they could move on and talk about work.

So she gave him as much information as she could about the whys of where she'd been and for how long. He'd been pissed off at how long she'd danced around the truth, telling her bluntly he knew she wasn't telling him everything. But it had to be enough. She couldn't tell him what she was and that was that.

So she'd apologized profusely and meant it.

She couldn't deny how much she'd missed him, but she'd had no choice and as much as she could, she tried to make that point clear. He couldn't know she'd made a kill so high level the fallout caused a shitstorm that embroiled her in meeting after meeting, hearing after hearing for months on end.

Stupid politics.

Hoping he'd find her apology enough, she jerked her head,, motioning toward her kitchen. "I need to talk with you about something I heard. You hungry?"

"I'm starving." He stood and stretched, apology apparently accepted.

Padding toward her kitchen, she waved him on. "Come on then."

She pulled out makings for sandwiches, piling them on the counter, and he settled in on one of the stools around the center island.

"So I heard some interesting news about a body you all just found." She continued working as she spoke, trying to be nonchalant. Most often he told her about the cases she asked after. He wasn't supposed to without official leave, but she often provided them with a lot of helpful information. Jack was a man who wanted to take out the scum who hurt people. If it meant sharing info with her, he would.

"You heard, huh? How is that?"

She put a plate in front of him and cracked open a beer for both of them before grabbing the folder and sitting down.

"I've got my sources. You know that."

He saw the folder and narrowed his eyes. "Goddamn, woman! How do you do that?" He tried to take it but she snorted and pulled her hand free.

"I'm special, what can I say. Now, just tell me already. It's not like I don't know. I want to hear your take on it."

He sighed and took a bite of the sandwich. "Two days ago we found a body just outside of town. Nasty bit of business. Head nearly ripped off. Never seen anything like it. I know, wouldn't be the first dead body we find outside town. But this body was nearly totally drained of blood."

This was the part that disturbed her the most. Her heart stuttered for a moment. "Wh…what? Like how?"

"I mean veins collapsed, nearly totally bloodless. No blood where the body was found. No blood on the wounds. Talked to our guy in the morgue and he says it's what a body looks like after they're prepared for burial and drained of bodily fluids."

"Fuck."

"Yeah. You got any ideas? There's nothing. I mean nothing. No fingerprints. No hair or tissue. She had sex, but a condom was used. There were no footprints leading to where this body was discovered. In the middle of an abandoned dirt field—there should have been tracks but there were none. No tire marks except for our own. We saw the body from the air. It was like someone dumped her from above but there's no physical evidence that the body was dropped. Looks like it was set down. But by what and how did they do it without making any tracks?" He shrugged. "You gonna give me that case file back?"

"No. Listen, it came to me from a concerned citizen. You know I'm not going to get in the way or make myself known in your investigation unless I'm called in officially to profile. But you have to understand I'm going to be looking into this myself."

He rolled his eyes and nodded. "Fine. Right now,

the higher-ups are just treating this like a run-of-the-mill murder of some dumb bimbo. But I don't know. I'd appreciate your eye, Rowan."

"Of course. You know I'll let you in on what I find. I may not be on your timeline but you know I don't sandbag indefinitely."

He nodded. "You shouldn't sandbag at all. Damn it, Rowan, this is dangerous shit. This is some fucked-up asshole out there. You're not a cop."

No. But what she was trumped that. Not like she could tell him what she was, though. "I'll be careful. You know that."

"I don't know shit, Rowan. For years and years I've known you but I haven't known shit. That needs to change sometime, you know? Why don't you trust me?"

She looked at him, pushing the bag of potato chips in his direction before putting the file in a nearby drawer.

"I do trust you, Jack. But there are things I can't say and you know that. Now eat your sandwich and stop bitching."

LATER, AFTER he'd gone, Rowan sat out on her deck, her bare feet on the railing, the warm wind in her hair, and let the night settle into her bones.

The realization that she was going to have to stake some Vampires again so soon after the last kill came over her. Her brain worked over the details of the murder—tears on the neck so severe the victim had been nearly beheaded. Wounds on the chest. The heart removed and tossed into the chest cavity, nearly desiccated.

This wasn't just a Vampire who'd gotten out of control on a feed. This was a monster and that was something altogether different and far more disturbing.

FOUR

AFTER BARELY FOUR hours of sleep, Rowan woke, knowing what she needed to do. She locked up, leaving her blade in the case in her back entry. Where she was going, she couldn't rely on it. It wasn't the place for weapons.

An hour later, she arrived at the nondescript ranch that housed the shrine to Brigid and her acolytes. As always, the Mother-Acolyte waited on the front porch, white-blond hair blowing in the heated breeze.

Rowan got out and approached, falling to her knees and bowing her head. "Mother."

The woman put her hand on top of Rowan's head and peace settled over her. "Rowan. Child of the triple Goddess. Come."

Rowan stood and followed the priestess into the house and down a flight of stairs. It was cool and dark but the way was lit by both the glow of power about the priestess and the altar in the center of the room, dominated by a large cauldron of flame.

"I leave you here."

Rowan nodded and removed her clothing. She cleansed in the ritual bath and pulled a loose-fitting robe over her head. Bare feet moved over the cool earth as she approached the cauldron.

Her fingers traced the marks on the altar, invoking the Goddess whose power she bore. Light burst through her and she let herself fall away from her body as she ascended.

"You've been away for some time. All is not well."

Rowan looked up into the face of her real mother and smiled, wishing she could touch her, be held by her. But still, she was thankful she had this rare opportunity to know her in any guise. Not all who served the Goddess were able to ascend in spirit the way her mother had.

She nodded. "You know of my slaying of the Scion here in Las Vegas. They removed me from my position while the matter was adjudicated. And now…now I'll have to slay another."

"This is your duty."

"It is. But something isn't right. I feel…I don't know, I feel like there's something else coming that I can't quite see. It's going to be very bad."

"Your father had a great gift. Cunning and intuition. Use it. I believe you'll need all your gifts to survive this one." Her mother paused a moment, gathering her words.

"My darling, I was merely a servant to her. You are her Vessel. Her blade is righteous in your hands. Do not forget that. I am proud."

"Thank you. I want so much to make you proud. To do what is right in her name."

"You're approaching your thirtieth birthday. You move from one cycle of life to the next. No longer a maiden. I expect you'll come into more of your power then, so be aware and listen when she speaks through you."

Rowan had a set of gifts inherited through her blood

and connection to Brigid. She presided over Imbolc ceremonies, marking Brigid's feast day and celebration, traveling to Kildare each year to do so. Each February first on Imbolc and Rowan's birthday, she gained more power. Gifted with battle and ability to kill when necessary, some years ago Rowan had come into some healing gifts. News that she'd gain some larger boost to her power on her birthday was of great interest.

Knowing better than to expect definite answers, Rowan remained for some time longer, listening to her mother's poetry and stories, letting her stores of power be refilled by the Goddess herself. When the small flaming arrow tattoo on her shoulder began to burn, she knew it was time to return to her own plane of existence.

"Be well. Be smart and be vicious if you need to be," her mother murmured as Rowan began to descend into her physical form.

After she'd changed into her street clothes, she went upstairs to the large kitchen and had tea with the acolytes who lived there. Rowan was always a revered guest in the house and it had ceased to make her uncomfortable after experiencing it for so many years.

As she left, they pressed apples—a remembrance of Brigid's Isle of Apples—into her hands and she took them with a smile. This was one of the few places she could be gentle without worry. Where she could give and accept love without wondering what the price tag would be.

THE DAY WANED as she drove into the city. She wanted to talk to Jack and she knew his on-again, off-again girlfriend and sort of psycho bitch from hell, Lisa, would be off shift.

"Hey, Rowan! Long time no see," Detective Don Styles called out as she walked into the room.

"Hey, Styles. Is Jack around?"

"I'm here. What can I do for you, gorgeous?"

Rowan looked over to where Jack stood, leaning in his doorway, and waved. "I want to borrow your brain, such as it is."

"Better than the one you got. Come on then." He waved her into his office and closed the door behind himself. "I imagine you came by to snoop so g'hed." Pointing to the files on his desk, he remained standing.

With a shrug, she sat and began to leaf through them. Once she'd read the autopsy report and seen all the medical data she knew for sure the murderer had been a Vampire. Nothing else could fly into a scene like that. Nothing else could drain the body of blood that way.

Gruesome stuff. They didn't have any real evidence. No skin, hair or fluid left behind but the victim's. The coroner was still holding on for some tox reports, but he'd noted needle tracks on her arm. Most likely a heroin or speed junkie. Which also meant she'd fall to the bottom of the case list because sadly, junkies turned up dead. Not *this* kind of dead, but they'd avoid the truth and stick to what they knew. Which was that junkies lost jobs and alienated family. They sold what they had, borrowed, stole and eventually ended up on the stroll. Any one of these things could get a person dead.

When she finished she rubbed her eyes and stood.

"Thank you for letting me look at this. I'm going to ask around. I'll get back to you when I hear something."

She started to walk past him but he put his arm up, blocking her exit. "You watch your ass. This is sick shit. Just tell me what you think. I know you know something you aren't saying."

"I have some ideas but I don't want to say anything until I do some checking out first. You know how I work."

"Yeah. Just don't let it get you killed. You come to me if you need me, understand?" The frustration in his eyes softened to concern and she tiptoed up to kiss his cheek.

"I gotcha. Thank you." She paused. "Really, I promise I'm careful."

He sighed, rolling his eyes. "You'd better be."

SHE BREEZED INTO her apartment and hit the speakerphone dial as she tossed herself onto her couch.

"Sangre International."

Rowan snorted at that. Damned Vampires thought they were so clever. Blood International? So lame.

"I need to speak with the Scion. It's Rowan Summerwaite calling."

There was a slight hesitation. "Of course, Ms. Summerwaite. I'll get him. Please hold a moment."

The girl probably thought Rowan kicked puppies and ate small children dipped in honey mustard sauce. Geez, you kill a few Vampires and suddenly you were the big bad wolf and all.

Some moments later she heard the call being transferred and Clive picked up. "To what do I owe the honor of this call?"

She reined in her annoyance. "I need to speak to you regarding an urgent matter."

He swore softly. "Really urgent? I'm expected on a conference call in ten minutes." Of course, his arrogant tone was still there.

"Look, do you think I'd be spending time with you if it wasn't really urgent? I need to have dinner anyway. Will you be done in two hours?"

"You're awfully accommodating."

"Stop acting surprised, asshole. You're the one who started the fight last night. I'm not all holy water and blessed blades through the heart you know."

"You've actually made me snort, Ms. Summerwaite. I don't like the general downturn in my behavior since I've met you."

"Yeah, yeah, I'm a bad influence. What's new? But?" She looked at her split ends and made a mental note to get a haircut.

"I do not admit to anything. But theoretically I may have started it. Although you're a very vexing woman and I quite believe you goaded me into the worst of it. And yes, I will be available in two hours. Shall I meet you in my home or would you prefer somewhere else?"

She smiled. The bastard was charming in his own uptight way. "Your place is fine. I love to scare your inferiors when I show up. I'll see you in two." She disconnected before he could answer and ran upstairs to change her clothes.

FIVE

THE HEELS OF her boots clicked like a metronome on the shiny floors as Clive's assistant brought Rowan up to his apartment again. The boots were favorites because they ferreted all sorts of weapons and lock picks and other various implements of up-to-no-goodedness in the buckles.

This time Mr. Stick-Up-His-Ass met her at the doors of the elevator. The smooth, regal female who'd escorted Rowan murmured to Clive, who nodded and dismissed her before turning to Rowan again. And she didn't fail to notice the way his eyes lingered on her breasts and legs.

"Ms. Summerwaite, won't you come in?" He might have roving eyes, but his voice was haughty and cool.

"Sure, Clive." She swept past him into the living room and sat down. "You've got a lawbreaker on your hands," she said without preamble as he joined her, sitting across the low table from her.

"What makes you say that?"

She tossed the pictures from the file across the table to him and sat back.

Annoyed, he picked them up and looked through them one by one until he put them down on the table again. Face a schooled blank mask, he blinked at her. "And what makes you think this is a Vampire?"

"Uh, because I'm not an idiot?"

"Must you always be so crass?"

She stood up. "Crass? Look at those pictures and the notes on them. Drained of blood. Desiccated heart that'd been ripped out of her chest. Throat torn out. You know what it is as well as I do."

He stood and got in her face. "You people are capable of this kind of violence too."

"But not in this case."

"You're biased where we're concerned, Ms. Summerwaite. It seems you're always looking for something to pin on us." He narrowed his eyes at her.

She threw her hands up in the air. "Always? You're an expert on my behavior now? You've known me all of two days and you know what I always do?"

The moment stretched as their eyes remained locked. Feeling something build between them, she moved away, escaping to the large windows overlooking the Strip.

"I know your history." His voice was a growl.

"And I know yours." Her reply was a whisper and suddenly he was right behind her. "You know what this is. The body was dropped some miles out of town in the middle of an abandoned field. No tracks of any kind around the body. No tire marks. Nothing."

He was silent for a moment. "It could have been an animal."

She spun then, eyes narrowed, mouth set in a frustrated slash. "You know what this is. Stop it! What is it with you people anyway? You just don't fucking care that one of your own has murdered this girl and left her body in the middle of nowhere. Animals wouldn't go near it. All the time it sat out there in the open and nothing touched it. I'm here to tell you that the cops are investigating and this will bring down a whole load of shit on your heads. I will hunt this lawbreaker, Scion. So wise up and get out of my way. I only came as a courtesy."

"Courtesy?" His face was close to hers, anger radiating from him. "You have no courtesy. Damn you," he murmured right before his lips found hers, taking her in a rough kiss.

Before the surprise set in and enabled her to pull away, desire, hot and forbidden rushed through her body as her hands fisted in the front of his expensive shirt.

The cool of the window at her back didn't matter as his lips owned hers, his tongue sliding into her mouth, shocking in the contrast of temperature even though it was only a few degrees different. It'd been a very long time since she'd kissed a Vampire. She'd been young then, a totally different person.

Wantonly, she writhed against his body, the hardness of him sliding against her breasts, her thighs. She kept her grip on his shirt, knowing if she let go, her fingers might wander to places best left untouched.

He had no such compulsion though. Slightly rough, as if he couldn't touch enough of her at once, his hands roved over her body, up her thighs, across her belly, skirting her breasts, through her hair. All the while he kissed and kissed her with a feral intensity that made her lose her mind.

He broke away, pupils dilated, breath heaving from him, his incisors gleaming in the low light, and a thrill skittered through her, even as she knew she should be ashamed.

He groaned and laughed ruefully. “This is so wrong.”

“Yes, it’s wrong.” Was he gonna do something with what he was packing behind his zipper or what? Why was he questioning it *now?*

“I already want to do it again. What are you doing to me? This is your fault.” He pushed away and began to pace.

It was her turn to laugh and thank the Goddess he’d acted like the prick he was to help her wrest control from her hormones.

“My fault? Who shoved their tongue in whose throat? You started it. You were all Frenching me and grinding your dick on me and stuff. I was just you know, um, stuck between you and the window.”

“Must you be so bloody vulgar?”

“Vulgar? You think that was vulgar? You’re a pussy. And anyway, you said bloody! I know that’s a bad word to you Brits.”

“You make me vulgar. Damn you.”

“Yeah?” She exhaled violently. “I’m already damned. Now, where’s the bathroom?”

He pointed and she snatched up her bag and sealed herself in the palatial powder room, staring at herself in the mirror. She gripped the marble countertop so hard the tendons in her hands protested.

Ruthlessly, she forced herself under control.

What had she done? What would she have done if

he hadn't stopped? He was the enemy and she was a traitor for even letting him touch her. Guilt and shame warred within until anger pushed it all away.

He'd had the audacity to blame her? Oh he was such a piece of work. All Vampires were so damned arrogant. He should be thanking his lucky stars she hadn't twisted his 'nads off!

She splashed cold water on her face and reapplied her lipstick. Clive Stewart needed to be kept at a distance. He was a Vampire. Underline, underline, bold and exclamation points. She knew, only too well, what they were. What they were capable of.

Methodically, she smoothed her clothing and fixed her hair.

There was no reason to have *anything* but a business relationship with him. The more he feared her wrath, the better. Wrath didn't include kissing and second base.

Looking at herself in the mirror again, she repeated that last bit, just to make it extra clear to herself because she totally *was* a bad influence, even on her own self.

Safely pulled together again, she returned to find him totally composed and sitting, looking through the file. Good.

"I should tell you you needn't worry about catching the virus."

She must have looked as confused as she felt because he pointed to her mouth. "I believe I nicked your lip. I apologize for that. And of course, Vampires can't carry STDs so you don't need to be concerned about blood exchange."

Her tongue found the spot he'd brushed with his incisors. A perverse need to poke at him built within her. A need to shake him and wipe that smug look from his face. "I know. You seem to forget I was raised by The First. I lost my virginity at sixteen to one of his lieutenants." The man who'd told her the truth about what really happened to her parents not six months later when they'd broken things off. When her godfather found out, the lieutenant had been executed. Another six months later and she'd escaped the Keep and landed on the doorstep of the Motherhouse in Paris.

He made a strangled sound, his fists clenching a little, before he sighed. "I do forget. Yes." He looked at her for a moment and then down to the photos on the table. "What are you going to do about this?"

"I'm going to hunt him down and slay him. You can help me. Or not. The outcome will be the same."

"You want me to help you kill a Vampire?" he demanded, incredulous.

"Don't pretend to be something you aren't, okay? I *know* what you are. I know what you do. This breaks the treaty. Period. You can't kill humans. You certainly can't torture them, kill them and dump their bodies. More than the fact that you seem to show no outrage over murder, you should be concerned that the human police are involved. They've asked me to consult on the case, as a matter of fact."

"If you tell them about us, it's you who've broken the treaty."

She shook her head and stood. Picking up the photos and tucking them in her bag, she looked at him for several long moments.

"I have not broken the treaty. Let's be clear here, you may wrap up what you are in a three-thousand-dollar suit and think you fool others about your true nature. But I don't pretend to be what I'm not. I'm a Hunter and I'll find this Vampire and kill him. I won't feel remorse for it. I won't tell the cops about you, but try not to underestimate humans for a change, okay? After a while, they're going to start asking the right questions and they may just figure it out on their own."

She moved toward the elevator and hit the call button. "In any case, it's up to you what you do. But never what I do. Remember that. I'm a Hunter. It's my job. I serve the Goddess, that's my calling. Justice will be meted out."

THE DOORS CLOSED behind her and he scrubbed his face with his hands, groaning at her scent. For a man who prided himself on never being out of control, he'd just had the most intense minutes of his life. In fact he'd never felt more alive than in the hours since she'd strode into his apartment the first time.

God, he'd kissed the Hunter. Against the windows. The one woman he should not want, should not have touched and he did it in view of the entire Las Vegas Strip. Worse, he'd do it again in a heartbeat. He'd have done more if he hadn't heard his phone ringing in the top drawer of his desk across the room.

Straightening his clothing he went and washed his face and hands, slightly disturbed that he hesitated at getting rid of her scent.

Pulling himself together, he gave a terse order to his personal assistant to set up a meeting with the others immediately.

SIX

NEEDING TO DO something other than dwell on what had happened between her and Clive, Rowan drove out to the scene where the body had been abandoned. It was out past the Desert Rose Golf Course, east of the city center, on the way to the Geological Preserve. Enough away from town to not call too much attention but still close enough that Rowan felt very strongly it was one of the Vampires who lived in Las Vegas.

The night air was still. Unnaturally so. She consulted the notes she'd taken and began to walk out into the open field.

As she walked, she opened herself up to her power. Took the energy and information the earth freely gave. In the middle of the field, she felt it. The sharp absence of life left behind where a dead body had lain. But there were no red splashes in the energy of the place. The murder itself didn't happen there. The body had been brought in from wherever she'd been killed.

Still, the trauma of the event hung in the air. Rowan found many humans had some level of psychic ability but most ignored it. She understood why they did. The world was complicated. Filled with things that upon close examination could scare the shit out of you but you couldn't do much to stop or prevent either. So most chose blissful ignorance.

And there were times—such as right then in the middle of that abandoned field in the dark of night, the death itching over her skin—Rowan wished she were just a normal human woman who'd grown up in the suburbs with a lawn and a basketball hoop in the driveway. Wished for the bliss of ignorance and the cover of an everyday existence where she knew nothing of the world beneath the senses.

Instead, she crouched, reaching out to touch the earth where the body had lain. The shock of it still resonated in the packed dirt. Rowan couldn't get much. The woman had been dead for at least an hour before the murderer had brought the body there. Sometimes if the spot was where the murder took place, Rowan could pick up sense memories from the victim or even the perpetrator.

Now she got nothing but the still and heavy cloak of death. So heavy it screamed unnatural causes. Of unnatural things—like Vampires. The earth was outraged in her own way. Rowan felt that. Felt also, that it received her and gave her strength.

Standing, she brushed her palms off on her skirt as she looked into the night. The moon was bright and she could see civilization all around her.

All that humanity within sight and yet no one saved the woman who'd been dumped out here like garbage. The senselessness of it offended Rowan deeply. Anger and frustration bubbled up from her gut.

Why? This was so much more than a blooding gone too far. Vampires were another species. One that preyed on humans and at some points in their history yes, they hunted and killed. But that had not been for a very long time.

And even at that, the depth of depravity of the kill stunned her. Vampires, even in the thrall of bloodlust tended to drain the human from one, maybe two pints and that was it. She hadn't seen the taking and draining of a heart and other internal organs in her lifetime, and she'd grown up in the capital of nightmare country. The only times she'd heard of it were references in books of the really bad old days before the Renaissance.

Could it be a Vampire that old? That kind of power would be dangerous, definitely unstable. The older they got, the more tenuous their grasp on reality was. Even then they sort of went into hibernation, they didn't turn into psycho killers for fuck's sake.

She shivered as she headed to her car. While she'd answered some questions, she now left with even more. Two things were certain to her as she started into town. She'd find the killer eventually. But it wouldn't be before he killed again.

CLIVE STRODE into the meeting room. He didn't need to hide his emotions as he sat at the head of the large table. Frustration and outright rage over the situation had pushed away his titillation and anger at himself over the kiss.

"I've had another visit from the Hunter."

The room erupted in grumbles and Clive silenced them all with a slight movement of his hand.

"Be quiet. There's been a murder and she believes it was one of us." He gave a quick look to be sure they'd keep quiet until he finished. They did. "And from my examination of the photographs and other evidence she had from the police file, she is correct."

"She's always looking out to get one of us killed. And who cares anyway? It's just one human. They find dead humans all the time around Vegas. Why immediately rush to the conclusion that it's a Vampire kill?" Wendela snarled and then was on the ground as Clive's hand, lightning-quick, made contact with her jaw, knocking her from the chair.

"Stupid as well as undisciplined." He used the linen napkin his assistant handed him to wipe his hand off. "I've been here six months and there's still not a day that goes by when I don't want to behead at least one of you. Perhaps I'll have to go back to that a few times to make my point since you all seem unable to retain your lessons. The answer to your impertinent and asinine question is because *I said* it was a Vampire kill. People, *listen to me!*" He slammed his fist down on the table and enjoyed seeing them wince.

"I've looked at her record. She's made eight kills, all legal. I've looked at the official complaints lodged against her by our people here and each time she was cleared by the Joint Tribunal. As for whether or not she's looking to get us killed?" He shrugged. "That may be true. It's clear she hates us. But she has a job to do and she does it. And from my examination of the files, she does it lawfully.

"Of course this is all beside the point. The *point* is that one of us has broken the treaty. *And* in an extremely public fashion and in such a way that marks it a Vampire kill. This makes me quite unhappy. Already the human police are involved and if they look too closely there'll be trouble. As the Hunter reminded me. Let me emphasize how much it displeases me to have the Hunter remind me of anything."

"It's got to be one of those damned idiots at the Vampyre Theatre." Alice had been Clive's assistant for thirty-five years. He trusted her judgment and insight.

"Well, considering the messes I've had to clean up down there over the last few months, that does seem to be a logical train of thought." Clive turned to his top lieutenant. "See to it. Get down there and talk to Marv. I want to stop this now, before it gets to the Keep." Clive stood. "And may I remind you all, the goal is *not* to kill when you feed. But if you do kill a human for God's sake, dispose of the body correctly. This Vampire is sloppy, that offends me."

SEVEN

ROWAN WOKE TO the sound of a ringing phone. Rolling over, she looked at the clock. 10:00 a.m. Sighing, she picked up.

"Rowan, darling, I'm returning your email. You know how I hate email. Please don't make me use the computer. Tell me what's up."

Pushing the hair out of her face, Rowan grinned as she sat up. "Hang on one sec." Leaning over, she hit the intercom and buzzed David, asking him to bring her up some coffee and a bagel.

Settling in bed, she tucked the covers around her legs and put the phone back to her ear. "Okay. Thanks for calling. By the time I got in and finished up my work, it was late there. Still, I wanted to fill you in before I crashed."

Susan Espy was Rowan's boss. Well, more than that really. Susan had been the one to bring Rowan into the London Motherhouse.

Rowan had arrived in Paris alone and emotionally exhausted. She'd heard of the Hunter Corporation and at that point, so soon after hearing of the real cause of her parents' death, saw them as her ticket to revenge.

And of course, they'd been overjoyed to have her there. She'd been trained by the Vampire Nation. By

The First himself. And she was a Vessel for the Goddess. It made her a threat on many levels. But they just saw her as a tool and it left her empty.

Until Susan had walked into Rowan's room and sat on her bed. After looking at her for long moments, the older woman pulled the seventeen-year-old Rowan into her arms, letting her cry it all out. From that point Susan had been her mentor, her mother substitute, her friend and companion. Brought Rowan to her own home in London and treated her like family. It was Susan who'd argued for making the very young Rowan a full partner in the Corporation. Once Rowan had that sense of connectedness, her commitment to the Hunter Corporation's cause had cemented.

Rowan filled her in on the death and her investigation up until that point.

"Well, puddin', you certainly do have quite a murderous bunch of Vampires on your watch. Must be all that daytime sun. Makes them quite cross. Do you need assistance?"

Rowan took a sip of her coffee. She'd considered it. "No. It's a pretty violent killing and points to one seriously fucked-up Vamp, but it's nothing I can't handle on my own. The Scion may not have wanted to admit it, but he knows it's one of his own. This one is different from Jacques. He's not likely to tolerate the possible exposure. I may not even have to stake the culprit if Stewart finds him before I do."

"Language, Rowan," Susan admonished with a smile in her voice. "All right then. We're behind you. Use whatever capital you need to. By the way, I do miss you. Having you around for all those months again was fun."

She held back a laugh at Susan's exception to the *F* word. "Sorry. I miss you too. But I'll be in Ireland in February for Imbolc and my birthday."

"Indeed you will. I'm looking forward to this one. Your thirtieth. Big things for you, I'd wager. Now I must off. You know how Rex gets when I dawdle on our bridge nights. I do love you, puddin'. Be safe will you?"

Rowan smiled at the thought of the vicious assassin having bridge night with her husband and their friends. "Of course. I'll speak to you soon."

After taking a quick shower, she dressed and headed out. Her office was in a fairly nice building on Paradise Road. Away from the Strip but not too far. She worked at home when she could but with all the gear she had stored in her penthouse, it was necessary to keep the public away.

Cindy, the harried and perpetually tardy receptionist, waved at Rowan as she strolled in. She'd considered firing Cindy, but in the end it would have been more work to find a replacement and the girl wasn't all bad. She never complained about being sent out for lunches or late dinners. Answered the phone without cracking gum and didn't ask questions about just exactly what it was they all did.

Everyone had flaws.

"Send Carey into my office, please?" Rowan asked, placing a mocha on the counter.

"Thanks, boss. Will do."

Rowan paused. "Take your vitamins, Cindy, you're looking pale."

"I think I'm coming down with something. I'm taking extra vitamin C."

"Go home if you don't feel better."

Rowan went into her office, booted the computer and began to read through her mail.

"Yo, bosslady, what up?" Carey Barker was her resident computer god, office manager and go-to-guy. He'd pretty much run the place while she was gone. He was also employed by the Hunter Corp. and was her right hand on the investigation side.

She tossed the folder to him and he looked through the pictures and her notes. "Holy shit, Ro."

"Indeed." She'd ceased to be bothered by his calling her by pet names. "So what I want is for you to work your computer magic and find out who this girl was. I want to know everything I can about her."

He stood up and nodded. "Got it. Your cop called three times today."

She sighed.

"Ro, he's human and he cares about you. He has no way of knowing you're like this super-human, Goddess-channeling Vessel of death and destruction worthy of one very cool Japanese anime series."

"Give me strength, dear Goddess." Rowan waved him away. "Get me the information, please. And close the door on your way out."

He left, chuckling.

She hit the button on her speed dial and called up her email while she waited.

"Elroy."

"You called?"

"Hey, Rowan, anything new?"

"Nothing yet. I've got Carey finding out what we can about the vic. I didn't see a lot about her in the file."

"Okay. Excellent. You know I'm going to warn you to be careful right?"

"Look, dad, I'm fine," she teased. "And you didn't say much about Lisa. Speaking of trouble and all. How are things going?"

Lisa, the psycho he slept with and hated depending on the day of the week, worked in the call center for the police department. She was batshit crazy and hated Rowan, always accusing Jack of cheating with her. There was something off about her, more than just crazy-girlfriend off. She had a toxic air about her at times and Rowan had begun to wonder, the last time Lisa had shown up to flip out over one thing or other, if she was sick or on something.

"The usual. We're sort of back together now. She relaxed a bit while you were gone. You need to give her a chance."

She put her hand up in defense but he couldn't see it anyway. "I wasn't saying anything bad. Oh well that trouble comment but that was really more about the general state of your relationship being on and off again. I was just asking."

"Sure. Anyway, you'd better call me. Hey, you free for dinner this week? I'll make pesto."

"Yum. I haven't had anything that tasty for months and months. Let me give you a call tomorrow to see what's up. Okay?"

They hung up and she looked at her screen. Lots of messages. Requests for research help, answers to questions, sharing of intel. The Hunter Corporation operated worldwide and had thousands of employees who did everything from weapons R&D and martial arts training to making up the army of attorneys at their beck and call. They had an extensive virtual library and several large physical libraries in the hub cities.

In Rowan's case, she was lucky Jack bent the rules and that the chief of police liked her. She had the kind of access that most Hunters had to gain through other means. Usually by theft, hacking or inside contacts at various police departments. She'd been hired to consult on certain cases, testified on several occasions. The time spent at the right hand of The First was far more informative than the training she'd received from her former boss, the FBI profiler. But there was no denying that those years and her degrees gave her the keys to work with the police on cases like this one. Still the cops wouldn't tell her everything. After all, she was a civilian and even with the credentials she had, they didn't trust outsiders. The attitude and the need to protect the integrity of the legal case created a necessity for her to bend and break the law when she had to to get information. That was a fact of her life and she didn't feel one bit guilty about it.

Carey came in at just before five and tossed some papers on the desk. "This is what I've got so far. Tammy White, twenty-eight. Born and raised in Barstow. She was a waitress there at a truck stop. Where she was staying here seems to be a mystery. Why she was here, how she ended up here?" He shrugged. "I don't know. Her medical records indicate she was moderately healthy except for what looks like a problem with meth three years back and then a year ago again.

I'm still working on that. Her parents live in Barstow, still married, have three other kids, all also living in Barstow."

Rowan looked through the information he'd pulled out of thin air for her, always appreciative of his deviousness. "How the hell did you find her?"

Carey leaned back in his chair and put his feet up on her desk. "I put in her photo and ran some matching software. All that shit that isn't supposed to exist comes in pretty handy. Anyway, I got a few pings after three hours, matched it with some of the dental record stuff and I narrowed it down from there."

"Impressive. I'm going to give some of this to Jack. The cops could use the help. After I go to Barstow tomorrow, that is. I want to talk to her parents. Why was she here, Carey? Why didn't anyone report her missing? Is it because she came alone? Or the person she came with did it? Or are they a victim too? Is there another body out there waiting to be found?"

"Dunno. But you'll find out and avenge her. You always get the bad guy. Want some company for the road trip?"

"I think I'm going to tap Thena, she's good at this shit. People tell her things. But I appreciate your offer. I know how much you love Barstow."

He snorted. "It's merely a testament to my utter devotion to you, Ro."

It was her turn to snort then. "I'm going to get out of here first thing so I can roll into town, snoop around and hopefully get home late tomorrow night."

"That's a hell of a lot of driving in one day."

She rolled her eyes. "Darling boy, I have a finely

tuned work of art on wheels, capable of very high speeds. Thank you for your concern but it won't be a problem if we can get in to see her parents and her co-workers. Find out who her best girlfriend is. Is there an ex?"

Sighing dramatically, Carey leaned in, pushed her hands away from the file and rifled through the stack, finally pulling out the sheet he'd been looking for. "Bob Price. They were married five years but the meth thing derailed it, at least from what I can see."

"Okay, another thing to check on." She stood and grabbed her bag and the sheaf of papers, shoving them inside. "I'll call from the road if I need you. Call me if you find out anything else. I'll be out the door by eight."

"You do that. I'll call you if I find anything out after nine when I get here. I'll work for another few hours tonight."

She kissed his cheek and breezed out the door after thanking him.

AFTER SHE CHANGED, she headed over to Thena and Martin's. Thena was a close friend, an acolyte to Athena as it happened, and a frequent help to Rowan. Martin was her fabulous husband.

Though she'd been gone so long during the investigation after she'd staked Jacques, she'd been able to have contact with Thena in a way she hadn't with Jack. After all, Thena knew what Rowan was. There was no need to hide from her.

But Rowan had missed seeing her friends regularly for dinner or Sunday brunch. She'd missed hanging out with them and going out for a movie or for drinks. Email and texting were only so good.

When Martin opened the door he pulled her into a tight bear hug.

"Rowan! How dare you be home for several days and neglect me so." Holding her away from his body, he looked her up and down. "You look well. Come on through, Her Highness is making dinner. You staying?"

"Who am I to turn down dinner? Plus, I came to see if I could steal your wife for the day tomorrow. I need her skills."

"You do huh? And what'll you give me for them?" Thena looked up from the cutting board and wiped her hands on a nearby towel.

"What's up?"

Rowan filled them both in briefly and Thena agreed to the road trip. "Why don't you stay here tonight and we'll leave first thing in the morning?"

"You sure? I don't want to put you out."

Thena rolled her eyes. "I hate when you do that. Of course I'm sure. You have your own damned room here. I'll set the alarm for six-thirty and we'll grab some coffee and hit the road."

They sat down to dinner and despite the seriousness of the situation, it felt good to be with friends doing something as normal as eating dinner and having a glass of wine.

EIGHT

THE SUN WAS already beginning to scorch the asphalt as Rowan tore onto the highway leading from Vegas to Barstow. Thena leaned her head against the leather seats as they sang along to PJ Harvey.

The drive was long, but even with some nasty traffic and a stop for gas and junk food, they still managed to make it through the front doors of the truckstop/diner Tammy had worked at.

Rowan hadn't invited Thena along solely for the pleasure of her company. Thena was blessed with the ability to get people to talk to her about anything. The only other person Rowan had known who'd been better at persuasion had been a Vampire. Whatever magick Thena had was similar to a thrall, but subtler.

Thena wove a conversation into something else. A web of sorts, Rowan supposed. She learned and gleaned and maneuvered until people told her things they hadn't expected to. Only later on they didn't really remember much and eventually their memory of the conversation would fade completely.

"Come to think of it, I haven't seen her around in a while." The waitress turned her attention from them as she scanned the diner. "I'm new so I don't know Tammy that well. We usually work different shifts anyway. But one of the other girls, oh there she is." She waved another woman over. "She and Tammy are real close. Kiki, these ladies know Tammy. Isn't that funny?"

The tall brunette eyed them warily. "That so?"

Thena nodded. "You have a few minutes to chat?"

Looking around at the now quiet diner, Kiki nodded and slid into the chair across from Thena, next to Rowan. The other waitress wandered off, saying she'd cover Kiki's tables for a bit.

"Kiki, we need to talk to you about Tammy. The other waitress said you two are tight?" Thena said, her voice soothing.

Kiki nodded and it was plain to see that she'd been worried about her friend by the way she wrung her hands. "I been knowing her since high school when we moved here. Is something wrong?"

Thena nodded. "We've got some bad news and we need your help."

Kiki paled but she didn't look surprised. "Bad news? Who are you people?"

"When was the last time you saw her?"

"It was that guy in Vegas! I knew it. Did he hurt her? Is she in rehab again or something? I don't have any money but I can probably get some if you need it."

Thena reached out and grabbed Kiki's hand and Rowan touched her shoulder. "Please, when did you see her last?"

"A week ago. We went to Vegas. Supposed to be a girls' trip, you know? But on our first night we met this dude and we let him buy us drinks and shit and he asked us, no, just Tammy, back to his room. And..."

Her voice wandered off and Rowan hid a sigh. Kiki's behavior was common among those whose memories had been wiped by a Vampire.

Rowan cut her gaze to Thena for a moment before she moved back to Kiki. "Where did you meet this guy?"

"Uh, oh God, I think it was at one of those theme dance places. Goths, chicks with wings. I can't remember the name." Kiki's brow furrowed as she tried to recall.

Rowan squeezed her shoulder again. "What did he look like?"

"I can't remember! I wasn't on drugs, I swear. I haven't used meth in nearly three years. The guy promised us some good shit. But I said no way. I have a kid, I can't be messing around like that or the state will take her again."

"I believe you. Do you remember anything else? Because, Kiki, Tammy is dead. She's been murdered. They found her body a few days ago. I'm sorry to have to tell you like this."

Kiki's face crumpled. Thena moved her hand in front of Kiki's face and murmured. She calmed. They'd have to wipe this part of the details so the cops could officially tell Tammy's family and friends but Tammy's friend deserved to know, even for a few short minutes. It might also shock her into remembering some small detail that might help them.

"Any details you have can help us catch the killer."

"When I said no, Tammy said yes. She was...weak. She still had the cravings so bad. You don't know how hard it is sometimes. Tammy didn't have a kid to keep her good. And her ex wrote her off a year ago. She left with him, the guy. I begged her not to but she wouldn't listen. I was pissed off and came home. I shouldn't have left her there."

"It's not your fault, Kiki. You couldn't have made her come with you. He's the one who hurt her."

They continued to ask questions and get some names of others around who'd need some looking into until the place started getting busy for lunch.

"We appreciate your time, Kiki." Thena stood and held Kiki's attention. "Can you walk us out to our car?"

Kiki nodded and they tossed down money for breakfast and headed outside. Thena wiped the details of the murder they'd given Kiki from her memory but left the part that they were investigators looking for Tammy. Rowan gave Kiki a business card and urged her to call if she remembered any more details.

They drove over to Tammy's parents' house and spoke with her mother and father, who thought that she'd fallen in with a bad crowd again and was using. They hadn't heard from her since before the trip to Vegas. More than anything, Rowan wanted to tell them about their daughter. Hated the necessity of letting the human authorities deal with it in their official way. It would be best for them to hear it from a uniformed officer and Goddess knew they'd want to know just who Rowan was and how she knew when the cops didn't.

The ex worked at a body shop on the outskirts of town and was openly hostile. It was clear he'd loved Tammy at one time but she'd burned him so often it'd turned into something darker. Rowan didn't get the feeling he was capable of violence but she doubted Tammy would have called him if she needed help.

By four, they headed out of town and back toward Vegas. They'd checked out Tammy's apartment and interviewed several people. Rowan took some hair from Tammy's brush and a snapshot of her and Kiki to show around at the clubs in town.

"There aren't that many clubs like that in Vegas. Not really a goth sort of scene. I can only think of two. And one of them is a place Vampires like to hang out." Rowan turned the music down.

The scenery blurred past as they discussed the details in their tiny, air-conditioned bubble of speed.

"I'm going to give Jack the name and tell him I was there today. He'll find out anyway when they talk to the witnesses."

"He's going to be pissed off you didn't tell him before you went to Barstow."

"I'm sure he will be. It's not my preferred method you know, hiding things from him. But you know the cops would not have gotten half that information out of Kiki. Now she'll know she talked to us about the details and won't hold back with the cops. What she can remember anyway. I'm so going to kick Clive's ass."

"*Clive* huh?"

"He and I still hate each other but I think he'll deal with this Vampire. He's on the ball." Rowan looked at the road. She was a natural liar, but Thena knew her too well.

"Hmpf. On the phone, just two days ago you told me he had a stick up his ass and now he's on the ball."

"He's still got a stick up his ass. He's the most uptight man—Vampire—I've ever met. And I've met a hell of a lot of them. But he's not smarmy like Jacques was. And if he's on the take, he's doing it with some sense of caution. Say, should we stop up ahead and grab some dinner? I'm starving."

Thank the Goddess Thena didn't seem overly suspicious and latched on to the idea of stopping to eat.

By the time they finished a leisurely dinner and left the restaurant, darkness had begun to fall.

As they approached the rear of the lot where Rowan's car was parked, she felt it. Felt the danger and the darkness of a Vampire approaching. She put her hand out to stay Thena. "I want you to go inside the restaurant right now. Don't come out here. I'll come in and get you when I'm finished."

Thena froze, knowing better than to second-guess Rowan. "All right. But if you get killed I'm gonna hunt you down and kick your ass. Stupid fucking Vampires."

Rowan stood still, listening, gathering, making sure Thena got inside safely. Then she moved quickly off the pavement to the bare ground behind the restaurant. She'd be better able to pull power from the earth there instead of on the asphalt.

In an economic movement, she reached back and grabbed the hilt of the blade. It warmed to her touch instantly, knowing her master. Rowan moved her wrist slightly, pulling the blessed blade from the custom sheath. The sound rang through the air. A beautiful, clear ring as it cleared the leather that bound it. That ring was the only sound now. No traffic. No insects, no birds. Nothing but death.

The Vampire approached on the wind. She'd be ready for it.

She rotated her wrist and the blade sang as it cut through the air. Rowan spread her feet apart and tipped her head back. Opening herself up, she took a deep breath, found her center and called to the Goddess. Reaching down and out, she pulled the strength and will from the earth and the air.

Everything inside her stilled. Her heart sped and then slowed, her blood thickening. Then, quicksilver, heat began to slide up her legs. Electric sensation made her fingertips tingle and her scalp itch.

White-hot light exploded outward and turned itself inside again, the power filling her up just shy of overflowing. A thousand voices filled her head, countless memories and visions swam across her vision. She was many and one. All and nothing but a servant of what was right and just.

When she opened her eyes, it was with the queer sense of double vision Rowan always had when the Goddess filled her. As if Brigid herself was just under Rowan's skin. And that was true in a way. Brigid blessed her with her strength and her presence and not a moment too soon because the Vampire alighted to his feet in front of her.

There was no wind but Rowan's hair moved on the breeze of her power. It surged through her body, building in her muscles. She'd be strong and fast. Unbeatable. And supremely pissed off. This Vampire had no idea what he was fucking with.

Which told her this was not her killer.

"Vampire, why are you here?" Her voice was deeper than normal and it vibrated with otherworldly strength.

The Vampire stared at her a moment, not knowing if he should be afraid or not. A trickle of bloodlust slid through Rowan's gut, anticipating his fear when she drew his attention to the blade. For the moment, she let him speak.

"You are meddlesome, bitch, so I've come to take care of a problem."

He didn't feel immensely old. The old ones like The First and those of his age felt so very cold and empty. And they had a certain scent, almonds. Even now that she knew the whole story of her parents' death, the scent of almonds comforted her. Still, this Vampire was dangerous enough and she wouldn't forget it.

"Have you now?" Rowan moved and with a quick turn of her wrist made the blade sing. A song of death.

The Vampire noticed and she laughed. "Ahh, he didn't tell you what to expect? Or does he not know? Hmm." She cocked her head as they continued to circle one another. "Lazy. You've come here expecting a feeble little human. You deserve to die for being so careless."

"You *are* a feeble little human." But his voice didn't sound so sure.

To underline her point she moved in and sliced through the tendons in his forearm. The blessed blade left a sizzling line of scarlet in her wake.

His scream only filled her with pity. She reined in her desire to mess with him and decided to question him instead.

"Now that I've got your attention, why don't you tell me who you are?"

He moved and so did she, warily dancing and looking for weakness.

"I'm Charles Rossinni. And you're going to die."

She stopped and wrinkled her nose. "Is that the best you've got? Listen, Chuck, since I'm going to have to slay you and all, I'll give you a tip. When in doubt and out of scary material, just flash fang. Less is more when it comes to this stuff. That's way more frightening than hackneyed movie phrases."

Angered, he lunged at her and she ducked neatly, slicing the other arm. The scent of his blood painted the air.

"You can do this the easy way. Tell me why you're here and I show you mercy and slay you quickly. Or the hard way, I slash and stab, stab, stab you until you tell me anyway. Oh, don't look shocked! I was The First's foster daughter. Any conscience I may have had over killing, he snuffed out at a very early age. Lucky for you, I got some mercy from my mother. Not enough to let you walk away from trying to kill me, but enough to kill you quick. If you cooperate."

He lunged at her again and grabbed her hair this time. Damn it, she'd have to keep it in a ponytail more often. One of his nails dug into her neck and she felt the warm ooze of her blood on her skin.

Her lip curled. "Gross. I hope your shots are up to date."

He moved quickly, knocking her off her feet but she countered just as fast and rolled, jumping to stand again in short work.

His fist shot out and connected with her cheek in a solid punch, raking his nails over the flesh as he pulled back. The sting made her eyes water.

Now she was really pissed off. He'd punched her and blooded her twice. His nails had delivered a nasty shot of Vamp chemicals almost like venom. She was immune to the killing effects of it but it still hurt like hell.

As he continued to attack her, circling and lunging, it became clear he wasn't going to tell her anything. Ah well, she needed to move this along then.

Preternaturally fast, he lunged, lifting slightly off the ground but she ducked, kicking out, rewarded with the satisfying snap when she connected with his knee. The air rushed out of him in an oath when he hit the ground.

Spinning, she connected the heel of her hand to his nose, knowing she'd broken it when she heard the crunch. She followed with the hilt of the blade to his windpipe.

His choking sounds in her ears, she turned, facing east, knowing the time had come. Murmuring a blessing, she brought the blade to her lips and kissed it at the hilt.

Sensing her distraction, he attacked her from behind but she was faster than he knew. A deft movement of her wrist and arm brought the blade up as she spun to the side. A croak of surprise came from him as the long blade embedded in his chest. The stench of his blood and burning flesh from the surface of the blade making contact filled the air.

"Die well, Vampire. I hope death brings the peace you could not find in life."

His shocked expression changed, softened, and his body turned to dust around the blade.

Rowan knelt on the earth and touched her forehead to the ground in thanks for the gift of strength, will and agility. She felt the Goddess drain from her, leaving behind healing and peace of mind.

Standing, muscles burning and jumping from the rush of possession, battle and Brigid's power leaving her body, Rowan realized the sounds of the world around her had returned.

Leaning down, she cleaned the blade on a patch of grass. She'd do a more thorough job when she got home but the earth would help cleanse the blood and taint from it in the meantime. Moving her hair to the side, Rowan slid the blade into the sheath and walked back toward the restaurant to get Thena and get back to Vegas.

NINE

FACE STILL STINGING from the nasty gashes the Vampire she'd killed tore into her flesh, Rowan stalked through the front doors of Fleur.

The maître d' rushed over in a vain attempt to keep her out, but his panicked flailing only amused her in her cranky state so she ignored him. She had quarry to run to ground and currently he sat at a table in a shadowy and yet visible corner wearing a designer suit and sipping a glass of wine without a care in the world.

Stalking over, her gaze locked on him until he looked up at her and started before narrowing his eyes. *Well*, that countered the sting a little bit.

"Ms. Summerwaite," he said, voice smooth but wariness edged it.

"I need to speak to you, Mr. Stewart." The people at the table with him were human and so she didn't want to make a scene and break the treaty. She did want to pop the smug right off his face though.

"Ms. Summerwaite, as you can see, I'm in the middle of a business dinner. You should feel free to call my assistant to set up an appointment for later on in the week and we can discuss whatever it is you need then."

When would he learn? She sighed.

She sat in the chair she pulled free and leveled a look

his way, just to be fair and let him know he was really in a shit ton of trouble "Well, *Clive*, I suppose you may have noticed the marks on my face?" She turned to face the other men at the table who watched her with slightly fearful fascination. "Terrible world isn't it when a girl can't even have dinner without being attacked by the Vampires of the world?" She shook her head sadly and narrowed one eye at Clive, daring him to continue to fuck with her.

She was almost disappointed when he heaved a sigh and stood. "Will you gentlemen excuse me for a few minutes? I would hate for Ms. Summerwaite to feel as if I hadn't defended a damsel in a time of need."

The maître d', who'd been dancing around in distress at Clive's elbow, listened, nodding like a bobblehead as Clive spoke in his ear. Without looking at her once he'd finished, he reached out, clamped his fingers around her elbow and steered her down an interior hallway.

Fleur was the flagship restaurant for the upwardly mobile Vampires in Vegas so Rowan wasn't surprised when he unlocked a door to a swank office and ushered her inside, closing and locking it again behind them.

"My patience with you is quite short, Hunter. I'm in the middle of something. What can't wait until tomorrow?"

"On my way back from Barstow, where the victim of your whackadoo killer Vampire's victim lived, I was attacked. Do you know how gross it is when venom gets in my system? Why don't you people clip your damned nails? It's gross. I know hygiene standards were not very high in the Dark Ages when you were a young lad and all, but if you can drive and use computers now, I expect you all to clip your nails. I had to pour holy water in the wounds, which hurt like a bitch."

He looked her up and down. "I take it you proved victorious?"

Rowan just stared at him for long moments. "If by that you mean did I drop off a very pissed-off friend, go to my apartment and wash Vampire blood off and change my clothes, which were covered in dust? Oh and did I have my valet pour holy water over open Vampire wounds which, yes, I'm going to remind you again *hurts like a motherfucker.* Yes. I killed your little buddy and I even had to file a fucking report about it via cell phone on my way over here after having to dance around your personal assistant's assistant for twenty minutes before she'd tell me where you were. One, I hate personal assistants. Two, I hate having to file reports. Three, I told you there was a problem in Whoville."

"My buddy? A random Vampire with a death wish attacks you and suddenly he's my buddy? This has nothing to do with me and why you think this merits disturbing me in the middle of dinner is beyond my ability to conceive."

"Look, stop acting like you're just this guy standing in line at the grocery store. You're their boss and this is your town as you so snottily informed me, remember that? So yes, he's your buddy. He's under your jurisdiction and you're responsible for him. You would be a totally sucky dad, just sayin'. You have a killer on the loose and that makes it your problem. I'm making it your problem."

"You said you killed him. Problem solved, thank

you." He crossed his arms over his chest and leaned against the desk.

"Problem solved?"

"Your killer is dead. Thank you for your service to the Vampire Nation, I'm sure your godfather will be very pleased."

"Are. You. Out. Of. Your. *Fucking.* Mind? He wasn't the killer! He was sent by the killer to dispatch me. By someone not even smart enough to warn his little assassin about what I was. The problem is *so* not solved."

"Did he tell you that?"

Unable to stop herself, she poked him square in the chest. "Did I say he was mentally defective? Why would he say something so stupid? This isn't an episode of *Perry Mason.* He didn't give me a map to the killer's house either. Pity, I should have thought to ask. Would you like his name? He did tell me that."

He grabbed her hand and moved it away, grasping her wrist. "You're very unpleasant. Please remove your finger from my chest. Go ahead and give me his name. I'll send it along to one of my lieutenants and they'll look into it. In the meantime I have a dinner to return to."

"Charles Rossinni. And if you don't unhand me right now I'll shove my boot right up your ass along with that two-foot-long stick you've already got wedged up there."

With a deft movement, he yanked her wrist, pulling her close. Her hormones surged as she realized, with nearly detached fascination, they were totally going to do it.

A tortured moan escaped him before his mouth

found hers. Her hands slid up into his hair, needing to muss it up and then grab it, holding him to her.

Shivers racked her as his tongue took possession of her mouth, the heat and wet of him echoing outward. Her nipples hardened to the point of pain until his hands found them through the material of her shirt.

Her hands left his hair to find the buckle of his belt and then the button and zipper of his trousers.

He spun then and picked her up, tossing her ass on the surface of the desk, sweeping the stuff on top off with a deft movement.

The quick violence of the movement brought an involuntary groan from her. She didn't want to be affected by him but she was. Her chest heaved as she struggled for breath.

"Pants. Open your pants, man!" she whispered urgently. Her nerves jangled as his hands stroked over her with a rough possession.

"Impatient!" Clive's words were sharp with his own hunger. Still the hint of a smile played at the corner of his lips as he ate her up with his roving hands and his eyes.

"Shut up and do me. My God you Brits with the talking!"

"Vulgar American women." He arched his now free cock into the vee of her open thighs.

"Yeah, well judging from the way you just tossed me up here like a fucking cheeseburger I think you're just fine with my vulgarity, fang."

She kicked off one boot but he didn't let her get any further. Instead he yanked open the waist of her jeans and pulled them down, only bothering to free one leg.

"I hope you're not considering doing away with the niceties like foreplay."

She arched as his fingers found her sex, pressing deep inside as his thumb pressed over her clit.

"As wet as you are, I don't think there's any issue of you not being ready. Are you playing hard to get with my hand between your thighs?" His gaze locked with hers, daring her to deny it.

"Oh we're going to fuck but you have to work for it, buster." Before she could poke at him any further, orgasm burst through her as she arched, her head hitting the desk.

"Hmm, how's that for working? Stand up and turn around. Please," he added when she cracked open an eye and looked at him.

"You don't even have calluses on your fingers. I doubt you work that hard. I'd give it a seven out of ten." She hopped down and turned to face the desk. He bent her forward and she widened her stance for balance.

He ran the edge of his teeth at the back of her neck and she tightened. "No biting! Sex, obviously yes, even if I am the dumbest woman ever. But no blood sucking. You people have taken enough from me."

He grabbed her hair, wrapping it around his fist and levered her head around so he could kiss her hard. "I don't want your blood. It would most likely be very bitter."

She couldn't help but laugh. Goddess, he was a pretty witty man, even if he was one of them. And she'd lied, it was way closer to nine than seven. But his ego was as swollen as his prick so she wasn't going to egg him on any more than she already had.

The blunt head of him pressed against the heat of her and then inside. She rejoiced internally that cross-breeding and STDs weren't possible.

That first entry was slow. Slow enough for her to arch back like a cat needing more from him.

Earlier he'd pulled up the hem of her shirt and shoved the cups of her bra down, and the cool of the glass top of the desk pressed against her nipples as he held her still with a palm at the middle of her back. Her face was just inches above the reflective surface and she couldn't close her eyes against the vision of the woman there looking up at her.

Wanton. Flushed. Lips swollen from kissing and wet from her tongue. She wanted this. Knew in the back of her mind this could happen even as they walked down that hallway. It was totally mental. Absolutely self-destructive and dangerous, but every inch of her skin was alive and on fire for him. She wanted to be angry with herself for it but she just arched to take him deeper instead.

She looked into her own eyes as he filled her up and retreated, thrusting into her with hard, feral digs. There was something deeply intimate about it, about seeing herself that way. Certainly raw and absolutely undeniably hot for the man whose body filled hers over and over.

The scent of how much she wanted him hung in the air along with the essential musk of his own body, the warm, sharp scent he gave off as his body heated. Heated for her.

"This is wrong," he gasped out.

"Seems like you're doing just fine from where I'm

at," she murmured as she moved to her toes to thrust back at him.

"Damn that's good. Your mouth is the annoying part when it isn't better occupied apparently. However, your body is as dangerous as that blade I'm looking at."

"Oh is that what you're telling yourself, Clive? Yes, yes, like that. Are you telling yourself my magic hoo-ha is why you can't be around me for three minutes without wanting to fuck me?" She laughed but there was no real mirth there.

His movements became less coordinated, his breathing choppy as she continued to watch herself. Was it voyeurism or exhibitionism? Both? Neither?

It stung, but just right, where his fingers dug into the muscles of her hips and ass while he pressed deep one last time and then came with a groan. What surprised her was the way he gently leaned down and kissed the nape of her neck before moving back and pulling out.

"Good lord, we just had sex," he murmured, tucking himself into his pants and then straightening his clothing.

"You're very observant. What are you going to do about this killer?" She finger-combed her hair before putting herself in order. She shoved all the voices in her head screaming about how stupid she'd been, *again*, aside.

"You killed the killer, Rowan. Problem solved. I'll ask around about Rossinni but you can't point to any evidence of him working with anyone else. He came to kill you because you got close to unmasking him. It's over. Stop looking for another Vampire to blame."

"Is that what you really think?" she asked, disgusted, hurt and then pissed off at herself for allowing his feelings to matter. Well, her godfather always said the best learned lessons were those involving pain. Apparently her pink parts weren't discriminating, but her brain sure as hell knew what Clive was.

"You've been officially notified, Scion. This isn't over and you know it. I've been doing this long enough to know. That Vampire tonight was *sent* by someone else but if you're too lazy to assert control over your people you'll have to deal with it."

She went to the door and unlocked it. "Be seeing you around."

DAVID GREETED HER when she arrived home. "*Déesse*, the Motherhouse has called twice."

She sighed. A simple phone message wasn't going to be enough. She knew it, but the last thing she wanted to do was deal with a video call after she'd just been tossed over a desk and fucked silly by the Scion.

David hesitated a moment before clearing his throat. "May I look at your face again? I'm concerned about infection and scarring."

He'd held himself together well when she came home covered in blood and the remains of a Vampire she'd dusted. Hadn't been the first time, but despite what the Vampires like Clive wanted to think, it was rare she actually had to kill.

She wasn't sure she was up to being tended just then, though. "I'm going to shower again. I'll come down and call Susan afterward. I promise to let you deal with the gashes then." She managed a smile to reassure him before disappearing upstairs.

Under the spray, with the sound of water rushing through the pipes, she allowed herself to break. The adrenaline of the fight was long used up. The anger at what had happened had burned out. The excitement of the encounter with Clive had bled into confusion and guilt.

Covered in gashes from one of them and she not only allowed Clive to touch her, she'd reveled in it. Goddess, what was wrong with the women in her family? First her mother and the dalliance with Rowan's father that had ended with both of them murdered and now this stupid whatever it was with Clive Stewart.

He was not for her. His reaction to the news and his quick jump to *problem solved* was further proof of that.

She let the tears come, letting that part of her connected to the Goddess take over and wash through her. A sort of sweet, mother-love flowed and soothed her aches. Most of them anyway and that was enough.

By the time she made it downstairs to her office to make the call, she was back on track. David tended to the gashes quickly and efficiently and when he returned from putting the first-aid supplies away, it was with a hot cup of tea and a lemon scone.

She swallowed the swell of emotion and thanked him before turning to the phone.

After midnight in Vegas, but the partners at the Motherhouse in London and their counterparts in Paris would be up several hours before dawn. Hunters worked when the sun went down far more often than when it was up.

Susan's face showed up first on the display, followed

by her husband, Rex, and from Paris, Celesse Blanc, Rowan's original trainer.

"We got your message, Rowan." Susan sipped some tea as she looked through her notes and then back to the screen. "Explain."

She told them the entire story from the trip out to Barstow to her confrontation with Clive. Well, not the sex part, but everything else.

Rex began to work, clicking away on his keyboard. He was the master of the Hunter Archives so she knew he'd be searching on Rossinni as well as looking for any references to the victim or her compatriots.

"We deem this a clean kill." Celesse's voice was smooth, but her past with Rowan wasn't. Still, they'd achieved a decent enough working relationship in the years since Rowan had left Paris.

"The Nation has already communicated this to the partners. The Scion of Las Vegas himself signed off. Good work, Rowan." Susan looked at the screen over the top of her glasses.

Rowan stifled her amusement at how Susan often took on the affectation of an older, mild woman when she was so very *not* mild. Rowan had learned a lot of masks from The First, but it was Susan who'd sharpened Rowan's skills and given her a direction.

"Why don't you think this is the end, Rowan?" Celesse raised a single brow, just ever so slightly. "The Scion underlined his belief that it was."

Yes, and Vampires were so known for their integrity. However, that was not a crack Celesse would suffer lightly. The woman was all business and frowned upon what she thought of as Rowan's bad attitude.

"I am aware Stewart feels that way. But I don't believe he's correct."

"Why do you think you and he are not in accord?"

Susan huffed her annoyance but Rowan needed to handle this herself.

"I believe that he, like most people, would rather take the easy solution than pursue the complicated one. I'm sure he wishes this were the truth and he's taking a gamble it will be." Rowan shrugged. "But I can't afford to live in the land of make-believe. Every instinct I have, as well as common sense, tells me the Vampire sent after me was a ploy, a poorly planned one at that. He was old, but not that old, and not very smart. He died decently enough, but the kill of the White woman was something more than run-of-the mill Vampire violence."

Rowan shook her head once, hard. "Rossinni wasn't the killer. I'll stake my reputation on that."

Celesse studied her for long moments and then sniffed delicately before one of those Gallic shrugs. "I believe you're correct."

"Keep us apprised." Susan shuffled the papers into the file before looking to the screen again. "Thank you for your service, Rowan."

And with that, shc turned the screen off and slumped in her chair.

"*Déesse*, you need to rest."

"I know, I know. Thank you, David."

TEN

THE NEXT MORNING Rowan walked out the front glass doors and headed toward her car. Instead she saw the cab and the life went out of her. *Shit*, Crazy Carl the taxi man.

She looked longingly at her pretty red Porsche and then back to the beat-up cab. Carl grinned and winked beneath the brim of his ratty orange cowboy hat. A grizzled handlebar mustache, the color of mud, punctuated his upper lip. He nearly always wore wrap-around sunglasses but she'd seen his eyes once or twice. Enough to know they were pale, pale green.

"Hey there, Margie! Come on for a ride. I got a few new pieces for you to check out."

She sighed and looked to David, who quickly covered his mouth with his fingers.

Carl hopped out and opened her door as she slid into the backseat of his cab and tried very hard not to stare at the stuffed baby something or other he'd attached to his dash. Whatever the fuck it was, it had a stuffed snake in its mouth. This had long day written all over it.

He got in and peeled out of the drive, swerving on a wide arc onto Las Vegas Boulevard. As per usual, there seemed to be no traffic to impede him until he got settled in to talk.

The whole interior of the taxi held a menagerie of stuffed dead things. Carl, in addition to being some kind of scribe, was also an amateur taxidermist. Stuffed snakes slithered along the backs of the seats, rodents of all sorts danced around and teeth hung from the rearview mirror.

Rowan knew better than to rush him. He'd get to the point in his own time and not a second before. She'd gotten into Carl's cab for the first time six years before and had tried to get right back out when the face of a small coyote leered at her over the seat. Carl had chuckled and locked the doors. He'd also told her, in his own roundabout, rambling way, she'd be staying in Vegas.

And so he showed up from time to time, could be a year between sightings and then three weeks in a row. Carl had his own schedule and his own way of delivering wisdom. While he may not always have been one hundred percent clear, he'd never been wrong.

Rowan didn't know what he was or even who he was, and he never got her name right. But despite her annoyance, she had deep affection for Crazy Carl and respected him, too.

Instead of speaking, he played the soundtrack to *Xanadu* and she knew without a doubt she'd be hearing ELO and Olivia Newton John in her head for days.

They hit traffic near the Mandalay Bay and she leaned back. He turned the music off and took a deep breath. "You got a birthday coming up if I recall."

"Yes. In February." She hoped all this bullshit with Vampire killers would be over by then.

As if he'd heard her thoughts, he spoke again. "Spending time with your kin is important. So many people only get to see one side of you. It's good to remember all your facets. And I never did know any girl who didn't like presents. And you, Carla, well if any lady needed some presents it's you."

Anyone but Carl and she'd wonder if he was insulting her.

He tapped a giant, mean-looking stuffed snake he'd artfully posed dangling from the mouth of the thing on his dash. "I went camping with my youngest last weekend, saw a diamondback. 'Course he—my son, not the snake—was such a pussy, cried like a girl when I grabbed it with the stick and held it out for him to look at. Takes after his mother that way I 'spose. Anyway, it's there right in front of you. Head the size of my boot!" He chuckled and Rowan leaned in slightly to look at the snake for a moment.

"Very nice. I thought your sons wouldn't go camping with you anymore."

"Told them I had cancer. My oldest wouldn't come anyway but the younger one fell for it. Now he's pretty hacked off at me. You'd think he'd have been relieved to know I didn't really have cancer. Stomped back to the car and slept in it all night long."

Rowan met a slice of his eyes just above the sunglasses in the rearview and shook her head at him while grinning. She'd thought her own upbringing was insane but with Carl for a dad? She couldn't imagine how much money those boys would spend on therapy. She'd once asked him why he could have children if he wasn't human and he'd just snorted and called her Mavis for the next hour.

"Well, I'm glad you don't have cancer, Carl. I'm

also glad I never have to go camping with you. I like luxury and the fact that no one shoves snakes in my face at midnight."

"You're no fun. You should come out with me sometime."

"I'll have to take a pass on that. I like running water, expensive sheets and room service. But I'd be happy to buy you a drink or dinner."

"Rhoda, I've been seeing mountain lions just north of the city. You know how rare that is? Still, ya gotta be careful. Even when you think you know the terrain and the animals won't hurt ya unless you hurt them, they're still predators. Predators know one thing. To hunt and kill. Sometimes the only way to deal with that is to hunt and kill them first, even if they are awesome creatures. Can't fuss about anything being what it's meant to be. Can't change it. You can only end it." He paused as if to appreciate the idea as she focused on everything he'd said, and not said.

Rowan's breathing slowed. She wanted to ask him to clarify but she knew he wouldn't. Sages did what they did and there was no cross examination or Wikipedia entry for it.

He met her eyes in the mirror briefly. "Thing about hunting is you have to trust your gut. I expect you know that. Tough girl like you, though, thinks her brain knows more than her gut. Perhaps they've trained you to believe so. Sometimes it's the best way to be. Not now though." He put the car in Park and, startled, she looked up to discover they'd returned to the drive in front of the hotel.

"Here you are, Sally. Have yourself a real good day. Twelve fifty, please."

Shaking her head to clear it, she thrust a twenty at him, and squeezed his hand when he took it. "Keep it."

He grinned. "You're a good girl. Watch your back and don't forget that the closer you are to home, the more dangerous your path gets." He let go of her hand and some tourists glared at her until she got out. Good luck to 'em. Carl turned on the stereo and suddenly Willie Nelson's voice filled the space beneath the awning as he cackled and drove off.

"Is everything all right?" David approached.

"I guess. He said a lot. Some of it I understand. Some I won't until whatever he's warning me about springs on me." She shrugged. "He warned me about the Vampire I'm hunting. So at least he believes I haven't found the killer yet. How long was I gone?" She noticed the sun had begun to set.

"Nearly five hours."

"Oh no! I missed brunch at Thena and Martin's."

"I called them for you, *Déesse*. Ms. Thena told me to inform you they'd make it dinner instead."

"Thank you, David. I'll be going now. Please take the evening off. Tomorrow too. I need to do some work so I'm going to hunker down here for a while."

He smiled, tipping his head in thanks and she took off for Thena's.

"THANK GODDESS those scratches are nearly healed." Thena put more potatoes on Rowan's plate as Martin poured more wine into her glass.

"I'd have gone postal if they'd left a scar. I suppose

carrying holy water around is good for more than just maiming Vampires."

Rowan told them about Carl's ride and briefly about the fight with Clive, *sans* the hot, furtive, guilty sex-on-the-desk part.

"What aren't you saying?" Thena narrowed her eyes.

"He's a self-righteous prick. The Vampire who attacked me yesterday was sent by the killer. This killer isn't going to be stupid enough to come to me himself. You'd think one as old as the Scion would know that. They're his own people, after all. Also he was easy to slay. Hello, this guy I'm looking for is not going to die easy." She shoved half a roll in her mouth and let the carbs soothe her anger.

"They're his people but he's not like this killer. For whatever else his crimes, what I hear is that this Vampire Scion is an honorable sort. For a Vampire anyway. He *would* do his own dirty work, or at the very least hire a decent assassin. But the real question is, why are you so upset he doesn't believe you?"

"What do you know about it?" Rowan glared at Thena.

"Oh I know you're not getting an attitude with me, missy." Thena raised one brow and Martin chuckled, relaxing to watch the interplay between them.

"I'll give you an attitude if I want to." Rowan snorted and swatted away the pea that landed in her hair. "It's the typical Vampire bullshit. He thinks he's so superior with his designer suits and hand-sewn Italian loafers. A human couldn't possibly know more than he does. He's dismissed my opinion—my expertise—out of hand because I'm not a Vampire. I don't tell him how to make investments, do I? He shouldn't tell me how to hunt lawbreakers. We all have our own special skill set. The only way he's going to see the light is when another body shows up and I hate that."

Thena dropped her fork and grabbed Rowan's hands. "You're *fucking* him. Girl, you like playing with fire don't you? Oh my Goddess. Not gonna lie, I've seen his picture and it's not like I can't understand why you'd nail him. How is he? Don't even tell me he didn't make you come and come."

Heart beating wildly, Rowan hoped she didn't look as guilty as she felt. "I am not!" Technically true, as she meant she wasn't going to tell Thena he had, indeed, made her come with barely even a touch of his fingers. Rowan yanked her hands back and wiped them on her pants. Thena wouldn't ever use her magicks to persuade Rowan to share something, not short of an apocalyptic emergency, but she was still intuitive. "Ew! In case you hadn't noticed, he's a *Vampire.* I don't do Vampires."

Gaze narrowed, Thena looked her over and then snorted. "You are so totally lying. But fine, I'll play your game for now. You'll come to me soon enough and then you will tell me every last juicy detail about what he's like in bed. In the meantime, I don't need to remind you how dangerous this could be for you—you know, if you *are* lying, which I know you are, about having fuckytimes with the Scion."

Rowan rolled her eyes but breathed an inner sigh of relief that Thena was letting the subject go. She wasn't ready to think about it much less discuss it with her friend. She didn't want it to be so exciting. Didn't want the memory of how he'd felt deep within her to make her shiver. She should hate him. She should hate herself for not hating him and what his people had done to her and her family.

She couldn't seem to control that. But she could keep her ass as far away from him as possible to avoid a repeat. No matter how much it made her tingle.

ELEVEN

DAMN THE WOMAN. Clive shoved a hand through his hair and clicked the phone shut as he got her voice mail yet again. She'd been ducking his calls for the last six weeks.

He knew she was in town. He'd seen her here and there, heard she'd been checking in on the Vampyre Theater crew. She was avoiding him, plain and simple.

Probably in a snit because he'd been right about the killer being the Vampire she'd slain in the desert. Or maybe because of his ridiculously quick job when they'd had sex on the desk of his office at Fleur.

He sighed at that memory. At his stupidity and lack of control when it came to her. Normally he was far smoother with women, but she tested him sorely. It was certainly her fault he rushed through it all.

Not that it would happen ever again. It was a stupid, stupid mistake, one he would not repeat. But he still needed to check in with her.

He turned his head at the sound of Alice tapping on his door. "Yes, come in."

The look on her face told him he wasn't going to be happy with her news.

ROWAN LOOKED AT the caller ID on her cell phone and sighed. Clive. She'd been ducking him and Jack both for the last month and a half. Clive more successfully than Jack.

Jack hadn't liked what she had to say when she told him she'd tracked down his vic and her family in Barstow. There was a fight. He'd been beyond pissed off that she'd gone without telling him until afterward.

But she missed Jack. Missed his company and having dinner with him. Missed his obsession with NASCAR and basketball. Just missed him plain and simple.

Worse, she'd sort of missed Clive's arrogant British accent and the way he smelled. She was so fucked up.

Giving in, she picked up the line. "What?"

"Oh to hear those dulcet tones again, dear Hunter. You've been avoiding me."

"You're not important enough to me to avoid." Thank Goddess he couldn't hear her heart speed up at the lie.

"Mmm-hmm. Well, as much as it pains me to admit, you may have been correct about Rossinni not being the killer."

"There's been another murder." Her voice was flat as rage, cold and focused, centered her. Suddenly all her tingly bits stopped their dancing and she wanted to kill something.

"Yes. I'm calling you because my people picked up the information on the police scanners. It appears to be the same situation as before."

Before she could give in to her anger and scream at his useless ass over the phone, she simply hung up on him and began to get ready to leave the penthouse.

Her phone rang again but when she saw it was Clive

she ignored it and let it go to voice mail. She wished she'd had the forethought to leave him a special fuck-you message. Maybe later, before bed.

She quickly dialed Mary, her source at the police station, and arranged to meet with her at their usual spot and then Carey to let him know they'd be working late that night and to meet her at the office.

MARY'S FACE WAS pale, even in the reddish tint of the lights of the bar. Pain marked her features, etched into her face.

Here at least, she could ease and help. Rowan sat and drew the other woman's hands into her own. Healing, one of her gifts from the Goddess, would be welcome here. She couldn't turn back time, or save whoever was murdered, but she could offer Mary some solace.

"It must be very bad." Rowan's voice was soft, gentle as she sent her power like a warm caress from her grasp into the other woman.

The tautness of Mary's features eased slightly. "I haven't seen it all. I don't have a lot for you right now because it's still very new. They found the body three hours ago. But it's similar to the other victim. Drained of all blood. But she…" Mary shuddered. "She's been torn up. They're trying to say it was ritual mutilation but, pardon my saying so, I've seen ritual mutilation a time or two and this isn't it. So much rage, Rowan."

"Ripped up? Like with teeth?"

"Her chest was ripped open like last time. But it looks like something took big bites out of her. Something with very sharp canines." Mary looked at Rowan, her fear giving way to professionalism. "You'll find this monster and take care of him." It wasn't a question.

Rowan nodded. "Will you get me the reports when they come in? Was she sexually assaulted? On drugs? Do we know who she is?"

"There's been a rush put on everything. She'd been dead for a day or so they think. I'll call Carey or you when I get everything. The file contains preliminary notes and some scene pictures. It's very near where the last body was found."

"Thank you for your service, Mary. Be well and I hope your pain is lessened. This murder is not on your hands. But I will make sure the monster responsible is taken care of."

Rowan stood, brushing her lips across the temple of the acolyte who'd been such a help.

She tried not to speed to her office where she knew Carey waited for her. She was surprised to see Cindy there on a Saturday. Clearly she'd been out the night before given the hangover face, but Rowan would take any help she could get right then.

Carey's face remained solemn as she briefed him but when Cindy left to go pick up a late lunch he let out a long sigh. "So, bet you're pretty pissed off at the Scion right about now."

"Not that I don't appreciate being right and all, because well, that's a given. But I don't appreciate having another human woman dying at this freak's hands because Clive underestimated me."

But what bugged her the most was how much she wanted, and *needed* to be at the scene right then but couldn't because it would be thick with cops. Rowan would need to wait until the very late night to go, maybe even the following day. The positive was that Mary would get her the rest of the info as it came in. But it wasn't the same as seeing it herself.

Cindy brought the food in, actually pitching in with copying and some basic data entry as they ate. Maybe they should use her more often for help with the investigative stuff. She wasn't entirely useless, though she was terribly lazy. But Carey hadn't been as driven when Rowan first met him either.

BY THE TIME she ended up back at the penthouse it was nearing two in the morning and Rowan was exhausted emotionally as well as physically. So it wasn't a pleasure to see Clive leaning up against her front door looking delicious and like a huge prick all at once.

She looked him up and down. "Why are you here? Do you have a death wish? I'm in a wish-fulfillment sort of mood so that would be win-win for us both."

"You're angry with me. I thought it best to discuss this issue like adults so we could avoid bad blood between the Hunter Corporation and the Nation."

"Ever the master of understatement, aren't you? How about this? I could kill you. I know I'd feel loads better." She walked past him and unlocked her front door. He hesitated at the entrance and she waved him in.

"I did not kill this woman, Hunter."

"Your inaction did. And your ridiculous belief that a human couldn't possibly know more than a Vampire." She moved to her back hall and got rid of her blade and other weapons before returning to where she left him in the living room. She wouldn't need them, it wouldn't come to blood. At least not yet.

"Why must you insist on knowing what I do or don't believe? It's very arrogant."

Rowan snorted, turning to stalk into the kitchen where she headed to get a beer. He wandered in, still haughty. "Want one?" She held a bottle up, mainly because manners dictated she offer, but also to see his reaction to drinking from a bottle.

To her surprise, he nodded. She popped one open for him and tipped her head toward the cabinet, asking if he wanted a glass.

He grabbed the bottle from her hand and took several drinks. "I'm not as uptight as you think I am, human."

"Puhleeze. You're so uptight I bet your boxers are ironed."

"What's wrong with that?"

She burst out laughing and began to make herself a sandwich. "Want one?"

"I've eaten this evening, thank you. Are you going to dance around this murder and talk about the state of my undergarments or can we discuss it like mature people?"

"You're not people. You're a Vampire. And the state of your starched boxers just shows what an uptight, judgmental bastard you are."

"I am not a bastard thank you very much. I know who my parents were and they were married when I was born. I don't deny I am rigid, that's what it takes to run my territory and keep my people in line."

"Oh yeah, so in line they rip poor human women

to pieces and dump them in the desert like they were nothing. Sounds like they're so well behaved instead of animals on the loose. What do you know about it? Tell me everything."

He narrowed his gaze at her and leaned forward, palms against the marble countertop. "It is clear there is a rogue at large. I agree. I have my people on it and I will share what I believe is important enough to share. But I am not a Hunter, it is not my job to do yours for you."

"It was clear six weeks ago too. The only difference today is that another human family has to mourn. Because of a Vampire."

He had the good sense to look away briefly, before he gathered his composure again.

"I came to you and told you you had a problem. You blew me off. And now two humans are dead. *That* is arrogant. Have you seen pictures yet?" Having stabbed that point home, she gave him her back and stalked out to grab the file. Proud of herself, she managed to slide it to him instead of throwing it in his face.

He looked through it and breathed through his nose. The anger rolled off him in waves. When his gaze met hers, she saw his emotions quite plainly. "Sloppy. This Vampire has no control at all. He's exposed us all. I will kill him."

"Not if I kill him first. There are bite marks here and here." She pointed at the picture. "They'll try to blame it on animals postmortem… If you're lucky."

"This messiness…it's beyond dangerous. Do they know who she is?"

Rowan shook her head. "Not as of the time this information came to me. I want to go to the scene but it can't happen today. It'll still be hot out there with cops."

"I tried earlier and yes, it's still filled with law-enforcement personnel. My people are more skilled at concealing themselves. One of my lieutenants is there and will report to me." He held a hand up to quiet her. "Yes, of course, I will share with you what you need to know. Rowan, it was not my intention to have another human die because I didn't trust your perceptions. Despite what you may believe about me, I do not want this rogue to kill any more humans. It's bad for us all."

"That must be why you keep accusing me of trying to find a way to pin stuff on your people just for shits and giggles."

He sighed and stood straight. "Must you be so argumentative when I'm trying to be apologetic? You're a very trying woman."

"Apologetic? I don't know where you were raised, bub, but where I was raised, by a monster no less, I was taught an apology goes something like *I'm sorry.*"

He sighed. She was going to make him say it, infuriating woman. "I'm sorry I didn't believe you. I will reiterate my belief that your intense dislike for my people creates a blind spot within you but I do not believe in this case you are wrong."

She took a healthy bite of her sandwich and plopped her rather delectable bottom on one of the chairs lining the center island. "That's a start, although you should have stopped after *I'm sorry.* The rest sort of negates the apology."

He wrestled a smile. So very hard on the outside and yet, he'd seen glimpses of a softer woman beneath the exterior. It intrigued him, made him want to know more even as he knew it was the very last thing on earth he should want.

"London." He sat across from her and took another drink of the beer.

"Hmm?"

"You said you didn't know where I was raised. I was raised in London. My parents were, *are* natural Vampires."

Surprise lit her eyes. He liked the way it softened her face.

"How old are you?"

"Cheeky."

She shrugged and he tried hard not to notice the tip of her tongue as it darted to gather a spot of mustard on her lip.

"Four-hundred-and-seventy-five more or less."

"Wow, the world has really changed in your lifetime. I remember Theo talking about seeing an aqueduct for the first time in Rome, lit by the moon. It's hard to imagine living in a time before electricity much less a time before running water." She looked up at his expression after her casual use of The First's name.

Pushing away from the island and moving to put her dish in the sink, she laughed with a shrug. "I forgot you people have all this reverence for him and rarely utter his given name. He was just Theo to me."

He heard the emotion in her voice and wondered, not for the first time, about the feelings she must have for the man who raised her and yet had her parents killed. It gave him a chill to imagine what it had been like for her. He rarely mentioned Theo's given name because to name a thing gave it power and the last thing Clive wanted was to invite The First into his life any more than he had to.

And then he paused because he wanted her to tell him. He wanted to know about her life and that was not a good direction.

She moved to stand at the doorway. She stood silent, her back to him for long moments. He didn't speak, sensing something was about to happen, not wanting to ruin it.

Slowly, she turned on her heel and leaned against the doorway. "I'm going to take a shower. Care to join me?"

Surprise momentarily stole his words. "What? You aren't going to goad me into a fight first?"

"I could. I *do* want to alternately smack you or fuck you. But as you did apologize and we both know sex is inevitable when we're in the same room alone for three minutes, I thought I'd kill two birds and take a shower first."

If she'd been nice, or even rational, he might have resisted. But something about her goaded him and that worked on levels he hadn't ever experienced before. Still, it wouldn't do to agree so eagerly right off. "You know this is a very bad idea." Not that he had any intention of stopping it.

"Yep." She turned and left the room.

He sat for a while and thought of the hundreds of reasons why having sex with her again would be disastrous but in the end he rose and followed her scent up a spiral stair and toward the steam coming from a half-closed door.

Their previous coupling had been so fast and furious he hadn't really had the opportunity to take her in. So as he divested himself of his clothes, he watched her through the glass enclosure.

She was long and lean, athletic but possessing the kind of curves a man's heart sped at the sight of. Her long, deep red hair was plastered down her spine as the water from the showerhead pelted her.

Not even looking up when he entered, she kept her eyes closed as she stood under the spray. He did sense a change in her awareness at his presence, the slight speed of her heartbeat.

He saw the Hunter's mark, a brand just above her right hip, balanced by the mark of service of her father's family on the inside of her wrist. A tattooed *fleur de lis* she'd most likely received at the age of eight or nine.

When her eyes snapped open and focused on him, the shock of it lit his every nerve. She wasn't classically beautiful, though her body was. She was striking. She drew the eye because there was something remarkable about her. Her strength prowled just beneath her skin with a raw energy that seemed to charge the air around her. Like Vampires had auras, she had something very similar.

"Decided to walk on the wild side?"

"Shut up and let me wash my back."

Laughing, she moved aside and let him get under the spray. It agitated him that she made him so discourteous. He was usually very solicitous to his sexual partners. Unless he was dressing someone down, he rarely lost his temper and even more rarely lost his control. With this human female, control was a constant battle.

She moved to leave the enclosure but he reached out and caught her about the waist and hauled her to his body. The heat of the water over his skin soothed the intensity of his need for her though not quenching it.

"Not so fast. It occurs to me, Hunter, that my cock has not been in your mouth and the idea appeals to me on two levels. One, how can any man not want his cock in that mouth? And two, with your mouth filled with cock, you can't carp, complain or agitate me."

"You're pretty bossy for a man who wants to put his johnson near my teeth."

"I have a feeling it may be worth my while."

"Come on then. I'm not going to get to my knees on this tile, it hurts."

She got out and tossed him a towel. It was then he noticed the scars on her lower back.

She turned and caught him staring at them. "Don't."

He shook his head, wanting to say more but letting it go. He'd have had scars too if Vampires scarred in all but the direst of injuries. Growing up at the knee of The First would not have been easy.

Instead of speaking, he followed her into a bedroom adjoining the bath. She jerked her head at him, indicating he should climb to the bed and he did.

He most definitely liked the view as she scrambled on after him and got to all fours over him.

ROWAN KNEW SHE taunted danger. Her own people would have a conniption if they had any idea and his people would be equally upset. Perhaps that's what fired her blood at the sight of him there, spread out below her.

Her fingertips followed the curve of his pectoral muscles, down the center of his chest, flirting with the sensitive skin of his belly just below his navel. The warmth of him rose against her body like seductive smoke. Vampires weren't cold unless they hadn't fed but this one had and the shower had warmed him too.

He was beautiful there below her. Eyes devouring her every move. Clive Stewart was confident, arrogant and cock-sure. Goddess help her, it was irresistible. So many men were cowed by her or afraid to fully own their own allure. This man did not have that trouble at all.

Dipping her head, her lips skated over his chest and headed south, scooting her body down as she kissed her way downward.

She meant to tease him, to make him beg but suddenly need rode her hard and she showed him it was very possible for her to carp at him and get the job done too. She was a multitasker.

She continued to move with him in her mouth until she was moved off him and found herself on her back.

A lock of his hair, usually so perfect, had fallen over his forehead, a gleam of feral intensity shone in his eyes as he loomed above her. Why it pleased her so much to muss him up, she didn't know.

He delivered tiny, sharp bites to her breasts and nipples. Not to feed, just for the sensation. His hands roamed over her bare skin, fingertips played over the Hunter's mark on her hip.

She writhed, helpless to do anything else as his mouth skated over her flesh. He knelt between her thighs, keeping her from squeezing her legs together to gain some measure of relief against the throbbing need.

And then he moved to make everything better.

THE BUZZING OF the intercom from David roused her sometime later. She leaned over and watched as Clive padded into the room, dressed and all cleaned up. Stifling her annoyance that she didn't get a chance to work on that neck tic thing anymore, she reached out to hit the call button.

"Yes?"

"*Déesse*, it's the policeman. He's here and he wants to see you. Are you indisposed?"

He must have seen Clive enter. All she could do was hope he just meant cleaning up a dead Vampire or still arguing with him.

"Give me five minutes and I'll let him in myself." Rowan got up and jogged into the closet, pulled on some clothes and brushed her hair into a ponytail.

"Policeman?"

"Yes and he's not one to be underestimated, Clive. He's very sharp and he's the lead on the case."

"Does he know about us?" Clive leaned in the doorway, watching her.

"I told you, I don't violate the treaty. I've done my best to direct him with the first victim but I'd never do anything to make him believe it was Vampires."

He chuckled and caught her arm as she passed. "No, I mean does he know we're…that we've…? Why is he going to think the man who runs the largest casino resort in town is here with you at three in the morning?"

"Goddess, this is not what I need right now." She sighed. "Walking and talking." She went down the stairs first. "Jack and I are friends. Have been for years and yes, some years ago we were more. But that's not what we are to each other now. He's very protective of me though. Frankly there's no way to explain away your presence here or the obvious fact that we've had sex recently. So, let me do the talking. Don't you need to go? The sun's coming."

He laughed again and tossed himself on a couch in her living room. "I can be home in less than a minute and I've got some time before sunrise. I'd like to meet Jack."

"Yeah, I can tell you're a real chatterbox social butterfly and stuff. Don't cause trouble or I'll stake you." She tromped over to the door and opened it, going into the hall to unlock the elevator.

Jack stalked in her door less than a minute later, fury on his face. "What the fuck is going on? There's another body. Of course you know this I'm sure."

He stopped and gaped at Clive, who sat on her couch all elegance and male sexuality personified. "Didn't know you were *occupied*." Jack's words held an edge meant to slice.

"Now you do. Jack Elroy, this is Clive Stewart. He was just leaving."

Clive stood, using that preternatural grace the Vampires had, and held his hand out to Jack. "I can certainly stay for another few minutes to meet your friend, Rowan."

He even managed to sound chiding, the bastard. Or prick since he informed her his parents had been married at the time of his birth.

Despite her annoyance, the memory of the way he'd said it made her smile just a little as she watched the two of them. Hands clasped in a handshake, they were currently engaged in a test of the relative manliness of each other's grip without squeezing too hard.

Momentarily she'd get pissed off at this testosterone-laced pissing contest, but she let them get on with it for a few moments.

"How long have you known our Rowan?" Jack asked, taking his hand back and checking Clive over.

"We've got friends in common but we've *known* each other for several months now."

"Rowan and I go back *years.* I never heard your name before."

"So, not to interrupt this moment or anything, but why are you here at three in the morning and mad at me?" Rowan turned to Jack but not before delivering a glare to Clive.

"I'll wait until your guest leaves. This is police business."

Any minute and they'd be measuring dicks and asking who she liked best. She already wanted to punch them both in the face for being so ridiculous.

There'd be no end to it until she shoved Clive out the door, and in truth, she needed some distance from him. She very much liked the way he looked in her house and she knew her sheets would smell of him too. These were not unpleasant things and they should be.

She could not be sentimental about him, not knowing what he was.

"Clive, I'll speak to you soon. Thank you for coming by." She tried to usher him out but just in the doorway he caught her, pulled her against his body and delivered a devastating kiss that left her knees shaking. Even as she knew what it was—a taunt to the other male in the room—it still left her breathless.

"I'll be in touch. You can bet on it, Rowan." He grinned and strolled into the waiting elevator and slid out of sight as it descended.

Steeling herself, she turned to Jack. "What is going on?"

"Why are you with the guy who runs Die Mitte? This is new."

"Another body?"

"You've been ducking my calls, Rowan."

"Jack, *tell me* about the new body."

"You can't take my calls but you can go on dates?"

She exhaled sharply. "I called you back several times. You can't seem to let go of me heading out to Barstow and the one time we managed to get together for a drink Lisa called and you scampered away. I know you're mad I didn't tell you, but I've explained I can't always share immediately. I've apologized for hurting your feelings and I'll do it again for good measure. I'm sorry. Now that we've reestablished that, will you please tell me about the other body?"

"Don't pretend you don't know. We found another vic earlier tonight. Very similar MO to the last one. You know the one you sandbagged me on until you questioned her family? What has your source told you? I know you have one."

"We already went over that. As far as I'm concerned it's done and I'm not discussing the Barstow thing with you from that angle ever again. As for the rest? My source didn't know anything. I was going to wait until morning and call you to see. I don't know anything more than another body was found with similar patterns to the first."

She sat on the couch and he followed, sitting across from her.

"Rowan, this is serious shit. These women were brutalized. You can't hold back on me."

"I'm not! Jack, do you honestly think if I knew who this killer was I'd not tell you? I want this monster taken out just as much as you do. Tell me what you know so I can help. I *will* help, you know that."

"Drained of blood. Left about a quarter mile from the first body. Same sort of thing only there were footprints, just the ones of the elderly couple who'd been out on a nature walk and stumbled across the body. She'd been dead about twenty-four hours before discovery and we don't think she was killed at the scene. Bites all over her, chunks of her flesh taken out. He must have left her exposed at another scene or sicced an animal on her. We think the bites happened while she was still alive. Sexual activity but again, a condom was used. No positive identification yet but her dental records have been sent out and there's a missing-persons check too."

He pulled a file out and tossed it across the low table.

"Thank you, Jack. I swear to you I'm going to do all I can to take this bastard out. I'll let you know what I find. Go home, you look like hell."

He stood and headed toward the door. "Don't you dare fucking hide any new information from me, Rowan. I'd hate to have to arrest you for obstruction."

She narrowed her gaze. "Fuck off, Jack. Get out and go home."

And she was alone with a file bulging with photographs of a woman who got in the way of something scarier than any horror movie she'd ever imagined.

TWELVE

IT HAD TAKEN another half a day for the cops and forensics people to clear out. She hadn't been able to sleep at all. After Jack had left she'd gotten to work again and before she knew it, it was already midmorning and time to head out to the scene.

The place filled her with dread when she walked through it. Something very, very bad had been on this earth. She bent, closing her eyes, her palms flat where the body had been. The shock of it, of the depth of the horror the woman had faced traveled up and into Rowan's senses with brutal force, nearly making her gag.

She stood, wiping her hands on the front of her pants, ignoring the small furry-animal part of her urging flight from the pain and horror.

The woman hadn't been killed there. But when she'd been dropped to the ground like a bag of garbage, it had only been perhaps five minutes from the time her heart had stopped beating. She'd still been alive during all the ripping and tearing. All Rowan could do was hope the victim had now found peace.

Thankful for the stupid amount of traffic, she headed to the office, using the time to chase away the dread. She'd seen death and torture. She'd *been* tortured. And still, there was something more about this case. What she needed was a paranormal profiler. She could call her old instructor at MacLean, but he couldn't profile a Vampire serial killer. He knew there were people like Rowan who dealt with the big bad unknowns of the world, but what she needed was someone who understood the Vampire mindset.

With an explosive sigh, she pulled into the lot at her office and realized *she* was it. Great.

She couldn't be like the world's premier expert on knitting or what beachside resorts were best. No. Not that.

She got to be the chick from *Silence of the Lambs*, Clarice Starling, only with serial killers who were Vampires.

Yay.

Though a nagging voice in her head reminded her Theo could give her some insight on this. Goddess knew he understood the whys and hows of Vampire bloodlust. She hadn't spoken to him in years. Moreover, she wasn't sure it would be a positive to include him on the case, or back in her life.

"We got an ID on the second victim." Carey didn't look up when she came in, engrossed in whatever he was reading on his screen. She moved to him, grabbing his coffee and taking a drink. "Name's Tricia Gale. Twenty-seven. Two kids living with the paternal grandparents. Worked here in Vegas as a cocktail waitress at The Golden Peacock."

Her lip curled. "The icky place way off the Strip? The one that smells like a delightful combo of pee and vomit?"

Carey laughed. "I see you've been there. That's the

one. She worked there for eight months. Before that she did three stints in rehab starting at nineteen."

Rowan sat on the corner of his desk. "Meth?"

"First time it was Oxycontin. Then crystal meth the last two times. Kids are with Grandma and Grandpa, have been for three years since Mom left them at home alone for four days while she was off on a bender. Dad's doing time for dealing. Wholesome crew."

"Lovely. Have the cops identified her?"

"Yes. Jack Elroy called here looking for you. He said the casino had called after her boss, also her sponsor's husband, went to her apartment when she didn't show up for work twice in a row. Had a key, but didn't need one. Door was open. Blood everywhere. They called it in and ID'd her as the vic."

"I've got to get into that apartment. I'll head over to see. Address?"

Carey handed her a file. "It's all here. All the info I could find on her. It's not pretty. She wasn't really on the straight and narrow, but it looks like she was trying her best. This Vampire, Ro, you need to keep an eye out. Don't let yourself be the next victim."

"Pfft. This fucker is going down. I will stake him myself."

"Don't be cavalier." He stood and took her shoulders. "Baby, this is crazy shit. Like *Natural Born Killers* shit. A Vampire serial killer is a whole shitload of trouble. You're strong and smart and all that stuff, but this Vamp is batshit crazy. Don't underestimate him, it, whatever."

She smiled, unable to be unmoved by his concern. "Thank you. But I know. I do. I'm not taking chances.

I don't anyway, but I get it. Yes, he's crazy and we have to stop him before he exposes them all."

"Might be for the best if they did get exposed. I'm a little sick of being seen as lunch, you know?"

Rowan wanted to laugh. But he was part right.

"What? Aren't you supposed to tell me it's our job to uphold the treaty and keep them hidden?"

"Frankly, I don't know what my job is sometimes." She briefly considered sneaking a cigarette, but she knew she'd get sick because the Goddess wasn't having any of that in Her Vessel.

It was what was best. What kept her strong of mind and body. Her blade must always be sharp. Theo said this, as well. When his *lessons* were finished, he'd patiently clean her up. Tend to her wounds with gentle hands, soothing her with words.

She hadn't understood at first. But he'd made the first scars. Had toughened her up. He'd broken her down and rebuilt her into something far more than human. The first time the Goddess had come to Rowan, she'd been ready.

Of late, she'd wondered if Theo hadn't known her future from the start. He had a touch of farsight. Manipulations and subtle maneuvering would put her exactly where he wanted her to be and she'd never know for sure if he'd done it to help her, or because he was an insane, violent man who did it because it had amused him to do so.

Carey waved a hand before her face, catching her attention. "Scares me when you lose your way."

She took his hand and squeezed, laughing. He wasn't the only one. "My way is not the same as my job. Or the treaty for that matter. My path is predetermined. I serve Her. I serve righteousness and that will always be. If the Nation doesn't deal with this rogue, they'll be exposed. It's most definitely *not* my job to save them from their own ego. If they end up on the front page, it's their doing, not mine."

And still, her gut churned at what a mess there'd be if such a thing happened. Exposure could bring any number of responses, most of them not good for anyone.

A cornered predator was the most dangerous kind.

She'd do what she was born to do. End of story. All the moping and poor pitiful me moments weren't going to change that. She stood. "Now, I'm off to her apartment. I'll call Jack on the way. Keep on it. I want to know where she went to rehab and if there's any connection with the first vic."

"On it already."

"Knew you would be." She paused when she got to the door. "And I appreciate it." That's when she noticed the front desk was empty. Again. "And where the fuck is Cindy? She didn't ask for a vacation day, not that she has any left. I thought she wanted to be more active with investigatory stuff?"

Carey sighed. "She called in sick. To her credit, she did sound pretty bad."

"Next time she calls in sick, you transfer her to me. Sick days are not for when you drink too much the night before, or for every Monday."

ON HER WAY over to the apartment, she put Jack's call on speaker. "Glad you could be bothered to call back."

"Get over it. You're acting like a fucking baby. Do you want to talk to me about this situation or are you going to pout more? I'm too busy to hold your hair while you vomit your issues."

He laughed. "You're such a bitch."

"HBIC, baby, all the way. Head bitch in charge. So tell me about her."

"I'm at her apartment now. Forensics is done and we're sealing."

Whatever. As if that could keep her out.

"Since we both know that won't stop you, I'll wait for you here and then you can take me to lunch."

"Fine. I'm about three minutes away."

Wow, her car did not fit into this neighborhood at all. Then again, no one would touch it, even if they had no idea why. She whipped it into a spot and stepped out, glad she'd opted for her heavier work boots. Stepping on something less than pleasant looked to be a certainty.

Jack waited for her outside the door to the apartment. She took the booties for her shoes, hating that she had to use another barrier between her and the surfaces inside, but understanding the necessity.

"Carey got me up to speed on her basics." She nodded her thanks as she pulled on the gloves and went inside after him.

And then she was glad she had a barrier between her and the surfaces inside.

It hit her, even as she had to pretend it didn't. Something very, very bad happened in the apartment. More than once, she wagered as the impressions were all layered on top of each other. Tricia had fallen off the wagon and had been engaging in some far less-than-safe behavior in this place.

"She wasn't killed here." Rowan bent to examine a blood spatter in the cramped dining space to the left of the equally cramped kitchen.

"Lots of blood for you to say that. Why do you think so?"

"This isn't blood from the murder. It's too old for that. She's shooting the meth up here. Or others are. There's a lot of fluid all over the place. But what was done to her, well that would be a lot messier." She curled her lip. Fluid. Ick.

"Aren't you glad you know what it looks like in a junkie squat instead of filling your head with recipes for meat loaf?" Jack's voice held a tinge of bitterness.

"I hate meat loaf." She stood, not taking the bait. "Tricia here, how long had she been using again? Have you spoken to her family? What about the sponsor?"

"How do you know this stuff?"

"You're a cop, Jack. Surely you figured that out the same way I did. Doesn't take a genius to look at this place and know she was getting fucked up regularly. And more. Was she tricking?" She paused to look at a picture hanging askew on the wall near the bedroom. The bedroom she really didn't want to go into. "She was pretty once."

"Once. Yeah. I spoke to the grandmother already. Grandma says no contact between Mom and kids for seven months. They've never been here. Tricia had been evicted, which tipped her into rehab the last time.

She couch-hopped awhile and then ended up here. The sponsor is ducking me."

"What about the boss? Tweakers aren't known for regular work attendance."

"We processed a warrant for all her records."

Yeah, she'd have a little talk with Carey when she left Jack, to get those records herself. If they were on a computer or could be bribed away, she'd get those records.

"What's up with the sponsor ducking you? There warrants or something?"

"It's bad in there." His voice was easy, a caution without being an order.

Bad wasn't nearly enough for what the bedroom was. Even before she'd completed the first step, it hit her. Blood. Lots of it. Pain. Hopelessness. Rowan dug her nails into her palms, willing her heart to slow and her breathing to regulate.

He had been there, in this small space. *Almonds.* So he was old and it was a he, she felt that too. Though, she bent to touch the bedding, breathing through her mouth now, another woman had been there, as well. A human woman.

They'd started it here. Images pressed against her closed lids. Impressions more than memories. What had been done to Tricia was an abomination. She would rid the planet of this vermin if it took her until the end of her days.

And still she managed to continue to comb over the room.

Jack spoke, jolting her from the vengeance coursing through her. "Sponsors are protective. They don't want to betray confidences and that sort of thing. But… they get tight and I can't think of a single time when a sponsor wasn't willing to do everything they could to help in situations like this."

He burst into movement, shoving a hand through his hair, frustrated. "Like *this*. Fuck. There's never been anything like this and I don't like it one bit that this woman is ducking me. This case is all wrong, Rowan. I can feel it. There's something I'm not seeing. I do know my gut feeling is this sponsor was doing the shit with her, or knew about it at the very least."

Rowan took a deep breath. And that right there was the crux. This was ten thousand kinds of fucked up. How she'd manage to deal with this Vampire and keep the cops from suspecting it was more than just a crazy dealer, she wasn't sure. Thank goodness for media, always playing up the gruesome in day-to-day life. Because of that, she might just make it out of this without any trouble.

She was sick to death of trouble.

"I agree. There's a point when silence stops making any sense. I'll dig and see what I see. She work at The Peacock too?"

"Yeah. First evening shift. Starts at six."

"I'm on it."

"Thanks." It was still slightly sullen, but it felt good to be in sync with him again.

Things got quiet as she focused on the details of the bedroom. The stench of dirty clothing, unwashed bodies, drugs, vomit and all manner of bodily fluid assaulted her.

"Looks like they got started here. Still, there's not

enough blood here for it to have been done in the apartment." She straightened, letting her senses unfurl and take in as much as possible. "Even in this neighborhood, unless our vic was unconscious when he did her, there is no way people wouldn't have noticed a murder like hers being perpetrated next door. The sounds would have been, well, you know what I mean. But he was here I think." Not that she could explain how she knew it.

"There's more blood and chaos than can be explained away, even by the using. And yes, we believe she was tricking." Jack put his arms over his chest and she knew he agreed, but was annoyed she came up with the same opinion so quickly.

Was she one of those humans who trafficked in blood to the Vamps? She'd have to deal with Clive. His people could find out that information far quicker than she could.

"Yes, something definitely happened here. But she wasn't dead when she left here. Whatever was done was finished elsewhere." Rowan moved to the door, needing to escape.

"And I'm wondering if Tricia did her rehab time with Tammy. Did they know each other?"

"You don't have that info already? Are you slacking off?" Jack's smug grin amused her as she kept walking toward the front door.

"Carey has it on the first vic. He had one of them on Tricia here and was working on the other two. But as you and I are here now, I thought I'd ask you. Did they know each other? Our two friends?"

"Lunch first. I'm dying of starvation."

"Fine."

THE COFFEE SHOP was crowded with locals who knew the food was plentiful, and affordable, as well. She and Jack often met there for breakfast or a late dinner so they were ready to order by the time the server reached them with a smile and some iced tea.

"You look tired." Jack had tried, and just missed nonchalance.

She snorted. "Yeah, so do you. But I'm going to sleep for a few hours after this. I have a feeling you'll be working for the rest of the day."

He stared at her for long moments, not speaking. Their food arrived and she began to eat, knowing she needed to, but not really feeling much interest in it. Aside from a nap after doing the mattress mambo with Mr. Vampire himself, she hadn't slept in well over twenty-four hours.

Not getting enough sleep pushed her buttons, took her back to one of Theo's lessons about human frailty when he'd routinely forced her to stay awake for days until she thought she'd lose her mind.

Maybe it was that small still-human part of her, maybe it was a flaw, but she got her fucking sleep and she didn't apologize for needing it.

"So, what's going on in your life these days?" Jack began to mow his way through a very large club sandwich. Not an ounce of fat on the man, but he was built like a tank. It wasn't so long ago that she'd been able to forget just how good he looked naked.

"Started a new workout that's totally kicking my ass. I need to go to the dentist. There's a whackjob on the loose. Same old same old." She knew he wanted to hear about Clive, but unless he asked directly, she was going to make him work for it because she was just that petty.

"When did this thing with whatshisname start?"

"Whatshisname? I don't believe I've seen him since whatsherfoosits was in town. Hey, and how's your delightful lady friend, Lisa, these days?"

He winced and she sent him a sunny smile.

"What's the story with you and Stewart? He's not your usual type." He said it like he had a stomachache.

"Usual type? You mean incredibly handsome, stylish, a great job, oh and a sexy accent?"

He laughed. "Yeah, I guess so. You seem to prefer them more rough and tumble."

A spark of what they'd had in the beginning danced along her skin for a brief moment. It was bound up in their friendship as well, an intensity of connection on all kinds of levels. It was what made them needle each other, what made her laugh, what had made the sex between them rather rough and tumble as he'd so rightly said.

"There's nothing to tell really."

He gave her a look and she laughed. "Really, I swear. He's an insufferable ass. He's not my prom date or anything. We fucked."

"I don't like that guy. What are his motivations?"

"Motivations? Are you worried he'll try to touch me in my no-no places or something? Little late for that. Anyway, you met him for like four minutes. I thought you two were too busy trying to give each other the macho handshake to chitchat much."

"The guy gets to town shortly after you disappear. I can't find shit about him except for generic stuff.

Articles about him in the British press. Plus, that Die Mitte place is hinky. I can feel it."

"You think Die Mitte is mobbed up or something?" Amused, she managed to put a little more gusto into her food. He wasn't that far off from the truth. The Vampire Nation was far better and had been involved in organized crime far longer than any humans had been.

"He's too slick."

"He's all right in his own way. But he's a powerful man. Just let it be. You don't need any part of what he is." Amusement at his jealousy was one thing, but Clive would eat him alive if Jack pushed too far. "Speaking of dislike and insufferable asses, again I ask how Lisa is."

"Just be careful, okay?"

"Always am. I can handle myself, trust me."

"Trust you, yeah." He paused, she knew weighing his words. "Lisa." He sighed. "She's, fuck I don't know. She's all over the place. Right now, this week, things are good."

What was she going to say to that? How could she judge him when she had her own baggage?

He drew his hand through the air. "Enough chitchat. The meth is probably a connection. Our vics were in the same facility, though not at the same time. We're looking into it, to see if they were acquainted another way."

She shrugged. It wasn't that junkies were strangers to crime. It was altogether possible they didn't know each other at all. But it was far less possible their killer wasn't connected to them both via meth.

Which presented a whole new ball of trouble. Or, rather a steaming pile of Vampire shit she'd have to scrape up.

"I'll call you later. After I make a visit to The Peacock."

"Don't hold back on me with this. This is serious shit, Rowan, and I don't want you getting caught in it. This perp is a monster. Creeps me the fuck out. Don't you go putting yourself on his radar. Got me?"

"I got you. I appreciate your concern. You need to watch your back too."

THIRTEEN

THE GOLDEN PEACOCK had never been glamorous in its heyday. There were, of course, many casinos that this could be said truly of, but The Peacock never had a heyday of any sort.

At six-fifteen on a Friday night, the old-school slots filled the air with their cacophony of bells and music. The air inside stank of cigarettes, stale sweat and rotting upholstery. Most likely from the moist heat of a shitty AC system. Which was the perfect backdrop, she was sure, for that lingering stink of urine.

She only barely managed to withhold the curled lip. It actually got easier when she imagined Clive's reaction to a place like this. *Ah, that was better.*

In her head again. Sneaky. She'd left him a voice mail right before turning her phone off and sleeping for four solid hours. Yes, it'd been cowardly, but she wasn't ready to deal with him yet, not after the night before, especially on zero sleep.

She'd kept it businesslike. Told him she expected to know if Tricia had been doing any game with the Vamps. She could have said please, but if she had, he'd have been less pestered and she still had to keep her eyes on the prize. That neck tic had a ways to go yet.

She headed toward the lounge area Karen Fisk ran

and where Tricia Gale had worked under her. A lot of connection to this place and these people. It didn't necessarily mean anything, but it raised some red flags in any case.

Rowan slid into a decent-enough-looking chair, close to the edge of the lounge so she could see the entire floor. Didn't take too long before a server came her way.

"I'm Rowan Summerwaite and I'm looking for Karen Fisk." She said it clearly, holding the other woman's gaze. It wasn't so much a supernatural power as the ability to get into people's attention and give them a direction. A slight bit of hypnosis. Vampires were masters at this, which was why part of the treaty was keeping them in check with who and how they used it.

Still, she learned it from them. Learned how to avoid it too. One of the more useful skills she'd gained as a child.

"I'm Karen. What's this about?"

Rowan used a variety of tactics when dealing with witnesses. Usually she went for the soft push at first. But this woman, no, this woman felt wrong. Soft would be useless with this creature with her flat eyes and her tight mouth.

"You know what it's about."

The woman's spine curved slightly before she squared her shoulders. "I don't know anything about what happened to her. She worked here. She was trying to keep clean."

"When was the last time you saw Tricia?"

"I got work to do."

"There's no one in here but the three drunks at the

bar. They're fine. But Tricia isn't and I can't figure out why it is you won't help her."

"She worked a shift four days ago." Karen licked her lips, eyes roaming, never staying in one place long. Rowan sincerely hoped Karen wasn't a gambler because she was a horrible liar.

"And that was the last time you saw her?"

"Didn't I just say she worked a shift four days ago?"

"Yes, but that's not an answer to my question. I'll ask it again, you know, in case you're confused. When was the last time you saw Tricia?"

"Like I said, I saw her when she worked that last shift."

Rowan sighed, cocking her head to take Karen Fisk in more fully. The woman had lived hard. That much was clear in her face. She looked easily fifteen years older than her thirty years.

The way she ducked Rowan's question told her more than the file had. She'd seen Tricia after that shift. She'd technically repeated the truth that Tricia had worked that shift four days ago, and that she'd seen her then. But she had neatly ducked the real question. Like a pro.

Karen here wasn't unfamiliar with lying or being questioned by the cops. And, unless Rowan's senses were wrong, Karen hadn't been a very good sponsor. The Goddess felt it, knew the muddy stench the woman poured from her pores was the same as Tricia's.

"Police report says your husband is the one who reported the scene at her apartment. You weren't there?"

"No. I was here. Working her shift because we were short-handed."

That much was true. But it also made Rowan wonder just why Karen hadn't accompanied her husband. Had she been unworried because she knew Tricia had been back on meth? Or because she knew the scene would be horrible?

"How long had she been using this time?"

"She hadn't. She was clean. She wanted to get her kids back. Talked about them all the time." What an automatic response. Karen was not the brightest bulb in Vegas, that's for sure.

Even if she wanted to, Rowan was sure she'd never have been able to hold her smirk back. "Really? What are their names?"

Karen froze and Rowan allowed a slight rise of her right eyebrow for the briefest of moments.

"I'm bad with names."

"Meth's bad for your brain, Karen. Now, why don't you talk to me about when Tricia started using again? Hmm?"

"I don't know what you're talking about." She tried to resist Rowan's hold, but she couldn't. She wasn't strong enough. The weak were the easiest to manipulate.

"Don't insult me any further." Lightning-quick, she grabbed the woman's wrist and held fast. "When did you see her last?"

Rowan pushed some of her power into the other woman, underlining her point.

"Night before last. She—she came in to get an advance."

"Did you give her one?"

"Bob did."

"Is there surveillance camera footage?"

Karen's mouth opened and closed a few times. Rowan opened her bag and slid the picture of what Tricia looked like in the desert, torn to shreds, across the table. "This is what happened to her. I know you're scared to tell me. You're afraid of whoever, or whatever did this to her. I'm trying to stop it, do you understand? Listen to me, Karen, I am trying to find this monster and put him down. No one, you least of all, will be safe until that's done."

"No footage. Bob got rid of it when Tricia went missing."

"Was she alone?"

Karen's brow furrowed. "I can't remember. I don't know. No, probably not."

"Who's her dealer?"

"She was going to score open air."

At that point, the hair on the back of Rowan's neck stood and she broke her gaze with Karen to find Clive watching from a slot machine nearby.

"Karen, what are you doing? Who is this?"

A pale, sweaty man stormed over. In the back of her consciousness, she knew Clive was flanking what had to be Bob Fisk, Karen's husband. The energy the two of them put out settled all around, sending those playing on nearby slot machines off to perches far out of range.

That connection of purpose, and maybe even of existence, zinged through Rowan's system.

Bob's eyes widened a moment as Rowan stood.

"Sit down, Bob. We're just going to have a quiet talk." Clive eased up to the table, a hand on Bob's shoulder guiding him into a seat. His voice was smooth. Calm and thick, like cream. It gave her a shiver.

"Karen was just telling me if Tricia was alone when she came here for money on the night she died," Rowan took over. Clive wasn't supposed to be breaking the rules this way, but like she did with other kinds of infractions, she applied common sense. They needed the info, he'd plant a powerful suggestion that they go to the cops to tell them what they knew and they wouldn't remember a thing about Rowan.

"No." He hesitated and shook his head. "Yes, yes she was alone. I think."

Rowan's gaze slid to Clive. He nodded slightly. There'd been some sort of tampering here, just like with Karen and the waitress.

Clive sat and listened to the humans talk. Watched Rowan's sharp gaze flick over the two, knowing behind it, her brain ferreted through information as fast as his.

There was no way he could hold even the smallest room for doubt. Another Vampire had done some pretty deep memory work on these two. Clive couldn't hold out even the tiniest of hopes his people weren't involved.

Moreover, he found himself admiring the way she worked, the subtle directions she pushed the Fisks as she attempted to make her way around the blank spots.

Her mind was razor-sharp. Her control excellent. He wished any of his team had half her skills. He saw The First all over her. He found himself wanting to collect her. Something he hadn't felt in centuries.

Avarice aside, by the time they'd finished up, he found a whole new level of respect and, he couldn't deny, slight awe, for the Hunter, and most definitely for Rowan Summerwaite.

He wiped the memory of their being in the casino and had Bob bring them the surveillance video of their visit as well before he escorted Rowan, her elbow in his hand firm enough to keep her in place, out the front doors. He knew she'd be heading out to the location Karen Fisk had indicated Tricia may have purchased drugs in the past.

A shiny red Porsche zipped up and stopped a little hard. She growled and sent the valet a look of such violence he shrank back and refused a tip. On the other hand, Clive found her little moments of violence fascinating. Liked the danger she exuded.

"You're still here why?" She yanked her elbow from his grip. Though she did have atrocious manners. Like a monkey.

"I'll need a ride." He got into her car, impressed with the luxury inside as well as out. "I considered this model last year."

"Huh. You have to be out of your mind to think I'd take this car to an open air blood-and-drug market. Or a *GQ*-looking Vampire for that matter." She whipped out into traffic, he suspected as fast as she did just to needle him.

"I have other vehicles at my request. I'll phone ahead and arrange one."

"No. I'll drop you at Die Mitte. I'll let you know what I find out. The parts you need to know that is."

"Who are you to decide this?"

"You told me the exact same thing just yesterday. Goddess, you are a baby. Why are all the men I know total babies?" She spoke to herself, as if he weren't even there.

"I am not a baby. Has it ever occurred to you that you're a singularly vexing person? That perhaps it's not the men you know, but you?" He sniffed, indignant.

Her grunt told him what she thought of that suggestion. "Why am I driving you anyway? I wouldn't be sitting in shitty traffic with a woman who thought about staking me every ten minutes if I had the power to fly my ass home in a minute."

He ignored that part, redirecting her around why he was there. He wanted to continue to pretend he didn't know either. "By the by, I do not appreciate being placed in the same company as your police officer. I assume he's the one I smell on that…article of clothing in the floorboard."

She looked down and the car didn't swerve even a fraction. As he'd suspected, she had excellent reflexes so her little stunt as she pulled onto the street had been deliberate. Provocative woman.

"Oh that's where it went. If you don't want to be referred to as a baby, don't be one."

He waited for her to explain why the policeman's clothing was there but she didn't.

"How'd you know I was at The Peacock anyway?"

"You're quite welcome for the help." Even *he* would have been hard-pressed not to mock the peevish tone he took.

"I could have handled that. I do handle stuff like that all the time. This time I got out without bloodshed. That's a good day. The backup was helpful, though I should warn you to keep the thrall to a minimum in the presence of the Hunter, I hear she tries to pin all sorts of things on poor innocent Vampires who are walking the elderly across the street or to church every Sunday."

She wiggled her fingers, winking at a male in the car next to theirs who'd been staring.

"Must you always do such things? I'd think part of your job would be to keep a low profile." Insulted by the human male's audacity to stare at a woman in another man's presence, Clive slid the tip of his tongue over the sharp edge of one of his incisors. He ought to snap the man's neck for such liberties.

"I can hear you grinding your teeth over there. What's crawled into your sharp-fanged craw now? Jealous of that little dingus in the car next to us?"

"I can't imagine how much The First enjoyed these tangents of yours." Once he'd said it, he regretted it. Fencing with her was one thing, being an ass was another.

Her mouth hardened for a brief moment before she shrugged. "He's big on small talk. Eats too many Cheez Doodles and watches the soaps on satellite. He gets that orange stuff on the upholstery and everyone rushes to scrub it off when he's resting."

She burst out laughing, he knew, at the way he'd recoiled.

"You should come up to my apartment. To fill me in on everything. I'm sure my people will have some information by now." He had no idea why he'd said it, but it was out there, hanging between them.

One of her brows rose. "You know what will happen when we get alone. Have one of your people email the data my way. That'll be best."

Well, of course he did. She said it as if he were unaware of the chemistry between them.

"You speak like a virgin maiden afraid to be ravished. I believe I can control my base urges." He examined his cuticles. "Unless you can't."

She sighed, bordering on a growl. The delight at ruffling her demeanor should have filled him with shame.

"I'm woefully under-informed. You left a brief message and of course I'd like to hear your thoughts on what happened at The Peacock."

Her brow furrowed as her mouth tightened. Just a brief movement, flashing her annoyance and consternation. The predator in him perked up, senses heightened at their exchange.

"Fine. I have an hour or so."

She stopped at a light and he stepped out as if he were not mad and in the middle of the street. "As you noted, I am gifted with flight. I will see you at Die Mitte." He tipped his head and slammed her door, walking up the crosswalk.

She knew he'd blink out of sight when he wouldn't be noticed.

Was she supposed to not know he was leaving now so he wouldn't be seen driving up with her? Truly, his arrogance was astounding, even for a Vampire.

Snorting, she changed lanes and headed home. She needed to send a report to the Motherhouse. Most likely, Carey would have ferreted out some new data, so she'd read that too.

And Clive could just wait until he figured out she'd just sent him the finger. Plan Neck Tic continued apace. Ha!

It was better she be alone anyway. Because the situation was so precarious she needed to do some thinking.

Closed in on all sides by this case, she changed course once again and headed out of the city.

The drive helped her begin to process all the threads of the case. The meth thing, well that was something she could easily work with. Nothing supernatural about drug addiction. The cops saw drug-related violence all the time.

Which was a point in her favor when it came to the next and far more worrisome step. This *wasn't* a crazy tweaker who'd be able to be arrested and incarcerated.

This murderer was a Vampire. An old one at that, and working with a human accomplice of some sort. *So* not something the cops in Vegas, or anywhere for that matter, saw at all.

Jack wasn't stupid. He knew the cause of death wasn't right. Knew it was something altogether unnatural. He'd expect her to know that too.

So then what? Where did that leave her?

Fighting the bitterness of resentment, she knew it was right to be there in this place so very far away from the city and her life there. Knew she'd get guidance here that'd help her find her center while surviving the assault of the anger that came. Feeling trapped, in over her head, out of control.

She parked, knowing the Mother-Acolyte would be there on the porch, waiting for her.

Rowan knelt and opened herself up fully to what she was. It hurt, sharp and bright, as the Goddess and all her aspects filled her, stretching as that energy took over and shoved out all else.

Greater calm brushed against her as the mother touched her head and bid her to stand.

"You need to visit with her." She took Rowan's arm. "Come inside. See her and then stay for dinner."

As she descended into the cool, toward the altar, Rowan let the ritual take over. Left it to her muscle memory to wash and kneel, to prepare and then to let go and ascend as the sound of the bell still rang in her ears.

But it wasn't her mother who awaited Rowan's ascent. It was, for want of a better way of expressing it, the Goddess herself. Though She was always a presence inside Rowan's heart and mind, She didn't often face her like this.

In fact, there had only been one other time in Rowan's life when this had happened. When Brigid had shown herself to Rowan outside. Vibrant and fierce, maternal and beautiful, so many things at once.

There were no appropriate words for what it was she looked at. So much light and energy. Intense and powerful enough that fear edged around awe and love.

Rowan lowered her eyes but before she got to her knees, She said, "No, Vessel, stand as your position demands. You walk a fine line just now, don't you think?"

Brigid sounded a lot like Shirley Manson—well, a more Irish than Scottish Shirley Manson, but the impression was there. The wisps of words Rowan heard from time to time, cautioning, urging or even chiding, had always carried the singer's features in her imagination.

"Goddess, I'm hemmed in. The Vampires have so far failed to deal with this threat. Another human woman has been murdered. The signs at the scene are not typical. They're not even extremely atypical of a murder scene.

"There are some troubling associations with a narcotic. For the police, it may be enough to keep them focused on so I can go around the more paranormal aspects of the case."

"But if the Vampires are involved in this human narcotic, what is their reason?" Rowan nearly saw one shoulder rise.

"They can't imbibe narcotics directly to achieve a high. Their wine is filtered through blood. There are some narcotics they can use via blood as well. Usually prescription medicines like Vicodin or Valium. It's the only way they can be medicated to have major medical work done. Which is so rare it's mainly only Vamps on the verge of death anyway so the risk is relative."

She paused as it hit her.

"So clever you are, Rowan."

"I apologize for wasting your time, Goddess." She bowed her head. So stupid, she should have figured this out already.

"The weight you carry can be heavy. No one makes it heavier than you yourself do."

Rowan had no words to deny this. Which only made her feel worse. "I am honored to be your Vessel. I only want to do what is right."

"You are uncomfortable in your role sometimes. You doubt the path you were set to walk long before you were born."

"I don't doubt my path, Goddess. I doubt my ability at times, but never my path."

"You are afraid, Rowan. And do you know what that means?"

She shook her head.

"It means you're no different from any other person faced with the same weight of duty you are. You're afraid because you deal with things that are frightening. Unnatural and wrong things and you do it all without anyone knowing you are taking the risk every day."

The Goddess began to pace.

"And yet, none of that matters." She faced Rowan again. "Your gift, and your curse is to be singular. You are special, Rowan. Special people guide the course of time."

Not that she'd asked for it.

Brigid waved a hand. Oh yes, they were connected deep enough to hear thoughts.

"What you are not, what you cannot do is meaningless because you will never be anything but what you are."

Rowan blinked quickly, smarting from everything Brigid had said. Every bit of it true.

"You would not be my Vessel if you were not worthy. That this is a trial is nothing you or I can change. You are what you are destined to be. To doubt yourself is to doubt me. You wouldn't dare such a thing, would you?"

Was she *teasing?*

"Never."

"Imbolc is fast approaching."

Guilt burst through her again. Presiding over Imbolc wasn't just something in her datebook. It was integral to her role as Vessel. But these killings were also part of her job, part of her role and it tore her up.

"That you feel so deeply about these women who've been so horribly used and killed as well as your place as my Vessel is more evidence of how seriously you take your path. I am pleased and proud."

"How can I leave the country with all this crashing down around me?"

"You are many things and yet one. Events are set into motion sometimes so far in advance, with such a small thing it is impossible even for one such as I to comprehend all the intricacies of fate. You are meant to go to Ireland for your birthday. For my day. Trust me and your path."

These words lifted weight from her shoulders. The fear of making the wrong choice.

"Thank you."

"I do not like to see you struggle so. It is my path to help guide you with yours. And so now I will tell you to leave here. I can feel how anxious you are. With this Vampire…another walk on a knife's edge. There is darkness, but then there always is, always has been. Balance is important."

And with a deep breath, Rowan stood on the stones again, Brigid gone, the fire in the altar low.

"I just totally got pwned by a Goddess," she muttered, still smiling.

FOURTEEN

ROWAN DIDN'T BOTHER with the valet. She had no intention of giving Clive Stewart any notice she was on her way. At least until she got inside the hotel.

She was angry at herself for not getting it earlier, but she sure as hell did now. This Vampire was using humans to get high. They'd broken through and found some version of crystal meth that Vamps could get high from. Until that point, they hadn't been able to use any street drugs but pot. She didn't know why, but she had no issues with it. Stoned Vampires just sort of sat around looking at the stars and stuff. They didn't rip people to shreds and leave them in the desert. But meth? What about heroin or cocaine? What happened when a Vampire ran out of money and needed a fix?

Such things fell under the designation, *very bad.*

Glad she still had her ass-kicking boots on, she motored up to the private elevators. The attendant looked her up and down.

"This is a private elevator. Guest room elevators are around the corner."

"Good to know should I ever actually stay. But I need this elevator to reach Clive Stewart. Go ahead and run along to tell him the Hunter is here. I'll wait."

She turned her back on him, dismissing him entirely.

If he didn't hop to it, she had a great deal of tension that needed working out. Punching someone a few times was always a great stress reliever.

Cheered, she turned as the elevator doors dinged open. His real personal assistant stepped out, looking even more pressed and steamed than her boss did. Until that moment, she'd thought it a feat totally unachievable.

"Ms. Summerwaite. I'm Alice, Mr. Stewart's assistant. Please, come with me. He was expecting you earlier, but got called into a meeting."

Rowan followed her into the elevator.

"I've taken the liberty of having some food delivered. I hope you don't mind. I imagine, given the report he just gave to his people, that you might need a few minutes to collect yourself and perhaps to rest and recharge."

It was hard not to appreciate Alice's thoroughness. But not overly difficult to remember what she was. And what they weren't. But Rowan did have manners, no matter what the other woman's boss thought.

"Thank you. Please inform him I will wait no longer than five minutes."

"I'll let him know." Alice smiled, just a brief flash. Rowan wondered if Alice gave Clive a rasher of shit and bet she did.

That amused her enough to settle in at the pretty and elegant seating area near the windows. She hadn't eaten in a while, not since lunch with Jack over twelve hours before. No harm in having at least two of those little tea sandwich things Susan loved so much.

She'd planned to have dinner with the acolytes,

maybe even spend the night at the ranch. She had a room there. They'd give her privacy. She'd be safe and taken care of and just for a few hours she could relax and let herself be. The lure of it had driven her out there in the first place.

But, she thought as she sipped the lovely mango juice Alice had provided, Brigid had been right. Once she'd come back to herself, she knew she needed to confront Clive.

Annoyance that she left behind peace and calm to come back to this mess of blood, politics, sex and violence was a fire she tried to ignore. It would do her no good to punch him in that perfect nose. Though she'd feel better for a little while.

She snorted. His five minutes were up. Heaving a sigh, she gave in and gobbled up several more of the smoked-salmon-and-cucumber sandwiches before she made to leave. She'd made it to the elevator right as he exited.

"Where in the hell did you hie off to? You were supposed to come right back here." He had the audacity to look cool and collected, even as he was being a total dick.

"Excuse me? Is there a dog or a cat in here you're speaking to? Because we both know what a terrible disaster it would be for you to ever talk to me like that."

His pupils swallowed the color in his eyes and she had to work to hold her ground. Their energy, like a live thing in the room with them, sinuously made its way around them.

"And then you come here and summon me," he continued as if she had said nothing. "I'm not a fan of being summoned, Ms. Summerwaite."

"Who cares what you're a fan of? How about you stick your shitty behavior right up your ass? Why didn't you tell me?" Annoyed, she stepped up to him, knowing how stupid it was, she did it anyway.

"Tell you what? What are you on about?"

"Are you stupid? Really? Because the only way I could possibly believe you don't know what I'm talking about is if you were stupid. You knew. You fucking asshole." She resisted shoving him, only barely, by turning on her heel and giving herself desperately needed distance.

"You came here six hours late to insult me?"

"You're not my boss, or my business manager. We'll get to that part in a bit. Back to why you're a total peen. You knew. You. Knew. How long have Vampires been getting blood highs from crystal meth?"

He sighed, heavily, and pinched the bridge of his nose. "This is Vampire business."

"Dead human women are Vampire business now? Oh good, I'll just send Jack your way the next time your little friend gets to work. I have a birthday trip to plan, I'd much rather be doing that than hanging out in meth-town messing up my manicure."

"You know what I mean by that."

"Maybe. Turns out I don't care either way. 'Cause, in case you forgot, I have a business too. It's to kill Vampires who make human women dead. This was something I needed to know."

"Why are you making this personal?"

She looked around the room and then back to him.

"Are we on a reality show? Next you'll tell me you aren't here to make friends. Then you'll drink too much, have sex with a stranger in your hot tub and puke. Maybe you and I can have a spat about how you never wash the dishes."

"What *are* you talking about?"

She made the time-out signal with her hands. "Don't pretend you don't watch all those skeezy shows with floozies and himbos. Anyway, about your astounding behavior. Can you honestly stand there and say this stuff to me with a straight face? This is key information! I have wasted time and effort I could have better used to take this Vampire out. You let me twist, all the while knowing and not telling me. There aren't words to describe how stabbity this makes me."

"I only got this information recently. Before the second murder. I have a request in to be heard by the Council about it. So I could share it with you."

"Excuses. I know you're powerful enough to give him a call directly. I also can bet he told you to help me out. You're wasting my time, dicking me around with this stupid shit."

"You know as well as I do, there are processes. I can't just give you everything. My people distrust you. I have to go through all the steps."

"And to think I had actually achieved a mental place where I could exist without driving a stake into your chest." Muttering, she stalked past him to the phone. She dialed the number she knew by heart and waited.

"This is Rowan Summerwaite, I need to speak to The First."

Clive made contact with her shoulder. That was his

mistake, but one she gleefully took advantage of, taking his hand and bending his wrist back, hard enough to make it hurt.

He moved away with a snarl, his incisors gleaming. Her mental illness sent a thrill through her. It was the only way to explain why every time the man showed his true nature she liked it. If she wasn't on the phone, she'd probably have done something totally inappropriate like kiss him. Or worse.

"What is your problem?"

"You are. Don't touch me or I will rip that arm off and use the stump to fuck your face up. Asshole."

"Ah, hello there, petal. How are you, sweetest?" The amusement in his voice was clear. "Who is this asshole and shall I help you fuck his or her face up?"

Both Rowan and Clive sprang backward, away from the other at the sound of Theo's voice coming over the line.

Petal, good Goddess, it had been a long time since she'd heard him speak to her in any affectionate sense. She missed him, even as she hated him, he was, despite it all, her father. Closest thing she'd ever have to one in this life anyway.

"Thank you for speaking with me." Father or not, even Rowan didn't mess around with Theo and his status. She feared very few people; he was at the top of her list.

"I am always available when you need me. What do you require?"

"I am attempting to keep the Nation from exposure, but am currently facing difficulties gaining all the information I need."

He laughed, rusty and sharp at the edges. "Do you expect otherwise? Why should we help the Hunters police us?"

She bit back her first response, which she doubted he'd have seen the humor in. *"Vater."* She swallowed, hard. Control was the only way to get what she wanted with him. If he made her lose it she came to him with nothing.

In her mind's eye she saw him. He'd be sitting in his favorite chair near the windows so he could look out at the world as he pleased. So very unearthly. Flawless. Pale, pale as moonlight skin, though his hair was still blond. His eyes were an unexciting sort of brown, but as bloodlust hit, their color deepened to port.

He'd be amused, it was why he remained on the phone with her. That and she knew he missed her too, in his own way. But also quick to cut her off and side with Clive.

"It is my job, the job of a Hunter to deal with Vampires breaking the treaty. Treaty notwithstanding, this Vampire's manner is so out of control, so openly *Other*, the risk of exposure is very high. I am not asking for this information without a pressing reason. Delays will only harm the interests and safety of the Vampire Nation."

He was quiet, she knew, half daydreaming and half playing over the issues.

"Is my Scion there?"

She knew Clive could hear every word of the conversation, not that she'd planned to lie.

"Yes. I'm standing in his, whatever you call this giant receiving room I'm sure no one ever uses."

Theo found this outrageously funny. For him, funny and insane were kissing cousins, so she always tread carefully, especially when he laughed. "Put me on speaker, or whatever it is that will allow me to address you both at the same time."

She sensed, rather than heard or saw, Clive's sigh. She merely rolled her eyes at his annoyed glare.

"I'm here, Sir."

Rowan did take a second to admire the way he presented himself.

"The Hunter has made a powerful case. What is your perspective?"

"Politically, this has the potential to be explosive. Our people here do not like her. She recently staked one of their own. They feel persecuted."

"They are as dumb as sheep. She should have staked the whole city, cleared the streets before you came in."

Rowan knew better than to celebrate just yet, but she did raise a brow, not looking at Clive, but knowing he saw.

"And still, you are right to keep such things in mind. Give her the information on my order. I will bring it up to the Council once this call is concluded. You will have their official response by the time you awaken tomorrow. If they believe I am playing favorites, they are correct. And yet, please do suggest your people contact me if they have concerns."

Ha! Not so much.

Clive's spine snapped rigid at the threat. "As you command. I will transfer the information to her immediately. We are sorry to have intruded."

"You might be, but Rowan isn't." His laughter made

her smile. "And I'm not either. It makes me very happy to hear your voice, Rowan."

Rowan bowed her head, revealing her wrist and her family mark.

Clive would have had to be made of stone to remain unmoved at the elegance in her submission.

The First couldn't have seen it. She did it automatically, like muscle memory. And yet, the weight of it was a tangible thing.

"Thank you."

The connection was severed and she took a deep breath. He watched as she put herself back together.

"Before you start a fight and the warm glow of this feeling evaporates under the bright glare of your bitchiness, I will tell you I found the way you presented yourself to him rather impressive."

She softened, just a tiny bit, before sliding her armor into place once again. "You give the best compliments. Now, let's get this done because I do not want to be here any longer than I have to be."

He'd made an error, not giving her the information. He knew that, but he had no choice. He wasn't overstating the trouble there would be if she appeared to be getting special treatment.

And yet, he'd done damage to their relationship. Or whatever it was they'd had. "Fine. You stood me up."

"You got out of my car because you didn't want to be seen arriving here with me. Now, I understand that, and had you simply spoken to me about it instead of your silly charade, I might have met you here."

"Had you not stood me up and then went over my head to my boss, your foster father I hasten to add, I might have told you that I was making the strongest recommendation to the Council that we share this information with you."

"Fine. Don't expect me to not be hot about this. Moving along. Spill."

"I received a report about the recent surge of Vampires who'd cracked the recipe for meth and had finally turned on the switch allowing them to get high from the blood of a human user. I put some people on it but all they found were several Vampires who'd binged and then fried. They were shells. Nearly dead. None of them appear to live very long." And his people had taken carc of any who weren't already dead. His vengeance had to be swift or he'd be the one being punished.

"Or so you thought. Who's the supplier and why isn't he dead yet?"

"Why don't we sit instead of having this tedious discussion standing?"

"I'm not here for a tea party, Scion. In case it hadn't occurred to you, I have a murderer to find and stake before the cops find him and suddenly I have to deal with the body count *and* the television cameras."

"My men are on this. He can't go very far. And the next time he makes a mistake, I will be there."

"The next time he makes a mistake means he's killed another human. That's a pretty unacceptable loss."

"What is it you want?" He shoved a file at her. "I've given you all the information I have. My best people are on it. I'm doing all I can. And yet you want more."

She sighed, running her hands through her hair. "I do. Do you know where his nest is? Or who the Vampire who cracked the code is? Have you questioned anyone?"

"It's all in the file. My lieutenant has made detailed notes on everything. We don't know who it is or where his nest is."

"He's old and working with at least one human."

"Yes. You knew this?"

"I'd planned to share it with you when we were alone." One brow slid upward.

Like a madman, he stepped the last inch between them and pressed his mouth to her forehead, impeding the movement of that ridiculous eyebrow.

The sound he made echoed against hers. That deep, full-body compulsion to do something even though you knew it was absurd.

He kissed her temple, over her ear. Her skin warmed as her scent ripened. Her power, whatever it was that came off her in waves, danger, violence, control—she was ruthlessly driven and it perfumed her skin. Nothing had ever caught his attention the way she had.

The heat of her blood pulsed with so much energy, Clive felt it as his lips brushed against the hollow just behind her jaw.

Her fingers left a butterfly of a touch against his side. He shivered as she caressed the curve of his ribs. Hissed when she dug her nails into his biceps as he licked over her jugular, teasing himself senseless with what he knew he'd never have.

In this, with his hands sliding up and over her breasts, with the indrawn breath and the exhaled sigh, with their mouths on each other, they were in sync. No tussling for control, no arguments. He was completely sure he wanted her. Equally sure she wanted him just as much.

One-armed, he picked her up around her waist, hauling her to him to take her mouth as he moved to his bedroom. He kicked the door closed, throwing the locks he used during the day as he rested.

His bedroom. Intimate. Vampires didn't allow many people into the place they slept. A French winged bed dominated the space. Sumptuously upholstered in a deep-as-the-ocean blue, it complemented the slate-gray walls and black-and-chrome accents. Luxuriously appointed, it was also classic and elegant.

This was the bedroom of a man who liked his sleep. All Vampires were hedonists. Every one she'd ever met had at least one thing they indulged in for the pure pleasure of it.

Clive Stewart may have been a control freak, tight-assed, all-business Scion outside this room, but here was where Clive the man lived.

He put her on the bed and stepped away while she got rid of the boots and he kicked off his shoes.

Rowan obliged, helping as he pulled her sweater up and over her head. Her bra followed. She liked the way he undressed her. As if he was warring between a need to see her naked and being a gentleman. But when he pulled his shirt off without bothering to unbutton it, as the sound of buttons hitting the bed and floor fell around them, all she could do was shiver at his loss of control.

He raised gooseflesh in the wake of his lips as they cruised from one nipple to the other.

"You smell of magick," he murmured against her belly.

None of that belonged here. She pulled at his hair to move him again and he went back to work, kissing her hip while he made quick work of her pants and panties.

And his mouth was on her, his tongue doing all sorts of delightful things. His hair cool and soft against the skin of her inner thighs. He drove her toward orgasm at a relentless pace.

When it came so hard her back bowed from the bed, his mouth still on her, she may have pulled his hair a little hard, but he didn't seem to mind as he wasted little time scrambling up her body, fitting the head of his cock at her entrance and pressing in slowly.

All there was was the slide of flesh against flesh, flex and bunch of muscle, slick, sweat-sheened thighs against hips and ass. His eyes went emerald, glittering with the desire to take her blood.

But he kept that control, even as that roguish lock of his hair dared to fall against his forehead.

His body was a thing of beauty. Lean, hard muscle hidden by the tailored clothing seemed a delicious secret. He certainly knew what he was about. He'd put those hundreds of years to good use, honing his sexual skills to a sharp point.

His sexuality was instinctually connected to hers in a way that unsettled her even as she couldn't seem to resist it. He knew what she liked, pushed her boundaries all while playing her every instinct like a magician.

He wasn't afraid he'd break her; he touched her exactly how he wanted. It was so bold and sure in that supremely masculine way of his it made the back of her knees tingle when he looked at her just so.

Arching, she canted her hips to get more, his near snarl when she changed angle and he got deeper sent a shiver through her.

She left her grip on his biceps to tangle her fingers in his hair, urging him deeper, harder, faster. He teased her, driving into her over and over only to back off with gentler, slower strokes.

Needing more, she angled her other leg and rolled him to his back.

"You're greedy."

She added a swivel of her hips as she came down on him fully. "Yes and I often eat my dessert first. I have many moral flaws."

"Impatient," he grunted as he grabbed her hips and drove up into her.

"Yes!" Her nails dug into his sides where the heels of her hands pressed hard for balance.

"Brilliant in bed."

Her next sharp comeback wisped away. Flattered, she fluttered her lashes before closing her eyes. "Thank you. A girl could get used to a man who's been taking lovers for over four centuries. You're quite adept yourself."

God above, she was magnificent. Her hair had come loose and lay wild against her bare skin as she rose and fell above him. Her blood raced just beneath the skin. So pretty, flushed with pleasure and her exertion, her lips swollen from their earlier kisses.

And when he began to tip over, she sat against him hard, arching her back, her head dropping as she came around him, crumbling the last bit of control he had.

FIFTEEN

HER MUSCLES WERE relaxed as a great deal of her anger at the Scion was burned off after the second orgasm. By the time he'd had a glass of champagne with her, some number of orgasms later, Rowan figured there might be a way to resist staking him. He made her laugh, she admired him and she forced herself not to think past that.

Later, Rowan wondered if all that post-naughty-business glow was the reason she didn't hear the female Vampire stalking her in the parking garage of Die Mitte until she was nearly on top of her.

Rowan barely kept her feet when the female rammed into her full on. She stumbled rather than being able to shift and toss the bitch to her ass.

"Stay away from him!" Vampira was all types of upset harridan just then.

"Whoa, crazy bitch, what is your deal?"

"You're going to die!"

"We all will, baby, we all will. Now why are you making me consider punching your ticket? Or is this a guessing game?"

"He's too good for you. You're using him and I won't allow it." She rushed Rowan again, landing a slice of her nails, snagging her sweater. The sting told her Vampira got the skin too.

"See, now you're making me mad. I'm warning you to stand down and get the hell away from me."

The Vamp hissed, so typical Rowan rolled her eyes in response. And then she punched the bitch square in the face.

"You can't have him," Vampira slurred as she spat out blood.

"You've said that." Briefly, Rowan considered saying, *And guess what? I have had him. More than once.* But that would create a whole new bucket of shit to deal with. "I take it you're speaking about the Scion? If you have issues with who he speaks with, you need to address him."

"Before you came back things were just fine. You have to go."

Rowan sighed, relaxing her muscles, keeping her stance easy. "I'm Rowan Summerwaite, the Hunter here in Las Vegas. Have been for years. Staked your last boss, remember? In my job description I sometimes have to speak with Vampires. You should get hold of yourself and realize a man like Stewart speaks to lots of women. If you get all upset over that, you're going to walk around perpetually annoyed."

She must be getting soft in her old age because Rowan didn't want to kill this bimbo, she just wanted to go home to report the new information on the blood barrier being broken to the Motherhouse and go to sleep. She had an early flight the next day and the last thing she wanted or needed was yet more drama with the Nation.

"I don't care who you are." The Vampire moved in again and Rowan narrowly avoided another claw to the face.

"You'd better care. You're what? Three years turned max? Bitch, I will clean your fucking clock and not blink an eye. I'm really getting agitated and after a certain point I *am* going to give you what you're begging for. So, if you're not going to run away like a smart girl, why don't you tell me your name?"

Good Goddess did this place have no security or what? There should be at least a security guard or two out here by now.

The female feinted left and clipped Rowan slightly on the right. A decent enough kidney shot.

"You don't need to know my name. Just that I plan to kill you. You're not meant for him. You're going to ruin him. And you can't hurt me. I'm not human."

The Vamp danced closer, gloating until Rowan popped her a solid right hook to the face. Then all her rainbows and kittens disintegrated with the fangs and the bloodlust eyes.

"Guess what? Neither am I." Rowan straightened and let her power shimmer around her. "You cannot best me. Not ever. Not to toot my own horn or anything, but I'm very good at killing Vampires who prey on humans."

Rowan delivered three more solid punches to Vampira's face. In return for this, she earned an answering pop to the gut and dodged the other lunge.

"It's embarrassing to keep referring to you as Vampira in my head as I beat your ass. So let's revisit the name thing. Given your fashion sense and astounding stupidity, I'd say you probably came to Vegas with one perfectly lovely name your parents gave you and changed it to something with all sorts of unnecessary letters to make it unique. By the way, in case I was unclear, I'd be making finger quotes right now if my hands were free."

"It's Kimberly."

"Like K-i-m-b-e-r-l-y? Even 'ey' would do."

Kimberly, who was most likely Khymberleahey with an umlaut or something, flattened her mouth into a sour line and Rowan couldn't help but snort.

"Don't worry about how I spell it. I can smell him on you. Don't deny it. And I don't care who you say you are. You broke my nose!"

Rowan sighed. "It'll heal. But I have this awesome sword, made with blessed steel. You won't heal from that so why don't you give it up, for fuck's sake. I don't want to do this with you. But I will. How about we skip the rest of this little jealous tantrum? I'm walking away and you're going to head in another direction. You got in a few punches to assuage your ego. Let it go or end up dead."

Rowan turned to go walk to her car, hoping to avoid the inevitable. By the time the female reached her again, Rowan was ready, her sword unsheathed. The female's incisors were fully extended, her mouth open and head cocked to rip Rowan's throat out. Her other hand was around Rowan's throat, nails digging in to hold her in place. Kimberly with extra letters and an umlaut meant to kill Rowan and that was not going to happen.

They met eye to eye, nose to nose when the steel sliced up and through her heart.

"Die well, Vampire. I hope death brings the peace you could not find in life."

She sighed and turned, heading home.

AS DAVID CLEANED and dressed the wounds on Rowan's neck, face and arm, Rowan contacted the Motherhouse.

Susan got on the phone immediately. "Darling, I think you need a vacation," she said, reading the report Rowan had David transcribe and send to HC.

"I'm leaving tomorrow morning. I'll be in Kildare and I can leave all this insanity behind for a little while anyway."

"I must tell you I wholeheartedly approve of your going to Ireland. I wondered if you'd try to skip it and I had a very lovely but stern speech about how your duty is also to Brigid prepared. I'll save it for some future date."

Rowan laughed. "I already got a lecture about it today. I'm supposed to go and I will. Even if I hate the idea of being gone for several days right now."

"Things seem to be very tense given this little stunt. You have Carey there. Thena helps often enough. If there's an emergency you'll know and return posthaste. Your head will be clearer in Ireland. You'll still be working on the case. I know you.

"As for this kill tonight? It appears to be a case of self-defense. We've just received an official complaint from the Nation about an unsanctioned kill, you should know."

Maddening. Why would he do that to her? "Tell

them you want the surveillance footage. It's a casino parking garage, everyone has cameras in Vegas." She rubbed her eyes. "I had no choice. I know this stirs up trouble, I'm sorry."

"Well I'm sorry they forced you into this yet again. They're like children, I swear. Is the report truthful?"

"Yes."

"You gave her a warning to stand down and she attacked you with your back turned. She attacked a Hunter and you defended yourself as you're allowed to. Trouble or not, this was a legitimate kill, Rowan. Do not let anyone make you think otherwise."

She smiled. "All right."

"Darling…you know you can always talk to me, right? Not as your trainer, or a coworker, but as your friend."

Rowan kept her sigh to herself. This thing with Clive was already far more complicated than she wanted. Careless, fucking him and trailing through the area when there might be Vampires about. The last thing she wanted to do was talk to Susan. Susan might say she should end it. Rowan knew she should. Especially in light of the attack and the Nation's response of complaining about *her.* But.

"I do know."

"Get some rest on that flight. Leave it all behind for a little while. And be safe. They'll be angry now."

"I have more. About the murders here."

Susan sighed explosively. "Let's get Paris conferenced in and you can tell us all."

By the time she'd told them everything about the meth and the blood breakthrough, she was ready to keel over. They all hung up and Rowan managed to kick her boots off and climb into bed.

And that's when hell broke loose…

ANGER COURSED THROUGH him as he pounded on her door.

Unfuckingbelievable! She'd walked away from his bed and killed one of his Vampires in the parking garage. Did she have no concept of the magnitude of trouble she'd created?

The assistant didn't bother to open the door, instead, addressing Clive over the speaker from the other side of the closed door. "Mr. Stewart, Ms. Summerwaite is resting and is not to be disturbed. I will let her know you came by and that you await her return call."

"She knows why I'm here. You have two minutes or I'm kicking the door in." He pounded again to underline the point.

And then she was at the door, her unbound hair floating around her body as if she were underwater. He saw it clearly, just how otherworldly she was, how much she was *other* just like him.

"You broke the treaty. You may turn yourself over to my custody."

She blinked at him, clearly surprised, and if he wasn't mistaken, a little hurt. Only a flash, because within a breath, she'd pulled her position around her like a cloak and she was as magnificent as that first evening he saw her.

"Is this about the dumb hooker I had to stake because she had a crush on you and felt it was all right to kill me because you prefer my pussy to hers?"

"Why must you be so tawdry all the time? And did you discuss our sexual relationship with one of my people? Are you mad?"

She cocked her head. "I have no patience left, Scion, so get the *fuck* off my doorstep before I decide to take out the trash. You got me? Your stupid fucking side piece bought herself a sword to the heart. I warned her repeatedly. I'm sure you have security footage, watch it, why don't you?"

Annoyed, he shoved past her into her apartment, which in retrospect was a monumentally stupid thing to do.

She went totally still, her power vibrating around her like a tuning fork. He felt it in his teeth.

"You have no leave to be here, Vampire."

He knew then it wasn't just Rowan and him in that front hallway. He was nearly five centuries old and what he faced was older than he could understand. He felt it, knew it with a deep certainty. She was death when she chose.

"One of my people has been killed on my territory. This cannot go unanswered." He kept his gaze down and his attention on the door just a few feet behind where he stood.

"My answer is this, Vampire, your fledgling overstepped. This is your mistake to own. She has been erased from the face of this planet. You are nothing to me, do you understand this?"

Even her voice was different than Rowan's.

"I have to answer to more than just you. With all due respect. I need to communicate with Rowan. This is not about you in any way. The Nation does not seek to upset you, Goddess."

"I don't need your respect, just your fear. I also have no cares for whom you have to answer to. You seek to harm my Vessel and I will not allow it. Do you understand this?"

This More-Than-Rowan stood before him, her fingers trailing over his shoulder. Ice filled his belly. "I do not seek to harm anyone. But your Vessel has broken our law. She cannot go unpunished."

Rowan pushed to the surface, he watched the change come over her just before he found himself shoved out into the hallway with so much force it knocked the breath from his lungs.

"Fuck you, Scion. Your Vampire attacked *me* thinking I was human. Which is a violation of the treaty. I warned her repeatedly. I tried to walk away and she attacked me blind like a coward."

She held the edge of her door so hard her knuckles stood white.

"Look at your own tapes. In the future, you can send your complaints directly to the Hunter Corporation Council. They're in receipt of your whiny little missive. I will defend myself with the truth. I've done nothing wrong and you can inform the rest of your band of thugs that they will meet the exact same fate if they come at me in the dark. And lastly, if you think to threaten my household staff again, you'll find my exhausted patience very painful."

And with that, she slammed the door in his face.

SIXTEEN

HER HANDS WORKED without much thought. Twisting and bundling, she aided the acolytes and the few nuns who tended the Goddess's flame in their own way. On the table, a small hill of Brigid's wheels rose. They'd be hung on or above doors to mark Imbolc.

This place, this time every year was her refuge and her spa weekend all at once. She'd arrived two days before. Harried and exhausted. She'd walked out of customs to find Susan there waiting with Sister Alma.

It had taken all her willpower not to fall into their arms crying. Instead, she'd cast it off. Every last bit of upset, anger, sadness. She'd sloughed it like dead skin and embraced her purpose once again.

And she'd understood just exactly why it had been necessary to come. All different things came to her, she used different parts of her brain, of her emotions and her skills. Parts she needed just as surely as martial arts or hand-to-hand fighting.

The train ride to Kildare had been good. Sister Alma plied her with tea and cakes while Susan had knitted and told them about her trip to Spain as they moved, rhythmic, soothing, down the tracks, away from her life as Hunter and to the center of her existence as a Vessel.

Here, in Ireland, she was blissfully happy. Her job

was sometimes difficult, yes, but this homecoming—this connection she had with the magical part of her life—it satisfied. Her agitation settled, smoothed away with an utter certainty of purpose.

Rowan's mother had died before she could teach Rowan to make the wheels, so it fell to Sister Alma. Sister Alma who'd shown up at the Keep along with the Mother Acolyte, Rachael.

They'd demanded Rowan be turned over to them for a set period of time every year. She'd come to Kildare because that is what her mother would have done for her.

None of them knew, at the time, that it had been Theo who'd ordered Belinda Summerwaite killed. Rachael had been doing her duty to raise Rowan as an acolyte as Belinda had been. But that she had barged in and demanded Rowan be trained, demanded it of The First, had been an act Rowan had admired all of her life.

And at that very first Imbolc, as the three-year-old Rowan had learned to make the wheels, they'd discovered she was not meant to be an acolyte, but was in fact Brigid's Vessel.

And then Rachael had moved to Germany where she was allowed contact with Rowan once per week for six hours. It had been in those sweet, all-too-rare lessons where Rowan had learned how much more she'd been. She was more than a descendant of a family of service. More than the favored human to The First.

He hadn't liked her divided affections. But to his credit, he'd never stood in the way of her training, not that Brigid would have allowed it. But he *added* to her training.

"A shadow crossed your face, Rowan. Blow it away, there's nothing but our flame here," Sister Alma murmured.

Alma had taken over when Rowan had left the Keep and started her life as a Hunter. Rachael had been getting older, less able to travel. There were pictures in an album at home, sisters to the ones she knew Rachael, Alma and now Susan had. Sitting at this very table. Year after year as Rowan had grown.

These women had been her mother in one way or another. Rowan smiled, relaxing after she pushed the memories of Theo's lessons from her head. She was home and surrounded by people who loved her. There were far worse places to be.

"Are you ready, Rowan?" One of the acolytes came to the door. She needed to go out to burn the old wheels and hand out new ones.

She stood. "Yes, thank you. Can you all please give me a moment?"

The others got up, gathering the rest of the wheels into the basket Rowan would carry.

Susan pressed a kiss to her forehead and they went out, leaving her alone.

She padded in bare feet over the smooth, cold stone floor to the hearth where a hearty fire played.

She willingly gave of herself, letting Brigid rush through her, letting the Goddess do the driving. This was for her, this was part of who Rowan was and she fell away.

As Rowan walked outside, the cold slapped at her

exposed skin. Sister Alma tutted at her, motioning to the boots near the door.

Properly chastened, she slipped them on and thanked Susan for the snow-white wrap.

A knot of people had gathered in the courtyard near the flame. Brigid was pleased to be remembered, pleased to see not so much the wheels themselves, but that the rituals had not been entirely lost or blotted out by others who came after and tried to downplay her importance.

Brigid, whether one wanted to call her the Bride or a saint, was the same as she had always been. She had little care for what other symbols were wielded around her, only that her memory did not die.

The acolytes, together with the nuns and several who'd come to Kildare to settle and live in Her presence, tended Her flame openly and reverently. Her shrine was near the well, miles from the old cathedral. Rowan had been happy to see just how many houses bore the wheels on doors, how many stores in town had been selling candles.

The events of that day blurred together. She visited with the people in town, was driven about the countryside blessing farmland.

Rowan only knew that when she slipped between the covers in the lovely, overstuffed bed in Sister Alma's guest room, it had been pleasing, the kind of day that chased all her troubles far away.

ROWAN LOOKED OUT the window at Las Vegas spread out beneath the plane. Lights everywhere. Life. Death. Everything in between.

Never in her life had she felt so totally connected to it all, the tides of life and death as they brushed against each other.

When she'd woken up on her birthday, before the dawn to ready for a long day of Imbolc activities, she'd felt a little uneasy. Anticipatory perhaps, though it was hard to remember what it was like…before.

Salt for purification.

All in white, she'd entered the field, each line she spoke, each time she stopped to mark another part of the ritual, the bell was rung.

And then she was washed away from herself. Away from all anchors. Frightened at first until she realized it was meant to be. She let go, went under and did not drown.

With a gasped breath, she came back to herself, full of wonder that she could stand after what felt like swimming forever and ever. But it was then, then as Rowan opened her eyes, that she realized this was what her mother had alluded to all those months ago at the ranch house.

Life. So much life pulsed within her she wouldn't have been surprised to find herself a kaleidoscope of color and pulsating energy. It hummed low, delicious. A counter to the sharp-edged power resting a little higher, that power that pushed her to take what she needed to make things happen.

When she bent to grasp the bundle of rushes at her feet, a line of green leaped from where she stood. Grass shot up several inches higher.

That had been two days before. Two days and she'd realized through much meditation and discussion with

Alma and the new Mother Acolyte, Lara, this was healing and life. This was fertility and sensuality. The maiden had matured.

She wasn't sure what to make of it, but had decided the Goddess would let her know just exactly what she was supposed to make of it when it was time. Rowan knew this because the connection to Her was constant in a way it hadn't been before. In the past, Brigid had ebbed and flowed as Rowan had needed her and called.

But now they were intertwined in a way that words failed to describe. Rowan only knew it felt right and that it would serve her mission.

Five days. She'd only been gone five days but it'd been revolutionary. All her life she'd had small and even some major revelatory moments, but the last five days had brought her a whole new level of knowing and understanding her path.

Certainty was a rarity in her life, so she accepted the way things worked, knowing that at least they did. So she didn't know what to expect when she landed, but she knew it would be something. But she knew she'd been led to this very point in this very way for a reason. And the closer she got, the more that something felt very, very wrong.

HER PHONE HAD seven messages when they landed. Suddenly her life as a Hunter came back in full force as she saw Jack's number over and over. She sent out a prayer that she could handle whatever this was.

She had the phone to her ear, trying to get through to Jack when she looked up gratefully to find David waiting with her luggage. Even better, he pressed a coffee into her hands, kissed her cheek and told her he'd be right back with the car.

And then he handed her a file.

By the time he'd returned with the car, she had gotten hold of Carey, who was already working on the information. He briefed her on the disappearance and she had moved on to calling Jack.

"I just got in ten minutes ago. I'm on my way to you. I trust you're at work?" She maneuvered through traffic, heading to the police station.

As she'd sent him home with her luggage, David had protested, telling her she needed to come with him to at least shower and change to be rested, but she knew Jack needed her.

"Where have you been, Rowan?" His voice sounded so lost.

"I was in Ireland for my birthday. With my mother's family. I've been on trains and planes for the last day. I was over the ocean when you called."

"I'm at work."

"Be there as fast as I can."

Once at the station, Rowan headed to Jack's desk and found him there, looking miserable.

"Tell me. I know the basics, but what's the situation?" She bussed his cheek and sat.

"Lisa didn't show up for work a few days this month. Or she'd be late and looking like shit."

Rowan had noticed the other woman looking rather worn and crappy over the last months, but she'd assumed it was just her attitude. Or Rowan's own hatred of the woman.

"We got into a fight on Wednesday. A big one. She..." He licked his lips but didn't continue.

"Jack, you have to tell it all. I can help you, I *will* help you, but the more I know the better. I know I'm not the president of her fan club, but I care about you and I certainly don't wish her any ill."

"I caught her stealing from me."

Rowan exhaled, hard. She promised herself not to let her utter contempt for Lisa show on her face, but it was a close thing. "Like what?"

"My credit cards."

It took all her restraint not to yell out, "Your girlfriend the cop stole your credit cards?" Instead she took notes and tried to remain detached. "What happened?"

"I caught her in the act. She tried to deny it, but she had my Visa card in her pocket. I confronted her and she lied to my face, even though there was no way she was believable there like that."

"Did she eventually share with you? I mean, is she in trouble? Gambling maybe?"

"She said she had money problems. I knew this, I've loaned her quite a bit of money lately. She said she was just going to use the credit cards for gas. But, well it wasn't the first time she'd stolen from me. So we had it out. Or rather, I did and she denied, clammed up and then stormed off after I made her give the cards back. I went through her stuff and she'd also lifted a silver box that had been my grandmother's."

Why hadn't he told her all this before? She felt like shit for whatever judgment she'd shown toward Lisa that had contributed to him dealing with all this stuff alone.

"What else did she steal?"

"You remember that time last year when I messed my hip up? I had some pain pills left. They disappeared a few months ago. I only noticed when I was looking for something else in my medicine cabinet. I wouldn't have even thought it was a big deal. Until I found the bottle at her place. Along with several others that didn't have her name on the prescription. Other things had disappeared before and I didn't want to think it was her. Stupid. God."

He bowed a moment, his head in his hands and she reached out, squeezing his knee.

"You love her. We all do stupid things for love sometimes." Rowan looked down at the paperwork in the file, allowing him to get himself together. "So you had a fight on Wednesday night and on Thursday she was suspended from work."

He nodded. "Fuck, Rowan, I haven't loved her in a long time. She's being accused of taking something from the evidence room."

"Let me guess, drugs of some sort?"

"Crystal meth, guns and a large amount of cash."

"What the fuck was she involved in, Jack? You were her boyfriend, yes, but you're a cop to your bones. Even I saw how ragged she was looking. I thought she had mono or something."

"I knew she'd...indulge from time to time with pills. I didn't care. Christ, if you do your job and pay your bills and stay out of trouble, I don't give three shits about what you do in your off time."

She waited for him to continue.

"But you know, so she starts having trouble paying

her rent. And Vegas is expensive, so I paid it for her a few times. She asked to move in with me, and God help me, Rowan, I said no. Maybe I could have helped if I wasn't such an asshole. I just couldn't have her living with me and fighting with me all the time. I needed the peace and now she's missing."

"That's dumb and you know it. Did you have any part in her disappearance? Did you hurt her, Jack?"

He snapped his head up, outrage on his face and she sat back, shrugging.

"Exactly. So you didn't want your crazy, ragey on-and-off-again girlfriend with sticky fingers and a pill habit living in your house. Makes you smart and also, human. You didn't hurt her, you tried to help her and so you know what? You and I are going to find her and that's that."

"It's meth, Rowan. What if she's caught up in whatever is happening to those other women? What if we find her like that?"

She put her things aside and took his hands. His turmoil rose and battered at her. All she could do was hope that wasn't the case.

Right then though, Rowan could help a little bit. She opened herself up to him, taking his angst and turmoil into herself and replacing it with calm. Soothing and hoping it helped.

His agitation seemed to lessen, his gaze glossed just a small amount. "They questioned me. I felt like a fucking criminal, Rowan. I know it's their job, I get it, but it sucked anyway."

"Just hold on to that. You have to know they're watching you. Don't take it personally and if it's necessary, get an attorney and don't hesitate. You got me? I'm going to get right on this. Carey's working on his end. Can I see her place? Oh and who is working her case here?"

"They're not even classifying her as a missing person yet!" He stood and began to pace. "They didn't search her place. They just did a cursory check to see if she was there and if it looked on the surface like foul play."

"Is this Fred's decision?" Fred was in charge of their unit and had the ear of the chief, but he was a smart cop and Rowan had an idea that there was more than just a few missed days of work.

"Yes."

Junkies disappeared all the time. No one cared about the other two women disappearing until they were found dead.

"Are you telling me everything? Have you been in her place?"

"She'd been put on probation here four months ago. She had been under suspicion then for some thefts of the evidence room before this last time. They removed her access, which is why she got caught. She used someone else's code, but it had been flagged. They found her loading it into a car outside. Eight firearms, meth with a street value of roughly fifteen grand, about thirty thousand in cash."

"*Your* code." It wasn't a question, she knew the answer. Lisa, the stupid bitch, had stolen his money and his meds and his work codes too. Now was the time to harden his heart a little bit because dead or not, Lisa was not someone he needed in his life. Not with the way she'd treated him.

Worse, those cases whose evidence had been stolen would most likely be tossed out now. Tampered evidence was the kiss of death. The chief would have been extremely pissed off, not to mention the prosecutors working the cases.

He didn't answer about the code. "I haven't been in her apartment. Fred warned me off. My union rep too. Fred promised me he'd keep an eye out. It's all I have to hang on to just now."

"I'm going to look the place over. I've got it. Fred is right. The last thing you need is to be involved in this any more than you are. Back to Lisa, what else aren't you telling me?"

"She got picked up two weekends ago. Prostitution."

Rowan just stood and went to him, hugging him tight. "I'm sorry. I really am. Did you know about the meth? You knew about the pills."

"I knew there was something. No one told me about the solicitation stuff." He shrugged, looking caught between lost and angry. "How could I have imagined she was tricking for drugs? That's not the woman I'd been with for so long, you know?"

"So what's the status of the solicitation charge?"

"Insufficient evidence. They didn't have enough so they kicked her. It was part of why she had been fast tracked for suspension. She told me she'd taken some vacation. Turns out she'd been using the process to buy some time. Then the stuff with stealing from me and then the evidence-locker theft. She's a lot further gone than I'd imagined. How could she have been so bad off and I just didn't see?"

When they found her, if she was alive, she'd still be facing a metric shitton of trouble and most likely the loss of her job to go with some jail time.

"Who would see that? I mean, now you have to face it, Jack. You can't fool yourself anymore. But who is going to jump from money problems to stealing from the evidence room for drugs? That's a pretty big jump there. Give yourself permission to have missed it."

She grabbed the file and her bag. "I'm going to look at her place. I'm on the case so consider me on retainer. I'll be contacting you with what I find out."

He began to interrupt with what she knew would be an insistence to go with her.

"No. Jack, you and I both know you're going to have to stay out of the investigation. This is hard enough as it is and damned if I'm going to push you any harder into the suspect box. So stay out of this and I'll be in touch."

He growled, but didn't argue. He did hand her some keys. "Her place is 4D, top right-hand corner. Her car isn't there, or it wasn't earlier today."

She tucked the keys away and headed to the door. "I'm going out now. Stay out of it or I'll kick your ass."

"Hey, Rowan?"

She paused in the doorway. "Yeah?"

"I'm so glad you're back. Thank you."

"That's what friends are for."

SEVENTEEN

STANDING IN LISA'S apartment, Rowan decided that love had made Jack blind. Unless this place had rapidly deteriorated in a day or three, no one could have stood there and believed anything but that a person in big trouble lived there.

Lisa's mental angst painted the walls as if it was physical.

Carefully, she looked the place over. Disorganized mess covered every surface and the floor. Paper, trash, all that jazz. The space on the stand in the living room was empty where a television once sat. Which most likely meant she'd pawned it for drug money, probably like everything else she'd once owned that held any value. In the bedroom Rowan paused at the scent of almonds.

Shit.

Shit. Shit. Shit.

Outside the apartment, Rowan ran into one of Lisa's neighbors.

"Excuse me, ma'am? My name is Rowan Summerwaite, I'm a private investigator." She showed her identification to the older woman, who looked Rowan up and down before she nodded and allowed herself a small smile.

"Do you know Ms. Walker?"

"Hmpf."

Okay then. "I take it you do? She's gone missing and I'm trying to find her. Any help at all you could give would be much appreciated. Can you tell me the last time you saw her? If there'd been trouble over there? Anything like that?"

"Her nice young man used to keep her calm. But he's been around less and less and her new friends more and more. I don't like getting involved you see, but a body can't hardly miss all the people in and out over there. They, her *friends* take the parking spots and won't move. Saw her, last Tuesday I think it was. She's not looking well. I think it's the drugs. Sad to say. I know she's a police officer and I was raised to respect the authorities, but that girl had fallen off the path, if you know what I mean."

Yeah, Rowan did.

"Anyone in particular you saw more often than others? Jack, her nice young man, is the person who hired me to look for her. He's very worried."

She described a few people, none of which sounded very familiar, but for one. One sounded a lot like Karen Fisk. The way the neighbor kept halting as she spoke told Rowan the Vampire had been there, as well. Something had been done to her memory.

Rowan thanked her and gave her a card, urging the woman to call if she remembered anything else.

And then she headed toward home.

"HAS Ms. Summerwaite returned?" Clive managed not to sound like he wished to throttle Rowan's assistant. Or he hoped he did. He felt like a complete and utter git standing there on her doorstep, her assistant blocking his way.

"As I've said, your messages have been passed along. When or if Ms. Summerwaite returns your calls will be up to her entirely."

They'd parted on terrible terms and he'd done nothing but think about her ever since. Had watched the video surveillance from the parking garage when he returned only to find everything she said was true.

Like an idiot, he'd let himself be inflamed by the hotel security people, low-level security people, and he'd set off over to her place without even viewing the footage.

So when he'd returned to Die Mitte, chastened and aware he had made a huge error in not bothering to look first, he'd done so with several of his upper-level people, including Alice. Even his own people couldn't deny the kill was righteous.

Moreover, watching Rowan move the way she did, with the same preternatural strength they had, with the speed and agility none of them had ever seen in a human and only rarely in a Vampire, had increased their fear of her. And with Vampires, respect and fear were inherently tied together.

"What are you doing here? I'm sure we discussed this before I left." Rowan breezed past and into her apartment. "No. I did not invite you in. Say what you need to, Vampire, and be gone."

Her scent teased his senses. She was delicious with that otherworldly magick she threw out. Even thicker now that she'd returned. She was…different somehow.

"I trust Imbolc went well?"

"Is that why you're here? I'm sure you can read about it on the internet somewhere. Your Vampire has chosen another victim, I have to find him because his mistake was that the woman happens to be Jack's girlfriend and a cop."

Her eyes held no warmth at all, not even the spark of humor she usually had. He felt guilty, which he resented, even as he knew he should feel that way.

"I have some new information. About the case."

"Great." She turned and walked away. "Give it to David and I'll look it over."

He sighed. "Rowan, do you really mean to continue on like this?"

"Like what? I have to figure out a way to talk to Jack without telling him anything when, to be totally honest, this is your fucking mess to clean up. As usual, you people think you're far too good to deal with the inevitable outcomes of your behavior."

"You people?"

"Yes, that's right. Vampires. The Vampire Nation has created this problem because you withheld information about the meth blood-barrier thing. And now you have some fucked up, tweaker Vampire serial killer and I'm the one having to tell my friend lies to protect you. I don't even like you. Him, I like. You? Not so much."

"We need to talk."

"Tell David the times you're available and I'll have him contact Alice to set up a meeting."

He made a move to come inside and didn't even see the assistant's move until it was too late. A sword, not as scary as Rowan's but plenty frightening when pressed to his neck, gleamed, holding him in place.

"No. Vampire, you have been given your answers and you have no bid to enter this abode."

"You cannot think to hold a sword to the neck of the Scion without repercussions!"

Rowan stopped, spun and headed back toward them. Glorious, beautiful rage marked her features. Far better than the flat expression she'd worn only moments before.

"David, please excuse us," she said as she got between them, nose to nose with Clive.

"If you're sure, *Déesse*."

"I am. Thank you. Please send the notes in that file on the table to Carey. Tell him I'll be expecting his update within the hour. I called in some help to look for her."

"Help?" Clive wondered what that meant.

"None of your business," she snapped, standing in the doorway to halt his ingress. "I warned you, Vampire."

"He pulled a weapon on me, Rowan."

"You attempted to enter my abode uninvited. That is all the excuse he needs. Now. Get. Out."

"Damn you, Rowan. I'm sorry. I'm sorry I accused you the way I did."

"Is that all?"

"No! Are you planning to punish me forever? I said I was sorry. I mean it. I overreacted, flew over here without all the information. I've damaged our whatever it is and I'm sorry."

"Do you really think this is about you? About punishing you? My friend, a man I care about, is going to have to face seeing his woman torn to shreds. I smelled him at her place. Same Vampire. Smelled him at the second victim's place too."

"Take me there. Let me see if I recognize the scent."

"Um. No. Run along, I have work to do."

"Are you really going to push us into a fight? I'm not leaving until you and I have dealt with this."

"What *this* are you talking about? There is no *this*." She pushed the door at him and he pushed back. The tension between them ramped up.

"Who did you ask for help?"

"The Dust Devils." She looked as happy to say it as he was to hear it. And then she shoved him into the hallway and slammed the door in his face.

Again.

He pounded on the door. Again.

"What?" She opened, looking feral and everything in his body perked up.

"The information I have. Don't you want it?"

"I told you to give it to David."

"It's not a dossier. I need to tell it to you."

She looked him up and down. "Wait here."

Again with the door in his face.

On the other side of the door he heard the assistant talk to her. "*Déesse*, you've been traveling for the better part of nearly two days. You need to take a break."

"David, I don't have that luxury now. I slept on the trip from La Guardia. I'm all right. I don't think Lisa is. I think I'm too late."

Her voice came near to breaking, but she held it together and though he should feel guilty for eavesdropping, he only felt admiration for her.

He was damned. No doubt about it.

"But the Devils?"

"I paid the price. They'll help."

A chill worked through Clive at hearing that. Such payment would have most likely been a magickal infusion, but it would have been painful. They'd have liked that too.

"Then you most definitely need to rest!"

"She paid it. The Goddess. I'm fine. I'm alive. I'll wake up tomorrow and the day after. Lisa, well, David, I don't think she can say the same."

"You can't make yourself responsible for this. She made her choices."

"I need to do my job."

The door yanked open and she stood there, her hair tied at the base of her neck, exposing the unique lines of her face. "Come on then. We're walking and talking."

"Where are you going?"

She only looked at him sideways until the elevator arrived.

"What is it you need to tell me?"

"I have a few names. Four of them seem likely as our killer. My people are looking for them now."

"I'll need their particulars. You can call my office." She handed him a card. "Call Carey and give him this information."

Thc doors opened and she darted out into the crowd. Growling, he followed.

"Ms. Summerwaite, I'm giving the information to you."

"I don't have time for this."

He took her arm once they'd reached the sidewalk outside.

"Make time. It's not as if I'm free to just flit around Las Vegas waiting for you to return. I have a job too."

"So get on with it. And then let go of my arm before I punch you in the nose."

"Would that make you feel better?"

She paused, surprised and then she laughed. "It totally would. But this isn't about me, asshole. Maybe later."

It was then he caught it. Not only the subtle changes in Rowan, which had been throwing him since he'd first seen her minutes before, but the scent in the air. Almonds.

"It's him." She said it low, so quietly he barely heard it.

Scanning the area, he saw several Vampires, but none who were nearly old enough to give off that scent.

He walked through the crowd, the humans parting like the seas. For so long he'd simply used his skills to manipulate them, it was second nature to create a path, to send out that little bit of confusion so they'd never suspect a thing.

Fragile and easily led. Humans never really came into his mind unless he was hungry.

But Rowan, dealing with her and seeing them through her perspective was interesting. Not that he'd come to care that much more about them, but she did and they must be worthy on some level.

In any case, the less they knew about Vampires the better off Vampires were.

"He's gone. But he was here."

She was at his side and he hadn't even heard her approach. "My, you're going to have to tell me about all your birthday…gifts."

"Not so much. Okay, then, I'm off. I have some information to track down."

"Don't go see them alone."

"I'm never alone, Scion."

But instead of her shiny sports car, a cab belched to a stop. A cab filled with stuffed beasts.

"Suzette! Come on then, I'll take your fare."

The door opened and she smirked as she got inside.

"Rowan, you can't take this person out there," Clive whispered.

"Keep your teeth on." The driver's smile was affable enough, but it was then that Clive realized he sure as hell wasn't human. "I been driving cab round these parts a long time. Miss Suzy here is gonna be just fine. Though." He cocked his head as he looked Clive over. "You got to be looking into your freezer situation. Open doors mean things spoil."

"We're not finished, Ms. Summerwaite."

"See you later, Scion." She waved and the cab sped away, the traffic parting for it much like the humans had parted for Clive earlier.

"HE'S SWEET on you. In his own way."

"Carl, it's good to see you, but he's not sweet on anything. He's incapable of sweet."

His crazy, wheezy laugh comforted her. "Well, we don't always get things the way we want 'em, Cloris. Fate's a bitch. Ha! Don't let her know I said that."

"Cross my heart. Carl, I need to go out of the city."

"Hold on to your hat. We'll get where you need to be. Tell me about your birthday."

She sat back and trusted him to get them where she wanted to go, not bothering to ask how he knew she'd been gone or that she needed to meet with the Devils. "I was in Ireland last week. Cold. I keep forgetting it gets cold in Europe. We had snow one of the days."

"Got some presents from Her I see. Good. Gonna need that in the next little while. Dark days a-coming. Serial killer in town I hear. Wowee. Always felt like those guys needed to be culled. Like rabid animals from the herd. They're sick and they'll infect the rest."

"I hear you. I'm looking for him. And when I find him, I will do the culling."

"Watch your back, Cloris. That fancy man over 'ta your place, he seems like a good one to have at your back in a firefight."

"Ha. I thought you were all knowing."

He wheezed again as he headed away from the lights of the city. "You oughta forgive the guy. He's a man after all. My wife always used to say that. Then I think I ran out the clock on that excuse."

"He's a predator."

"As are you. Predators would get bored with a fluffy bunny type, know what I mean? Can't say I ever saw much of a future with you and the cop or those others you were with."

He pulled to a halt in the parking lot of a shitty bar on the side of a road barely wide enough to be considered a highway. She hadn't even noticed he'd gotten them this far.

"Meter's running, Jenny. Don't take too long."

She took a deep breath and stepped out. It was windy. Cold. The night was so quiet it ran against her skin like the reverse nap of fabric. Not right at all.

When she walked in, she saw Rex right away, leaning against the bar. Cleaning his ear with keys. *Gross.* Who did that? She shuddered as she headed toward him.

Brigid filled her hard and fast, the cold shock of it bringing her steps a little slower as she attempted to swallow all that power without letting anyone know she was struggling. Danger was to be had here, Rowan knew it, but this was something else. When the Goddess pushed her way into Rowan that way, it was akin to an internal defense system.

He paused, cocking his head and looking her over. "It is good to see you, Bride. It's been some time."

Not in her own voice, Rowan spoke, "Rex Price, we are appreciative of your assistance in this matter."

Deep within, Rowan wondered about the connection between the Goddess and the Devils, but she kept quiet. If She planned to answer, She would.

"This thing hunts in our ground. This offends us deeply, Hunter."

Brigid receded enough for Rowan to come forward. She inclined her head, just enough to show respect but not give any position to the other man. "Price. It is my aim to find it and kill it."

He pushed a sheet of paper across the bar. "We grant you access to our ground."

Which was good. Hunting in the areas controlled by the Devils without their permission was a very bad idea. She rarely did it if she could avoid it. This meant, too, that this Vampire had edged out of the main part of town and into the darker corners.

Price licked his lips and she saw the flash of *other* in his eyes. That flash of magicks older than most anything left on the face of the planet. The Devils were a physical incarnation of chaos magicks, like the Wild Hunt. They were the keepers of the balance, though their methods would most likely never make sense to humans, Rowan understood and feared what they were. Brigid respected them and the taste of her power she'd given them in return for their cooperation had been a small price to pay.

Or so Brigid thought. Rowan was merely grateful she couldn't really remember much about what transpired. But nothing came for free in the world, especially not between beings of great power like the Goddess and these Devils.

She just considered herself lucky she had something they wanted.

"We're looking too." Price's second approached and pushed a beer her way across the scarred bar. "They leave an absence of things in their wake. Better than a footprint, as it happens." A flash of a smile brought a glimpse of sharp teeth and a repressed shiver.

One had to be careful when thanking beings so old. It had to be done right or you could end up offending, or worse, being in the wrong kind of debt with them.

Inside, Rowan's connection to Brigid was brighter than it had been before the trip to Kildare. She knew the Goddess waited, watching how she handled this.

Rowan inclined her head again, opting for that rather

than words. It seemed to satisfy both Brigid and Price, which was enough.

Though she wanted to leave and get looking again, she knew she would be risking offense if she left without drinking the beer they'd offered.

"What think you of the Scion?" Price had wandered off, but his second remained. "Not the one before. The one you ended—" again the flash of teeth "—he'd be worse than useless against this killer Vampire."

Ah, more politics here. If she said the right words, they'd turn on Clive. Which should have pleased her given what a giant prick he was. But she couldn't bring herself to pull that trigger.

"From what I can tell he's done a great deal to bring the more troublesome of his number to heel. Jacques, the one before, wouldn't have even been aware of this issue." She kept her language formal. It was useless to appeal to their feelings about humans or even a sense of fairness. These beings lived on balance. They thrived on chaos, but an ordered chaos. The kind that kept them secret from humans. Without that secrecy their ability to go about their business was impeded and no one liked red tape.

"Humans watch too much television. One of these days they will find enough to push the majority into believing."

And Rowan didn't want to think of what sort of punishment would be meted out to whoever provided that last bit of evidence.

"Is he cooperating?"

She shrugged. "In his way. You know how they are."

He snorted. "Vampires have always been like this.

More self-centered than humans. For all the mess they leave, they have zero affinity for cleaning it up."

Which, in its own way, served the Devils because Devils clean up messes of the sort Vampires left.

Rowan wondered if this Vampire left the bodies close to people to keep the messes from being cleaned up on purpose.

Brigid warmed from that place in Rowan's belly. She was on to something. She drank the rest of her beer as fast as was permissible before inclining her head again.

"I must be off to continue my hunt."

Mick, the Devil she'd been talking to, handed her a business card. "My contact information. We are available to you on this matter."

Nodding, she put the card in her pocket and left the way she'd come, never turning her back on the bar completely. Mick flashed a grin and winked, bringing a reluctant smile to her lips.

She half expected Carl to be gone, but what she hadn't expected at all, was to see Clive standing, leaning against the passenger door of a sleek sedan, waiting.

"What did you do with Carl?"

"Carl? Is that what he calls himself these days? He saw me pull up, walked over, extorted your fare from me and drove off. Said to tell you to watch your back. Which given the circumstances we're in, seems good advice."

"Why are you here?"

"This is my problem too, in case that has escaped your notice."

"Notice or not, you don't need me to find this Vampire. You're the Scion, you don't need me at all. You have people to do your bidding."

"I do. It's a good thing." He opened the door and indicated she get in.

Most likely she could walk into that bar and get a ride to town. Most likely she could do it in a way that would not offend or end up having her owe more than she wanted to pay.

But if Carl had left, it was saying something specific about what she needed to do.

She got in and only sighed at the warmth of the heated seats once Clive had closed the door to walk around.

"Where are we headed?"

She sent him a raised brow he wouldn't see as he paid attention to the road like he was supposed to. "I thought your people had info on this Vampire. Or at least a few of them."

"They told you nothing? What was the point of this trip out here if they told you nothing?"

"Too bad I'm not actually strategizing with you." She nearly added *fuckface* at the end, but he heard it either way. "The Devils aren't workmen for hire. That attitude would be a colossal mistake. I can hunt on their ground. Head back to town so I can get my car."

"We'd be more effective working together." He ignored her comments and headed east. "If you've received their permission to hunt, let's head out to one of the spots my people identified as a possibility."

"I have permission. You don't. Also, you're a jackhole and I don't want to be with you."

"I'm in your company, doing your bidding. Of course I have permission. It's implied."

She snorted and then cringed inwardly. "Do you think the Devils play lawyerball by Vampire Nation rules? Because I don't. Just FYI if they get on us about this shit, I will throw you under the bus so fast you won't even see it coming." She turned to him, smiling sweetly. "And I'll enjoy it."

He muttered under his breath.

"We withdrew our complaint. I just thought you should know."

She did know. Susan told her before she left to come home.

"If you hadn't I would have known because you'd have received the official missive from Hunter Corp referring to the close circuit video footage you claimed not to have but my assistant was able to hack into your system and find."

She let him chew on that for a while before speaking again. "And I think your holding that back and pretending you didn't have it was a totally pussy move. Vampires, Goddess, you're all fourteen-year-old girls. How did that happen?"

She was pretty sure she heard the click of his jaw as he clenched it. It was then she remembered her project and made a promise to redouble her efforts to get that neck tic back in play.

"It was internal business. We rescinded our complaint before we refused to turn over the footage."

"Were you an insufferable asshole when you were younger? Or did you learn it over time? You get a gold star."

"I'm trying to apologize and explain."

"You need a fucking dictionary then so you can look up the word *apology.* As for your specious excuse about internal business? Only if you define internal business as evidence of your appalling lack of security and control over your side pieces. Really, Scion, you need to control your women better."

"Side piece? Is that vulgar slang for lady friend?"

"That's me, always keeping it classy. However, men I fucked once upon a time are not trying to kill people in parking lots because I moved on. I prefer vulgar to that. Anyway, you're not that awesome in the sack that I'd be killing people over your penis. Also, she wasn't your lady friend. You had sex with her, but not enough that she was your anything. Just because she was gullible doesn't mean I am."

"She was young and stupid. It was an overreaction on your part to kill her."

She couldn't hold back the head whip at that bit of stupidity.

He sighed. "She was young and stupid and infatuated. I admit that. She wasn't worldly and when my affections faded, she was unable to handle it. It was my own failing."

Did he think that was an apology? Not bloody likely!

"You saw that footage, I practically begged her not to take me on so don't make her stupidity my fault." And now she was mad all over again. "You piss me off, Stewart. Just drop me at my place, suddenly I have zero desire to be anywhere near you unless I'm driving a blade through your chest."

The road was dark as they sped away from town and

all the lights and people. All she saw out there was the shadow of the mountains in the distance and the occasional reflective buttons in the road when the light from the moon hit them just right.

Of course he needed no headlights. Neither did she really. But she played along and used her headlights when she drove. Stupid showoff Vampire.

Suddenly, she slid in her seat as he pulled off the main road and sped down a dirt track. He didn't reply to her as he continued at an alarming rate of speed down that shitty little road.

Rowan hoped his alignment was FUBAR.

When he slammed the brakes on and got out of the car suddenly, her anger spiked and she followed. "What is your problem?"

With a growl, he stalked to her, hauled her close by the fistfuls of her sweater he grabbed and got in her face. "It would appear that you are."

Her heart sped. Not from fear. No that would be too simple and too normal. Heaven knew normal was not on the plate for her.

Adrenaline spiked as his mouth hovered above hers. She tried not to pant, worked to control her pulse, knowing he could hear the rush of her blood through her veins, knew he would hear the way she swallowed a moan of desire.

"That's not my problem. Your murderous Vampire is. And if this goes on any longer, he'll be the problem for a camera crew. The media is here. Serial killers get great coverage you know. Also, the stupid fucker took a cop's girlfriend. Lastly, you are all far too cocky if you think you can just get away with this level of violence."

He heaved a sigh. Heavy, threaded with frustration.

"Don't you think I know all this? I've got my people on it, double shifts with human help. This Vampire is not registered so we're having to go through nest by nest to find him."

Most of the old ones were reluctant to register and be part of the larger nests. They liked to be left alone and do their own thing. She didn't blame them really, after all, who wanted to be three hundred and be told what to do in any way?

"I don't know *what* you think. Half the time you're trying to get into my pants, the other half you're accusing me of being part of some grand conspiracy to frame Vampires for crimes they didn't commit."

"I said I was sorry for accusing you."

"Sort of. And yet, you do it all the time."

"I'm sorry." He licked his lips. "She was young and silly and she's dead. Her parents are still alive. I had to tell them. I saw the footage. I saw you try to walk away and I saw her continue after you."

She got it then. It wasn't really about her, it was about his own sense of guilt and failure. Tenderness brushed between them for long moments as they stared at one another.

He kissed her then, hard, possessive, his fingers digging into the muscle at her hip.

STILLNESS RUSHED OVER the landscape. A wave as suffocating as water, as heavy and disorienting. Clive's fingers left their grip at her hip as he moved away lightning-quick, crouching and looking up. Rowan's gaze had been locked on him for just a moment, long enough to miss the source of the dull thud.

Spinning, she coughed slightly at the dust still hanging in the air. Just a moment before that cough strangled in her throat, tangled and caught as the body sprawled on the ground became visible.

Within moments she'd unsheathed her blade, the ringing of the metal clearing the sheath breaking that dread silence. Gaze now locked on the sky, she attempted to catch sight of the Vampire, but got none. She turned to Clive but he'd launched himself upward already, leaving Rowan earthbound and reaching for her phone. Goddess knew how she'd explain this, but it had to be called in.

There, lying in the dirt, arms and legs akimbo, eyes dead, pain and terror etched into what was left of her face, was Lisa. Though Rowan had expected this, had known it would most likely come, the sight of the woman Jack had loved so fiercely was still a shock.

Though she knew Jack would be angry, she called Fred. It'd be better for Jack in the long run that she called someone else first, even if he wouldn't see it that way.

As she had no idea how to explain it all, she opted for curt and blunt.

"Fred? This is Rowan Summerwaite. I'm out in the desert west of town and I'm looking at the pretty fresh body of what once was Lisa Walker. Same MO as the others at first glance. I figured you would want the call first rather than 911."

Fred cursed and then sighed. "I was hoping like

hell she just ripped Jack off and blew town. Did you call him?"

"Not yet. I called you first."

"I'm going to ask you to let me handle Jack. Can you do that for me?"

"Yes." She considered telling him to be gentle with Jack, but Fred had been a cop going on twenty years; he knew his job. More importantly, Rowan knew the man cared about Jack and considered him a friend as well as a good cop. "I'll be here until you arrive."

"Oh and we found Karen Fisk dead. House fire. Her husband is missing. Thought you'd want to know."

Damn it! Rowan had known the Fisks had been involved in this somehow and now it was too late to get anything from them.

After thanking him, Rowan gave him the coordinates from her phone and promised not to contaminate his scene.

But that didn't mean she couldn't get all the info possible before scene response arrived. After she hung up, she drew her camera from her bag and began to photograph the scene and the body. So much rage. Lisa's body was barely in one piece, much of it had been shredded by tooth and nail. Her face was a ruin of torn flesh and blood. From what Rowan could see, some internal organs were missing.

Brigid took over, Rowan knew it the moment the nausea passed and calm seeped through the anger and dismay. After that it was easier to photograph and record her notes as she made a call back to Carey and began to send the data to the office.

She'd moved away from the body and back to the

car when Clive landed, looking mussed up and highly pissed off. His eyes…her heart stuttered a moment as she took in the eerie glow she'd seen in Theo's gaze in times when his people had angered him. Usually right before he ripped their heads off.

The blade rested in her palm as he approached.

"I didn't find him. But I scented him and I will know him by sunset tomorrow night." His voice had lost the cultured cream. Now it was rough as he wrestled with his control.

"He left some physical evidence." She held up a vial containing a tooth. Vampires very rarely lost their incisors because they were retracted most of the time and because they were immune to tooth decay. "Stupid. Lucky for me."

"Give it to me. My people will run it through the database."

"Back off. I'll be awake during the day and I will get it through the database. By the time you're awake, I'll have a name."

"Don't you think I want to catch him as much, if not more than you do? I have a far more complete database and my people work during the day, we just don't go into the sun."

With a muted growl, she handed the vial to him. "I can't afford to take any chances. The cops are on the way. Go. I'll drive this back to town. David will have it delivered to Die Mitte."

He paused, cocking his head. Surprising her more, he was against her body before she took another breath, the blade between them. "This thing between us is not done."

She had to agree. But what she thought that meant and what he thought it meant were likely to be two very different things.

"How will you explain being out here? Do you need an alibi?"

She shook her head. "I'll work it out. There's a trail obviously with me leaving town with Carl in his cab and then going to the Devils' bar so I can't lie about that. This is further out than the other scenes. This is your car so I'll say you loaned it to me."

He blew out a breath as he stepped back. Sirens sounded in the distance.

"They'll be here in moments. This thing between us will get out. We need to talk, about a lot of things."

"Go. I'll let you know what I say. You're a smart man, cagey, so stay out of reach until I get back to you."

He looked as if he considered arguing but the sirens got louder and louder and he had no choice but to take flight and begone.

Rowan looked at the sky as she put her blade back into place and put herself in order, waiting for the police cars to arrive.

That's when she caught sight of the telltale dust cloud and knew she wasn't alone. "I have leave to be on this ground," she called out. "I claim this woman so that I may turn her over to the human authorities."

The blink of red as the Dust Devil, remaining utterly motionless, watched for seconds longer, finally moved away as the cars arrived.

EIGHTEEN

SHE'D BEEN WITH the cops for several hours, first as she filled Fred in on how the body came to be out there and then with the what-were-you-doing-out-here issue.

She hated that she couldn't give him the whole truth. It hindered his investigation and in truth, that was a good thing. But it sucked to lie and say she got a tip and drove out here just looking and happened upon the body.

They hadn't believed her, but what else could they do? Say she'd done it when none of the physical evidence pointed that way? Like most humans when confronted with something paranormal, they accepted it rather than look too closely at something they might not want the answer to. And it wasn't like this thing was ever going to trial anyway.

The sun was rising on the horizon when she finally finished up at the office with Carey and headed back to her place.

Where Jack waited on her doorstep, curled in a ball.

"Was it her? Why didn't you call me first?" The questions fell from his lips even before his vision began to clear once his eyes had opened.

"Come on inside. What are you doing out here?" Keeping her voice gentle, she helped him stand and braced, readying against his anger. But what she saw wasn't anger, it was the chaos of guilt, despair, relief, confusion and loss.

The door opened, and David stood aside to let them through. He'd known Jack was out there then, most likely had tried to cajole Jack inside.

"I need to know, Rowan." His fingers dug into her upper arms as his gaze locked on to her face. "Please."

"Yes."

He allowed her to steer him through the door and into a chair. David materialized with the bottle of Jameson and a pot of coffee. "I'll return momentarily with some food."

"Fred wouldn't let me go out there. Was it like the others?"

She sighed, looking for the right words, trying for the way to tell him without tearing him apart further. Knowing none of that was possible.

He had to know and there was no way to save him from the truth. No matter how much she wished otherwise.

She poured him a shot into the coffee and pushed it his way. "I'm going to tell you all I can, but you have to eat. You're no good to me, or her, if you fall over and end up in the hospital." David materialized with some simple sandwiches and fruit. She plated a little of everything for Jack and slid it next to his coffee mug.

Automatically he shoved a bit of apple into his mouth and gulped the coffee. At his acquiescence she sipped her own coffee.

"Yes. It was her and yes, the MO was the same. We did catch a break in that we found her hours before the others had been located. There's more evidence this time."

"But the location?"

"Further out than the other two bodies." Which led her to believe that there were most likely more bodies out there in the desert they'd never find. If the body was in Devil ground, they might inform Rowan or they might not. But no one would find any evidence if the Devils didn't want it found.

"Yes. Twenty-seven miles outside town. Far off the road."

He'd dropped it there for her. To taunt Rowan, just as he had when she and Clive both had scented him outside the building.

"Torn up like the others? Worse?"

She considered lying but in the end, he'd find out the truth and it would be harder. "Worse. You don't need the details, Jack, so don't bother asking anything else. It was bad. He's losing his control."

He shot up from the chair and began to pace. "How'd you know where to find her?"

"Tip and a hunch. I'd driven around awhile before I found her." How naturally the lies fell from her lips.

"Tell me all of it. I need to know." He tugged at his hair and a wave of his anguish hit, souring her mouth.

She moved to him, slowly, like you would a panicked animal.

"No, you don't." She took his face in her hands, gently but firmly.

Tears welled up but didn't spill over. His mouth twisted, lips trembled as he fought his grief. "I wasn't there to help her. She must have been afraid. No one helped her."

That way lay madness. She knew, having been down it many times over her parents.

A line was somewhere. A line she shouldn't cross. He needed to grieve, everyone did. Grief was part of life, part of the continuum between birth and death and to rob anyone of it was to disrespect the human experience. If she deadened it she'd help him today, but it wasn't her place to steal it from him entirely. She'd be betraying her own path and his too.

At the same time, there would be a place she could step in and help him find some peace. She had to listen for it, to be patient and wait for it, even though she wanted to fix him now. She knew this with utter certainty, just as she knew equally surely, just exactly when she'd intervene. The gifts of her birthday had sharpened her intuition as well as many other things.

"I have to know."

She shook her head. "You don't. You'll only torture yourself. She's dead. Can't change it. You can wish it and wish it different and it will never be. She's gone. How she died can't change."

"It wasn't normal. What is it, Rowan? Don't lie to me! I know you see it too." He drew from her reach.

"You know serial killers aren't normal. Sure these scenes are freaky and horrible, but this monster can be killed."

His gaze locked with hers as he understood she'd just said she would kill a murder suspect. She waited, mostly sure he'd agree with it.

"Is he using animals? Come on, this is some high-level creepy shit! The bodies are…what's been done to them isn't normal, not even for a serial killer."

"If you go trying to make sense from what a severely violent, mentally ill person does you're always going to fail."

"Coroner says he's never seen that sort of damage. I tell you that?" Jack's gaze went far away as he began to pace again. "I read through the reports and nobody wants to say it out loud but goddammit, this is not normal!"

"Who's arguing that it is? Was Dahmer normal? Huh? Human zombies? What *is* normal about a serial killer? There's a soap opera in their brain and no one else knows the storyline but them."

"I should have known. About the meth. I should have seen how bad she looked lately. I should have connected the killings with meth sooner. She didn't have to die."

She let him go for a bit as he ranted and raved. He looked so exhausted she was surprised he was still walking.

"Did you know it would end this way?" he asked suddenly.

There was no use lying. "When she disappeared and you told me all the connections, yes, yes I feared she'd end up like the other two."

"You didn't like her."

"No, I didn't. But you did and I care about you. Even absent that, no one should go through that. This killer is an abomination of the worst sort."

"You know more than you're telling me. You always know more than you tell me. You can't sandbag me on this. Tell me what you know!" He was on her in moments, still slow enough she braced herself for impact and kept her feet when he latched on, gripping her upper arms. "Tell me!"

It was time.

Slowly, she let the heat build from within. Let the Goddess fill her up from toes to scalp. This new gift came to her far more readily than some of the others had. She let calm emanate from her skin and into Jack. Deliberately, she avoided the sharp edges of his loss, those were his to exorcise, but she smoothed away the animal panic of his fear, the wildness of his feelings of failure. She let that sweet, healing heat slide from her body and into his.

He needed to let it go, needed to release his hold on the tidal wave of tears he'd tried to brick off.

"I will take care of this. I promise you."

"Tell me, damn you."

She needed to get permission and only one person, scratch that, one Vampire could give it.

"Jack, you need to let Fred and his team do their job. Keep out of it. I'm going to be working it from my angle. Fred knows this and he's okay with it. So what you need to do is trust the people who care about you to get this done."

He sighed, long and hard, and fell to his knees. She followed, taking him into her arms and rocking as he cried. Deep, ragged sobs of a man who wasn't prone to a great deal of emotional expression.

Each time he drew air into his lungs to sob again she felt his spine ease just a tiny bit more as she fed him comfort and wisped away what sorrow she could.

Finally he seemed done and lay his head on her shoulder, his breathing calm but for an occasional cry-induced hiccup.

"Why don't you stay here? I have a guest room. Sleep awhile. Wake up, shower and eat and I'll fill you in on whatever I find out in the meantime. You're running on empty and you're not doing anyone any favors being so exhausted. You're going to miss stuff this way."

"I can't sleep."

She stood and helped him up. "I have several meetings to attend. I only came home to change clothes and check in."

"Are you involved? What are you hiding?"

She knew it wasn't personal, or even serious, but it hurt anyway.

"You're no good to me like this. You need me, Jack. The cops aren't going to let you in. You know it. They can't. So if you want to hear what's going on you'll get your shit together, man up and deal with it. I'm it for you. Me and my access to the case. So shut the fuck up with that and go take a few hours' kip."

David must have been at the ready because in two strides he was in the room and at Jack's side. "Mr. Elroy, please, this way. I've laid out some pajamas for you."

"I can't sleep! Why isn't anyone listening? Lisa is dead and her killer is out there right now. How can I sleep?"

"Like this." David whispered into Jack's ear and escorted him through to the guest room. David had his own form of powerful magick and Rowan had no doubt Jack would be in a deep, dreamless sleep for a few hours.

She moved to the phone in her office which had started to ring as she approached.

"The First is on his way to you."

"He is?" Rowan couldn't help her surprise. Not only at the news of Theo being on his way to her—he'd have had to procure a special dispensation to set foot on American soil—but at the sound of Enzo's voice. Her third cousin and the man who'd taken over after Rowan had left the Keep.

"You have reason to hate him. I know this. But he loves you in his way."

"He had my parents murdered, Enzo. And then he raised me like a foster father. He pretended to mourn my father's death as deeply as I did."

The level of that betrayal—of the way she'd laid herself bare for him in her grief and rage at missing people she'd never known, all as he'd played along—stung to that day.

"Your father broke our oldest rules. There was nothing else to be done."

"How? By falling in love with my mother? She wasn't connected enough?"

"Do you think Theo would have cared for that? Are you so blinded in your upset that you can't see reality, Rowan? Never had I met a human more vicious and whip-smart than your father. Until you. Be his daughter."

"I have no fathers anymore. Theo killed the one who gave me life and finding that out at sixteen killed the one who'd taken on that role."

"You're too old to think like a sixteen-year-old. Your father had been promised to another family. This is the way of the Human Servant and has been for thousands of years. Your mother was on another path entirely. What he created with her set our entire existence on its head. You were not anticipated. He *had* to kill your parents or he'd have lost his position. More than that, our family and the family of the female your father was supposed to join with would have lost everything. Hundreds of humans would have been at risk.

"I loved your father like a brother, but he took a risk when he acted on his feelings for your mother. He took my life into his hands. My mother's life, my sister's, the children I'd have some day. I forgave him that. But he acted *knowing* the likely outcome. The First had no choice. But he saved you. He raised you and trained you. You are the fearsome woman you are today *because* he loved you when he shouldn't have."

She didn't want to hear this. Didn't want to try to understand Theo or what he did to her all those years ago. She sure didn't care to empathize with the man who had her parents murdered.

"I'm asking you to look past his mistakes, past the things that make him so very different than we are, and to see he comes to you, keeps a watch over you because he loves you. And you love him. Your father, my cousin, would not want you to miss this fact. Even as it hurts to see it."

He disconnected and she scrubbed her hands over her face.

It was daylight so she had a while at least before she'd be summoned to wherever he'd decided to nest.

CLIVE ATTEMPTED TO sleep but knew it would evade him for some time yet. He'd given the tooth over to China and she was on it. Once they'd examined it closely, he'd noted the decay there. Vampires didn't lose teeth like human children did. That this killer had wasn't a good sign at all.

On top of that, he'd received word that The First was on his way to Las Vegas with his lieutenants in tow. Explicit word that The First was coming to see Rowan Summerwaite.

Rowan most likely had a very full agenda with the cop's girlfriend ending up dead in the middle of the desert, and now this. As tough as she wanted to appear—*as she was*—Clive saw through her when it came to her foster father. He'd seen and heard the way she interacted with him and knew there was a great deal of complicated affection between them both.

That Clive had a part in what must have already been a tense emotional time for her only made him feel worse.

In the time she'd been gone he'd come to accept the very inescapable fact that he liked her. He enjoyed sparring with her. Admired her intelligence and strength. Her viciousness only sharpened his hunger for her. It shouldn't have surprised him as much as it did. After all, she was the product of thousands of years of service to the Vampire Nation. Vampires were, he could admit, prone to shallow behavioral tendencies. They liked pretty things and pretty people. It wasn't a surprise that the Human Servants, who served the Nation for as long as there'd been Vampires, were attractive to them.

But she was more than a pretty shell. Blast it all she wasn't even beautiful! Not like the ridiculous perfection of the female form she'd killed in his parking garage. It was that essential spark within her, the surety he had that there was simply no one else in the universe who was like her, that drew his attention to Rowan Summerwaite over and over.

Not just the sex, though it was extraordinary, he had to admit. If it were just the fucking, he'd do it over and over until he lost interest. No, it was the whole of her.

He enjoyed being with her. Found himself wondering what she'd think of this or that situation as he moved through his day. This was an entirely new situation for him. He had to admit that when he'd found out about the killing in the parking garage, so soon after they'd broken the rules yet again and had sex in his penthouse, he'd been knocked off balance at the clash of the different aspects of his world.

He'd felt guilty. As if he'd betrayed his people by his attraction to her. And he'd gone to her and made it all worse by hurting her when he knew he was wrong.

"If you're going to resist resting, at least feed." Alice strolled in.

"I did." He waved her away but she only sent him a raised brow as she sat to watch him pace.

"Are you truly worried about what he'll do when he arrives?"

"No. It can never be ruled out entirely, he is who he is after all. But I'm doing all I can." He would have received permission to be in Las Vegas but his people couldn't hunt. And, he realized, The First wouldn't do it for fear of weakening Rowan's position. Most likely Clive's, as well. Vampire politics never ended.

"He's coming here to help her. You know that."

He nodded. "Yes, I suppose so. He feels loyalty to her. To her family. They served him for a very long time."

"More than that. She's captivating in her own way."

"Doesn't matter. She's not a Vampire."

Alice laughed. "She's more than that. She has all the affectations of a Vampire. Quick. Brutal when necessary. Vicious. She is a predator with a sharp mind. And she's a Hunter, which makes her irresistibly forbidden to you. On top of all that, she's a human Vessel for a Goddess. I did research before we arrived here. There have only been four documented cases of this in all recorded history."

As if he was unaware of how singular Rowan Summerwaite was. It still didn't change anything. "What is your point? I'm aware of what she is."

"My point is you want her and you're trying so hard to deny it you're going to bollocks it all up. She is, beneath all the other trappings, a woman. If you continue to pretend you aren't interested in her you may just succeed in making her think that's the case."

This was not the discussion he should be having with his assistant. "If I don't stop this killer, we're all at risk of being exposed. For real this time."

She raised one perfectly manicured brow at him. "Yes. We will be eventually. With cell-phone cameras and Twitter and media at your fingertips every moment of the day it's bound to happen. Don't avoid the subject,

Clive, I've known you too long for this silly evasion. You need her for more than just this case."

"The last thing the Scion needs is to be romantically associated with a Hunter. I have enough complications in my life."

Alice waved it away as if it were inconsequential. "She's every inch your match. No Vampire could ever be. Too complicated. Too many politics. No human can, they can't keep up and eventually they all get crushed by their association with us. So what then? Weres? Sure if it weren't for that whole we hate them/they hate us stuff. Other paranormal beings like Dust Devils and mages? Face it, Clive, the two of you are perfect for each other. Doesn't matter what anyone else thinks about it, the truth is the truth even if you pretend not to believe in it. Lastly, you're quite strong enough to hold this seat, no matter the challenger."

She stood. "Now if you're sure you don't want to feed, I'm going to advise a sleeping draught and some rest."

If he gave up on this, she'd cease talking about Rowan. "Fine." He held his hand out and took the mug she'd proffered and then gulped it down.

"Go on then. You'll be notified when he arrives. China has all the preparations covered. Extra security is in place now."

She walked out with the same brisk, efficient manner she had coming in and he headed to his bedchamber, locking the door and settling in.

Even before sleep took over he thought of Rowan as she'd been that night. Her blade in her hands, muscles coiled for action, the light of her mission seeming to glow from her skin. Magnificent and furious. It didn't really matter that she wasn't for him. He wanted her anyway. He'd have her anyway.

NINETEEN

"ROWAN," David murmured as he shook her awake.

She straightened, having fallen asleep at her desk. A quick look at the clock told her she'd only been out about an hour and a half, but it had to be enough.

"He has sent a lieutenant."

"He's here?" She stood, alarmed. Jack was there, what if he saw The First before she got the chance to warn him? Theo could handle himself, and it was Vegas after all so strange-looking people weren't exactly rare. But she'd rather not have that moment.

"No. He's sent an envoy." David shuddered. He tried to hide it but she saw it anyway.

"Don't tell anyone, but they're not as bad as they make people think. Especially if you're not their quarry." She spoke while she brushed her hair and efficiently braided it to keep it out of her face. He refrained from saying anything else but handed her a warm washcloth, which she took gratefully.

"She's awaiting you in the formal living room. Mr. Elroy is still sleeping. What would you like me to do about that situation?"

"Keep him asleep until I'm gone at the very least. If he does awaken, strongly suggest he stay here because I need to speak with him."

"This meeting with… The First is about Mr. Elroy?" David paled.

"It's more than that." She paused a moment. "Not just for him, but for the investigation."

He nodded once. "Of course. You're right. I'll watch over him to keep it that way until you are gone. Is there anything else I can do for you? Do you need an escort of some kind?"

If she couldn't handle this without an entourage or bodyguards, she wasn't fit to hold her position.

She gave herself a quick once-over in the mirror and then looked back to David. "No, thank you. I'm fine. I'll ring if we need anything, but I imagine I'll be going to meet him somewhere. He'd be in there scaring people if he'd come along. He's not really the wait-in-the-lobby sort."

The look of amazed horror on David's face cheered her up.

"I'll be fine. If he was here to harm me, I'd be harmed." True enough.

A quick bow and he left, she knew to be away from their visitor.

Nadir hadn't changed much from the last time Rowan had seen her. Among the oldest of Theo's staff, she was the only one of his lieutenants to ever speak in public, though they all did in private.

Nadir wasn't her real name of course. No more than Theo was The First's real name. But beings as old as she tended to reinvent themselves at least once every few centuries.

She turned to face Rowan as Rowan entered the room, bowing slightly, a smile marking the far corner of her mouth. “You’re tired. You know how you get when you need sleep.”

Rowan took Nadir’s outstretched hands, squeezing them, exposing the mark on her wrist. “I’d be getting more sleep if Vampires stopped killing humans. The paperwork alone steals hours a night.”

“We’re incorrigible, I’m told. Good thing you’re around to keep us in line.”

Rowan snorted. “I think you scare them more than I ever could.”

“I’ve got a few years of practice on you. He’s here, staying at Die Mitte. He’d like an audience. Can you meet with him now?”

Though it wasn’t really a request, Rowan appreciated that Nadir made it sound like one anyway. She nodded. “Of course. The honor is mine.”

Nadir paused as Rowan slid the blade home and straightened. With one long assessing look and a slow blink, she told Rowan she was pleased. It warmed her even as it shouldn’t. The feelings of Vampires shouldn’t mean a damned thing to her. But what should be was irrelevant.

“Shall I meet you there?” Cars had always made Nadir nervous, Rowan remembered that. And frankly, if Rowan could fly, she totally would.

“That would be fine. I will be waiting to escort you to him.”

Ha! Awesome. Rowan nearly laughed out loud imagining how uncomfortable all the Scion’s little toadies would be with one of The First’s lieutenants lurking about.

She’d gone over her talking points already, all she

could do was make her arguments and hope he listened. She'd have to give something up, she knew that. What it might be only Theo knew.

Using the time it took to travel over to Die Mitte, Rowan centered herself, got herself together and pushed her emotions as far down as she could. It was important to remember he was a Vampire. Theo would not be swayed by passion or upset, even anger.

He'd raised her to be one of the best, and so she'd be.

CLIVE AWOKE LONG before the elevator doors opened to admit Alice. He'd showered and dressed, preparing himself for what would likely be a trying evening. He'd even fed. The First had most likely brought his own people and would offer some to Clive as his host, but it never behooved a body to gorge on a gift.

More importantly, it paid to be well rested and fed before one dealt with a being as powerful as The First.

Alice entered the room in her brisk, efficient way, a phone in her ear, instructions being issued in a clipped voice, her gaze taking in every detail even as she took notes on her ever-present yellow lined pad.

"Be sure to keep the hotel stocked with donors for our visitors. Yes. Of course he brought his own, that doesn't mean we won't extend our hospitality. Really, do not make me educate you on something you should know by now."

Clive relaxed, finding her utter implacability comforting.

"Settle their donors on the same floor. Keep the kitchen on the eighteenth floor fully stocked and staffed. The rest of their retinue will be arriving in three hours. I expect to be hearing from you within the hour when you report all these details have been taken care of."

Absently, she tapped the button to end the call and shook her head. "I do say, some of those boys downstairs are not terribly bright." Alice looked him up and down before nodding smartly. "Nice choice. The chocolate in the tie brings out the green in your eyes."

He sent her one raised brow.

"I don't see why that observation is such a bad one. She'll be here momentarily. Nadir will meet Rowan in the lobby and escort her to The First's apartments."

He paused to admire the way she managed to work in that bit about Rowan, even as she gave him pertinent information. More than his employee, she was his friend. His family in a very real sense. There were very few people he ever let this close to his life and she was one of those few.

"I do appreciate you, Alice. Thank you for the job you do. I'd be rather lost without you."

Her laugh made him smile. "You would indeed, Clive Stewart, and so I must stay. Everything is in place. China has taken care of all the extra security. Their rooms and suites are all being prepared. We've got the transportation on the way to the airport now. The First will meet with the Hunter alone. You'll be sent for when he's ready."

He knew he frowned, even as he told himself not to. Such a shoddy emotional mistake would get him punished if he wasn't careful.

"Will she be alone or attended?" He knew the answer, but asked anyway. If she came with any attendants she'd be meeting with her foster father as one of his protected. But she was here as the Hunter. She'd come alone and in doing so, tell everyone she had no fear, no doubt in her own abilities to kill any one of them if threatened.

It fluttered his pulse for a brief moment.

"She'll arrive shortly. Alone." Alice took another phone call before turning her attention to Clive. "Imagine what it would be like to face him after all this time."

He had thought of it.

"How many Nation Vampires will be staying in my hotel and for how long?"

Alice sniffed delicately but slid a file his way.

THE LARGE DOUBLE doors slid open silently as Rowan and Nadir approached. The First's guards were there, waiting. Recht inclined his head as she passed. He'd been good to her in his own way. Had protected her when he could.

The others looked on, a small group, most likely just part of his retinue. Theo rarely traveled, but when he did it was with no less than fifty people. Because his ability to hunt and travel around the area would be limited by whatever agreement he'd made with Hunter Corp., he'd most likely be traveling with more rather than less.

Enzo stepped toward her, taking her hands. "He's waiting for you through here."

He sat near the fireplace, the golden light licking over his pale skin, casting shadows on his face and against his hair. At first glance he appeared to be an older, distinguished gentleman with nice clothes and some money. He wore soft leather loafers she knew were hand-crafted in Italy. The jeans were designer of course, the sweater would be cashmere.

He'd posed himself for greatest impact and even knowing that fact didn't dim it for her.

Longing hit, twisting in her belly as she remembered that once in her life she'd been undaunted, despite his erratic behavior, she'd trusted him. He'd been her father, even as he still remained utterly not human.

He stood, all his energy gathering and flexing around him as he did. He was beautiful to watch, powerful and graceful. Old enough that his charisma and attractiveness were a snag, even without him trying. It was impossible not to watch him when he was in the room.

She dropped her gaze, turning her wrist outward, exposing her family mark. *"Vater."* She'd given him that because it would have been offensive to them both to pretend her being his foster daughter wasn't a huge part of why she had this very unusual access.

A ghost of a touch at the top of her head. He murmured in a language older than any spoken today. He'd gone off into that dreamy place he did sometimes. When he'd been overcome with nostalgia.

"Leave us." He switched to German.

No one hesitated, they simply moved toward the doors in an orderly fashion as they'd been ordered to.

"Sit. I've ordered tea. Enzo will bring it soon with those little cookies you like. You're thin." He sniffed as if that were some deliberate thing on her part to annoy him.

She sat. "Have you rested enough?" she asked out

of habit. Out of true concern. A wholly different part of herself came out in his presence. It puzzled, comforted and alarmed all at the same time.

Enzo brought in the tea and, automatically, she began to prepare and pour out. As she had three times a day from the age of four. The scent of the bergamot in his Earl Grey mixed with the cream and sugar she added. The heat rose with each circle of her spoon. One tap and she handed it to him along with the saucer.

He wore a far-off smile for a breath or two, pleasure on his features as he drew the delicate flavor of the tea in. A sip. "Perfect. You haven't forgotten. It's a trial, petal, to get someone who understands the subtlety of a proper cup of tea these days."

She let her breath out and began to make her own cup of tea. "I'm sure Enzo does a fine job. He's the one who taught me, after all." They'd been bred to serve. Generation after generation. Tea making was only one of the things Rowan and her kin excelled at.

"Before work, I would speak to you about some things."

She looked up, letting him have her gaze and her attention, knowing he could take her over whether she looked at him or not. She had to trust he wouldn't.

"You left without saying good-bye, Rowan."

Ruthlessly she shoved all her emotions away. "You had my parents executed, Theo. Good-bye seemed to be imputed when I left."

One imperious brow rose, disgust on his face plain. "Do not waste my time by hiding your emotions. You are human, no matter that you share your consciousness with a Goddess at times, or that you are from a long line of servants to my House."

He wanted to see emotion? Fine, she'd give him some. "I will not play for your amusement. You killed them and then you lied to me about it for nearly sixteen years. I found out and knew I could no longer give you my service willingly. And so I left. There was no need for farewells."

"And do you think I had my beloved Augusto killed to torture you? For, as you'd say, kicks?"

When he said her father's name, she didn't want to hear the affection there. "I think it doesn't matter why you decided to kill him, or my mother. The outcome is the same, is it not?"

He nodded and something that looked an awful lot like sorrow crossed his features.

"But it does matter why. To me. To you. To them. Would you like the whole of it?"

He hadn't made her beg. This surprised her. And though she wanted it not to be true, it moved her too. Being with him left her off balance. They were both on shaky ground and that above all things was why she was there.

"Yes, I would. Please."

His irises flared just a bit.

"You know that the Servants have rules. An ages' old history and complicated set of rules to keep things running. Your father knew the rules. He had an intended, the woman who was supposed to bear his child and strengthen the progeny of his line.

"He met her, your mother, while accompanying me on a trip to London. She was there with the Mother

Acolyte apparently and they took up an affair very quickly."

His eyes focused on something a long time ago. Her heart beat so quickly she felt a little light-headed.

"We were there for four months and by the time we left, you were in your mother's belly and Augusto could have left it alone. But she came to a nearby hill town and he continued to see her. They got married and still I never knew." He laughed a moment, jagged.

"It wasn't until you were born that I began to suspect. His scent had changed, you see."

"Because of her?"

He focused on Rowan, blinking his surprise. "Because of you. Power has a scent. Servants from lines such as yours, well, you all have a certain scent to us. Your father had grown up in my household. I knew his scent. Could have picked him out of a crowd from three miles away. Your mother didn't change his smell. She had her own of course, but I have those with magickal abilities in my retinue."

Enzo brought in more tea and withdrew just as quickly. Rowan poured out as she worked for calm.

"But when you were born he changed. His *power* changed. He was not only my protector, but biologically driven to be yours as well. His loyalties changed in a way my bond to him recognized."

He stood, unfolding himself with effortless grace. Even as he paced, the power swirled around him.

"Did you confront him?"

"I'd received an official complaint and inquiry from the family of his intended. I came back to my rooms to speak with him, but he'd gone out. I'd planned to have him followed, but he was so stupidly in love, he led me straight to her. And you."

He paused a moment and looked back her way. "When I saw her, when I saw them together I knew why he'd done it. There was much love and devotion there. And then you. He knew what he'd done. Augusto asked me to spare you and I agreed. She, Belinda, made me give my word that I'd allow the witches to get at you when it was time. This was a difficult promise to make. But over time, as you grew and I could see just how powerful you'd become, I knew I was right to assent to that too."

She licked her lips before speaking, choosing her words carefully. "You're The First, none question you. How could you kill him? You still didn't get a child between his line and the other one. Killing him made no difference in the outcome."

"I am The First, but you lie to yourself if you think I don't have to answer to anyone. We have rules. Those rules have protected us for thousands of years. That system of regulations has kept us safe for generation after generation and no one, least of all me, had the right to disobey. You know this. He took an oath and he broke it. Knowing the punishment for such an infraction. I had no choice but to do exactly what I did. He was an extraordinary man and I loved him very much. Don't strip him of that strength and intelligence to paint him as a hopeless innocent, Rowan."

It was easier to think of them as star-crossed lovers who'd been innocents.

"I knew one day you'd look at me with eyes filled with the dreadful knowledge of what I'd done. I made mistakes. Many of them over the millennia, but you were not one of them. I could not save them, but I could raise you in the tradition he was raised. I do not—*will not*—make excuses for what I did. And you have made me proud, even as you've torn my heart out. This is what it means to be a father."

Nothing else he could have said would have impacted her more. It was the longest speech he'd given her in decades. It wasn't closure really, but that was impossible anyway. He gave her the story and in doing so, part of himself. As he had here and there over her life, he'd given her glimpses of his weak spots, trusting her to not exploit them.

And while she'd left him and a part of her hated him, she never had used anything he'd given her so freely to harm him.

"In any case, it is good to see you. Good to see how much power flows through you now. I expect to see more of you in the future. You are the Vessel, without a doubt. And a Hunter. But you are also my daughter. No matter how much you try to deny it."

He sat again and she knew he'd say no more about it. But what he had said was important.

It would have been nice to have one simple and uncomplicated relationship in her life. But she had what she had and it was more than many others. Complicated and dark it might be, he did love her in the only way he could. Messed up as it was, she loved him in return, even if he remained alien to her in most ways.

She handed him the plate of cookies and he took two, a smile lurking at his mouth for just a moment.

"Tell me what it is you need."

She sipped as she gathered herself again and then told him about the situation. Laid it all out toward one goal, getting permission to tell Jack.

He listened until she'd finished and she readied herself for the questions she knew he'd batter her with until he was satisfied.

There was no denying he was brilliant. The ultimate predator. Dangerously intelligent. Provocative. He led her in a dance of his own choosing as he sailed his inquiries her way.

But he'd taught her well. They'd danced this way before and she found it was rather like playing Monopoly—it came back to you.

"You say yourself that he did not see any evidence of this human woman's true descent into her substance addictions. This shows poor judgment. You said he was full of grief and anger. This shows an unbalanced emotional state. How can I in good conscience give this unbalanced, emotionally unstable police officer access to information that could bring harm to my people?"

"He's not stupid. He sees that these murders are supernatural. So far he's pretending he doesn't, but now that his woman has been taken, he won't sway from the truth. He'll *have* to know. It'll become his holy mission."

"What is that to me?" He brushed lint from the front of his jeans.

"I know a little something about holy missions. He will avenge her. And if that means he'll expose you all and bring death to himself, he'll do it. If that means losing his job and being hunted forever, he'll do it. Give him the truth of it, let me share with him just how much is being done and I can diffuse him. I need the information he can give me."

He looked at her sideways and made a sound. "Is that so? You are unable to procure this information without him? How have you done this before? I'm told your investigative abilities are peerless. Are you telling me this is a lie?"

She wrestled her annoyance.

He rapped on the wall and Enzo poked his head in. "Send for the Scion. I'd hear what he has to say for himself." Theo looked back to Rowan after he'd given the order.

"I'm a good investigator and I have other avenues for information, as you well know. However, I'm involved openly here. I've been working closely with Jack on this case and he knows I'm not telling him everything. In this instance, his assistance is helpful. I could procure it elsewhere but that would take more time and invite more examination of me and who I work for."

"And think you I should care about that? About the Hunters being inconvenienced?"

"You'd best care about the Vampire Nation being exposed once and for all and not at a moment of your choosing but as serial killers. Bloody fangs and torn-up human flesh. The treaty will be a small inconvenience compared to humans in a blood frenzy as they hunt you." She poured herself another cup of tea. "It's going to happen. Really it's a matter of time. But we both know you'd be far better off coming out in a coordinated public-relations-friendly way instead of this."

"Finally you loosen up, petal. I've been waiting to see your sunny side shine through." As she processed his silly comment, he turned toward the doorway. "Now, what think you, Scion?"

Rowan didn't look up. She sipped her tea and kept her breathing and heart rate even. She would not give either man the pleasure of getting to her. Or knowing it at any rate.

In one easy movement, Clive went down to one knee and offered his throat. His suit didn't even get mussed up when he did it. As always, it called her to muss him up just because. "It is a pleasure to have you here, *Ovilius.*" *Ovilius*, the Latin word for *shepherd* and the formal term of address from a Scion.

Clive stood and moved to the chair next to Rowan's. "Ms. Summerwaite." He nodded and she blinked his way.

"I believe the Hunter is correct. And if I might offer something to this discussion?" Clive waited for Theo's nod before he went on. "I am of a similar opinion about this human Ms. Summerwaite speaks of. He is unstable. However, she is correct that in this particular situation sharing information with him could be crucial."

"You will be with her when she informs this human. If he makes any indications that he will share what he learns or that he cannot handle what he is told, you will wipe his memory of the information. And do be sure to impress just how dire the consequences should be if he exposes us. My lieutenants won't leave a body for any humans to find."

Rowan used every bit of her discipline not to react. She got what she wanted, she needed to hold on to that. Even if Clive would be there, which would totally muck things up with Jack. She could still tell him and that was a win.

Theo watched her carefully, waiting for any slip in her behavior and she'd give him none. At last he smiled and sat back. "Now, as to what you'll do for me in return." He steepled his fingers, bringing the urge to smile to her lips. He'd taken to that move after watching the Francis Ford Coppola *Dracula* movie. An inside joke between them.

She waited, outwardly patient. He knew, of course, exactly what he planned to ask her for. Or rather tell her to do. He'd known before he'd arrived in Vegas. He'd probably planned this for years, just waiting for all the pieces to come together just so. It was why he was who he was.

"I believe you are correct about the reality of exposure and our need to control such a thing rather than be known hand in hand with some event which places us in a negative light."

Rowan refreshed his tea and decided to confound Clive a little by making him a cup, as well. The surprise and then wary curiosity he wore on his features amused her.

"I also believe, as do my advisors, that perhaps a closer alliance with the Hunter Corporation is in order. I don't like the partner we must deal with. She bothers me and is generally unpleasant to look upon." He sniffed and then sipped his tea. "We need more than a person to make complaints to. We want a true liaison who understands the world of the Vampire and the world of humans. From the perspective of an Other. You will be our liaison. This string of events only makes it more clear to us that as Others, we need to find ways to stand together. I've sent my formal request to the Joint Tribunal so you should expect to hear shortly."

Wonderful. The politics of such a move would be a pain in her ass. Celesse would be angry that Theo would have elevated Rowan's status in such a way as to circumvent all her plans for her own people. They'd assent. After all, this sort of access to the Vampire Nation would be a coup.

Moreover, it would make Rowan more powerful than all but the top few partners. Some of them would like that, and some would feel threatened. It would take a great deal of internal scuffling, but she'd be fine in the end. Still, it was a huge time suck. She'd need to seek Susan's advice. Her mentor and chief protector would have useful advice.

Rowan may not have been a Vampire by blood, but it was enough that she thought like one and because of that, she had zero doubt in her ability to weather this storm and come out stronger for it.

TWENTY

"YOU'LL BE quiet and let me explain the situation to Jack."

Clive made a face as he followed her into the elevator. "I don't need your permission to speak."

"You do in my house. Jack is my friend. He's suffering and I aim to help him through it. He doesn't like you and he sure doesn't trust you so I need you to keep your mouth closed and let me do the talking."

"I have to take his blood. Just a little. It'll enable me to wipe his memories easily if he reacts badly."

She sighed. "I know. Just keep that to yourself for a while, please."

Because she said please, and because he knew she'd be raw from the meeting with The First, Clive backed off.

She showed him into a small, formal living room space. "Wait here. I need to talk with him first."

He paused, thinking it over and she touched his arm.

"Whether you do or not is going to boil down to whether or not you trust me. So make up your mind now or we can't do this."

Did he trust her? A silly question, he realized even as he thought it. He'd had her in the heart of his home. In his bedchamber. If she'd meant harm, she'd have made a move by then. She was certainly capable and fierce enough.

"All right then. I'll wait."

He watched her leave and took that time to put away the look on her face when he'd entered The First's quarters. So much energy in that room. He'd tasted her sorrow, her anger and her grief. But also her love and respect.

She and her foster father had had some sort of emotional breakthrough. He'd seen it in both, stamped all over their body language. He'd thought himself above and beyond the ability to be moved by the simplicity of something like that, but he'd been wrong. As off balance as she and her foster father were, Clive too had been turned sideways.

His respect and like for Rowan Summerwaite had grown. And now, he had to find a way to make this situation with her ex work out. He'd sooner punch the cop in the face for making Rowan so upset, but that would only make matters worse.

Clive stifled what would have been an undignified snort. It was more like he hated to think about making her life any more difficult than it already was. Which he'd given up wrestling with, he realized.

Alice had been right. Damn it all. He could remind himself all night long of just how inappropriate she was, how bad she was for him and obviously vice versa. And yet, none of that seemed to matter.

ROWAN SHOVED AWAY the rawness from the exchange with Theo and searched out David, who led her to Jack.

"Where have you been? And no more fucking lies,

Rowan. I've had it with lies. You know something you're not saying and my woman died because of that."

She sighed, wrestling with her own guilt. "I was getting permission to share the information I have with you."

He stood quickly, on shaky legs.

She barely stifled a snarl of disgust. "First thing first, get your fucking head out of that bottle. You're useless to me *and* to Lisa if you're drunk."

"I just had a beer with some food." His mouth turned into a sullen frown and she realized, not for the first time, just how many men in her life got pouty of late. She really should look into hobbies that included happy people for a change.

"We'll pretend I don't see three bottles over there on the counter, shall we?" Bracing herself, she faced him fully. "There's really no way to prepare you for this one so let me just say it. I can tell you, but that's not without strings."

"What sort of strings?"

"Clive Stewart will walk you through this next part. But I want to assure you I'll be with you the whole time. I wouldn't allow you to be harmed."

"Like Lisa?"

"Now it seems to me that when someone has gone out of their way to help you, it's unconscionably rude to treat them so poorly. You wouldn't be here right now if Rowan hadn't risked herself on your behalf." Clive strolled into the room and she wanted to hug him and hit him at the same time.

"If she'd shared with me right off Lisa would be alive right now."

Clive raised a brow, every inch the arrogant Scion. "Blaming Rowan for your girlfriend's drug addiction is absurd. Why her and not you? Hmm? How is it that it's everyone's fault but yours, Mr. Elroy?"

"Enough." Rowan stepped between them. She looked into Jack's eyes. "This is how it has to be. I answer to people, just like you do. So do you want to know or not?"

"Fine." He had no idea of course, just what was about to happen, but how could he?

Clive moved closer. Close enough that she caught a wisp of his scent. Those pheromones would help calm Jack, but *hoo-boy*, her hormones liked them too. He'd use just enough to bespell Jack so he could take blood. Rowan wished she could just tell Jack, what she was allowing was, in its own way, a violation of her own rules. But she knew it couldn't be controlled any other way. This would keep Jack alive, even if he freaked out at what he heard.

Knowing there was no way around it still didn't make her feel any better about it. Knowing that the easy way they had, the years of friendship might very well mean nothing to him once he knew. And yet she had to do it anyway. For him.

"What I'm about to tell you can't be repeated. Not to anyone."

"Is this about the mafia or something?" Jack's eyes had blurred just a little. Clive's thrall was ridiculously strong to work so quickly and with such a small push.

"Something like that. But if you repeat it, it will get you dead. And I can't protect you from that. I had to make promises of my own."

"She risked a great deal on your behalf, Mr. Elroy."

Rowan turned to Clive to find he'd put on part of his glamour. Good Goddess, he was irresistible enough on a daily basis, but when he went all vampy he was a thousand times more. More everything.

Jack's face lost some of its tension as he looked to Clive. "If this is illegal how can you expect me to turn the other way?"

Now he was going to play morally superior? "Like you did when Lisa popped pills and stole from the evidence locker? We're running out of time, Jack. Can you put your misplaced sense of judgment away long enough to hear this or not?"

"I said fine. Do what you need to do. We're wasting time with this bullshit."

She took Jack's hands and let a little of her magick slide between them. Warm and comforting. She'd helped him the day before, but the next part would most definitely need some assistance from her special skills arsenal.

Ha. Like Batman's utility belt?

His spine relaxed and the fury faded from his gaze.

"Clive has to take some blood from you," she murmured as Clive glided around them both, silent and graceful.

Rowan watched, caught up in the spell of it, as Clive bent his head and broke Jack's skin. Caught up at the sight of the bright red bead of blood and then of Clive's tongue sliding over the slice to heal it.

Jack drew a breath, laced with pleasure as Clive straightened and moved away, back behind Rowan again.

She waited a few more beats as the thrall wore off and Jack came back to himself. His eyes widened as he tried to pull his hands away from her hold. "What the hell just happened to me?"

"Clive took some blood from you. Just a few drops. It had to happen. I'm sorry for it, but that's the truth. Come on, Jack. Do you really think what's going on out there is because of a human? You said it yourself, the scenes aren't normal. Not even for a serial killer. If you want to know, you have to realize there's way more to the world than you think."

"Why? Why does he need my blood to tell me the truth?" It was only because she'd calmed him and Clive's exceptional thrall that Jack hadn't run out of the room. It wasn't fear in his eyes, but pain.

"Because I need a way to wipe your memory if you don't react well to what you're about to hear." When Clive smiled, his incisors gleamed in that way they did.

"Jack, I'm asking for your trust. I won't let any harm come to you. But if you want to know the rest, this is the only way. I had to get permission to tell you all this and the price was their ability to wipe your memory if you reacted badly." She licked her lips, uncomfortable with what she'd done, but knowing she had no choice.

"ARE YOU one of them? Is he a Vampire like on television? Are you one too? No. I've seen you in full daylight. Is that a lie too? Are you both just freaks?" He pulled his hand away. "Where did he bleed me? Am I going to be one now?"

At her back, she felt Clive tense up at the insult.

This could get out of control so easily. Vampires were not easygoing and Jack danced on the edge of sanity.

"The wound is gone. He only took a very small amount. It won't cause you any pain or harm. No, you won't turn into a Vampire. No, I'm not one of them but I know many of them. Yes, he's a Vampire but *not* like the ones you see on television. And most of what you see on television is a lie in any case."

Clive had to admit she handled the human well. Considering her basic personality, she must have really cared for this human. He didn't want to be jealous over it, it was clear they had nothing sexual or romantic there. But he was and it only annoyed Clive further. Perhaps he found being annoyed sexually alluring? Every time he was around her she annoyed him and he still got hard. Damn it all.

Clive wanted the whole thing to be over. Having this rogue out there so bent on exposing them made him look bad. On top of making him want to rip heads off. This human cop was in over his head and he was too macho to know it, or accept what Rowan was trying to tell him.

"JACK, sit down." Rowan pushed him into a nearby chair and perched close. "I couldn't tell you before because I'm bound by honor and blood not to. So here's what I know so far. The three women we've found were all murdered by a Vampire. What they call a rogue. Someone who's gone outside the internal system of laws that keep Vampires in check."

"*In check?* You're telling me there are Vampires and

this one killed. No, not killed, killed is too mild a word for what he did to them."

Clive resisted his urge to curl his lip. "Believe it or not, Mr. Elroy, we don't kill humans for sport or for fun. We have far lower rates of violence among our citizenry than you humans do."

"This is not helpful." Rowan shot him a look. "Sit down, please, Clive." She touched Elroy's hand to snag his attention. Clive realized anew just how much magick she had in her own right. Elroy's gaze snapped to her immediately.

"Yes, the Vampire is out of control. I'm on his trail. Clive's people are on his trail. We'll find him and take care of him. But I need you to understand that you have to let me do my job."

"Tell that to Lisa. Yeah, fine job you've done so far."

Clive saw the barb hit home as her spine stiffened. "Off sides, Mr. Elroy."

"You can't defeat this Vampire, Jack. No matter what you think of me, that won't change. He's not only a Vampire, which means he's faster and stronger than even the fastest, strongest human, but he's an old one. This makes him *even* faster and stronger. You can't stand against him and win. The cops on this case can't either. This is why I'm telling you."

"But *you* can stand against this freak? You say you're not a Vampire so how is it *you* can do it and I can't?" Jack crossed his arms over his chest, defensive.

"Because I'm just that special. What I am doesn't matter. What matters is that I am trained to kill Vampires. It's what I do."

"When you're not fucking them?"

"You're a vulgar, ugly man, Jack Elroy. What Rowan sees in you I cannot say. She's trying to help you if you'd put your ego away for a moment and listen." Clive wanted to punch the human for so deliberately harming Rowan when she'd gone so far out on a limb to help him.

"For all I know you and she are out there killing women for thrills and this is just a way to keep it all quiet."

"Really? Is that what you think?" She shook her head.

Seeing her composure crumble even just a little bit only made Clive angrier at Jack Elroy.

"I don't know what to think other than *you* know all these details and you have this whole time. *You* hang with these monsters. *You* found Lisa. How do I know you didn't kill her yourself? You hated her."

Rowan licked her lips. Hurt. Knowing he wasn't in a right state of mind. Knowing he was in great pain and loving him as a friend, wanting to help him and yes, being cut to the bone by his behavior.

"If you really think I'm the one who did this to those three women—" she indicated the phone with a wave, "—go on and call it in. Report me for it."

She waited and he burst up from his chair and began to pace. Staying away from the phone but clearly agitated. "You're a fucking monster and you're catting around with one too. Great. Just great. You brought this to Vegas, didn't you?"

Rowan sent Clive a look warning him to keep his mouth shut. She couldn't handle him being protective just then.

"My job is to protect humans. It's why I'm here. You don't have to like me, but you really need to think a bit on what your best chances are. Not only to find this killer, but to keep your ass alive. You won't survive even half a minute with this Vampire. If you don't keep your mouth shut about it, others can be harmed. I'm doing my level best to find this killer and put him down. If you believe nothing else, believe that. This Vampire is a monster and he will flick you off like a fly."

"Damn you, Rowan. I can't believe you kept all this shit to yourself. This thing…why? Why is he…it killing? Just for kicks? I can't believe I thought it was the meth."

Bracing herself, she took a deep breath before speaking. "It *is* the meth." She looked to Clive, wondering how far she could go with the information about the blood barrier and drugs issue. From his response of narrowed eyes and the quick shake of his head, she guessed it was a big shut-up-now. Stupid. "Just because he's a Vampire doesn't change the rest of the fact pattern. Don't let yourself get too distracted by the Vampire thing. I'll handle that part. It's the drugs. You have to know this, Jack."

Jack spun, features hard. "No."

She sighed. "Jack, each of the victims had drug problems. They went to rehab and in Lisa's case jail or rehab were only a matter of time. That's just basic police work. If we can keep our focus there, find some known associates and narrow, that would be something the cops could do and stay safe."

"They were all three women. All three human. Why

assume? Maybe he's, well fuck, how do I know what the hell an abomination is or why it does what it does?"

"Jack, get hold of yourself, for fuck's sake!" Rowan stood and went to him. "You're too close to this if you can't see the connections. You saw them yesterday. We talked about the drug stuff."

"Lisa wouldn't use drugs with a…a monster! If that happened, he forced it on her. She wouldn't do that."

"Really? What high ideals for a junkie." She knew it hurt him to hear it, but it had to be said. He had to hear it and understand it. Rowan was not doing him any favors to pretend Lisa was perfect.

"How dare you!" He got in her face and the room arced with electricity as Clive moved so fast Rowan didn't register it until Jack was pressed against the far wall, Clive's hand at his throat.

"How dare *you?* You have no concept of what this woman has risked for you. And from what I can tell you're not worth it."

He flustered her just then. He wasn't supposed to be defending her honor. He was supposed to be insulting her and being a prick. When he was, well, nice to her, she didn't know how to keep him away. Not that she did much of a good job on that front, but still.

"Let him go, Clive. He's upset."

"I should arrest you." Jack glared at Clive like the idiot he was.

Rowan threw her hands up before stomping over, grabbing Jack by the shirt and tossing him into a chair. If she hadn't separated them, it would have only escalated matters and she didn't have the time or energy for it.

"Sit down and shut the fuck up. We're done playing nice with you. If you can't get yourself together then get out of the way. The fact is, whether you want to admit it or not, your girlfriend was using. In a bad way. It led her to make desperate choices. She stole from her employer. On more than one occasion. She was on the verge of losing her job. Her apartment is a clear indicator of how far she'd fallen. This pattern isn't unique. How many files a year cross your desk with a story about a girl who never would have done this or that doing just this or that because she was jonesing for meth or something else?"

"You did this to her." Jack shook as he said it, but she could tell he believed it. Or at the very least wanted to believe it enough to make it so.

"Whatever you think, I'm the best hope you have. If you can't get yourself under control and give me your word to keep this secret, you won't leave here with the memories intact. I'm sorry. But that's reality and you had best deal with it."

"Why should I trust you? You're a…well you're not human and you never told me and you fucked me for God's sake!"

Now that was something she would not let him bully her over. She leaned down and got in his face, speaking very quietly. "I'm not a thing, asshole. I am a motherfucking killing machine who also shares her body with an actual, real-life Goddess. So you should be on your knees giving thanks that I fucked you. Now, grow a pair and deal with reality. Your mewling won't solve this case and I've had enough. You took your shots.

Back up before I'm forced to defend myself and fuck your shit up."

She straightened and turned her back to him, giving space between them and deliberately not looking at Clive.

"You're a what?"

"Doesn't matter. What matters is that I'm more than equipped to deal with this killer and I will. I need you to keep the cops off my case while I do it. If for no other reason than to keep them alive, I expect you to deliver. Can you do that, Jack? Can you get your head out of your ass long enough to help me find this killer and put him down? You can be disgusted by me and my otherness all you want, just keep it to yourself along with everything I've just told you."

"Do I have any other choice?"

She turned, heavy with sadness at what she knew would happen, but hated anyway. "Sure. You can leave here and go fight crime against an enemy you can't find or beat." She shrugged. "Or you can be a man, suck it up and hold your nose while you choose the lesser of two evils like everyone else on the planet. Up to you. Believe it or not, Jack, I care about you and I want to help. I'm *trying* to help right now."

He stood, wiping his palms down the front of his jeans. "I don't see that I have any other choice. Keep me updated but otherwise I think it's best if you stay away from me. I'm protecting your secret, but not for your sake."

Clive cleared his throat as he smoothed down his tie. "Be sure you keep that oath, Mr. Elroy. You're bound by your word."

"What's it to you?"

Rowan was sure she goggled at him for saying it. Jack was so angry he shook with it. But he wasn't usually stupid. One look at Clive just then should have told anyone with half a brain to keep quiet and get away.

"The real question, Jack, is what it is to *you.* You gave your word. In my world, your word is your bond. And this is about my world, so don't make any mistake thinking otherwise. If you break your word, I will come for you. If you're lucky it'll be me. There are others who'd be less…quick than I'd be in removing your life from your body. Others Rowan faced to help you. You should try some gratitude."

"Like I should thank you monsters for bringing this shit into my town? For getting my girlfriend killed? Yeah, fuck off. I'll keep your secret, but you won't get any thanks from me." He stalked from the room, slamming the door in his wake.

And she tried to pretend she didn't feel so very alone. Tried to pretend it didn't matter that this person she thought of as her family had just torn her to shreds and she deserved a lot of it.

TWENTY-ONE

"DON'T," she said as he moved nearer. He knew she struggled to keep her composure. Knew it and it felled him all the same.

"Are you afraid I might see your soft underbelly, Ms. Summerwaite?" He'd planned to sound more teasing, but to his hearing, it sounded as raw as he felt.

Slowly, as if she were afraid, she turned, tipping her chin to look at him better.

He drew a fingertip along the line of her jaw. Warm. Vibrant. She was fire and a riot of color. Sunset. Dark and seductive even as she was so very bright and bold.

Clive knew pity would be scorned. And what he felt just then wasn't pity anyway.

This fierce woman was vulnerable. In the slow, sticky moment between them, he saw her to her foundations. Jack's rejection of her had hurt her far deeper than he'd first imagined. And it only made him angrier at the man for doing it.

"He doesn't understand what you've done for him. But that doesn't mean what you did is meaningless. Or small."

She leaned into his palm, just for a brief moment and he used it to get closer. What they had, their electric, snapping, hissing, unavoidably magnetic attraction rolled through him and then over him.

Her eyes widened as she gasped in a breath, her fingers twitching. So very attuned to her, he swayed closer, sliding against her and moaning as the sensual *shuss* of his suit jacket against her sweater filled him to nearly bursting.

"What you do to me, Rowan." He pressed a kiss to her temple. "I find myself totally unable to stop thinking about you." Another kiss just lower, against her ear.

Her spine loosened as arousal flooded her, the scent of it rising between them, catching his senses, snagging him. He wanted her until he ached with it.

Her hands pressed flat against his belly and into his suit jacket. Encircling his waist and drawing closer.

"Why are you being so nice to me?"

His amusement was spiced by the way he seemed to go wild for her when she was extra prickly.

"You are a magnificent woman. Strong. Sexy. Powerful. I like you, even when you're being a wretched bitch."

She gasped a little laugh when he nipped her lip and kissed the corner of her mouth, drinking in the way it curved up so perfectly.

"I'm not a wretched bitch, Scion. I'm a fierce bitch. There's a huge difference."

Surprised, he laughed, swooping down to take her mouth in what he'd meant to be a teasing kiss. But her nails dug in, bringing him close, his cock pressing hard against her.

"My body, embarrassingly led by my penis, seems to come alive any time you're near." He licked over the hollow of her throat. "And, despite your habit of killing my people and leaving big messy paperwork piles for me to fill out, I like you."

Her breath caught as he slid his hands up her sides and over to her breasts. "Yeah?"

"Even your grammar is atrocious. But I can overlook it, I suppose." He struggled not to smile as she peered up into his face.

It would never be safe with her. Not in the way he was supposed to want. It would often be fractious, because while sexy and intelligent, she was also a pain in the ass. Unmanageable. A political nightmare. He'd certainly not be able to bring her to any professional events.

And yet, none of that seemed to matter to him.

"Ferocious," he said out loud before taking her mouth again, tasting her capitulation. "It will rarely be easy with us, you know."

She tipped her head back and laughed as he steered her toward the couch. "Because we're the odd couple of the paranormal universe perhaps?"

"Word will get out eventually."

"I notice this isn't stopping you from taking my shirt off." The last part was muffled a bit when he pulled the sweater off and over her head. "Is this your way of declaring your intentions, sir?"

"I don't know quite what it is we have, Rowan. But most assuredly we have something. Something I'd like to explore."

Her fingers, nimble and clever, had already opened his pants and tiptoed their way up his cock.

"You know you don't have to butter me up to get into

my pants." She said this as she shoved his suit coat off and began to work on the buttons of his shirt.

"I've not used butter in many decades. They've got so many better ways to make a woman slick. Frankly, I'd prefer to work for it."

She stilled, cocked her head as she took him in and then laughed. "Even though you're an uptight prick, I keep forgetting you're nearly five hundred years old. Also, it amuses me when you get vulgar. I feel far more productive in my role as bad influence that way."

He had a clever retort, but swallowed it when she shoved his pants down and wrapped her legs around his waist, grinding against him.

"I need you in me."

He paused a moment to look at her breasts as her hair spilled across her nipples.

"Always a pleasure to obey such an order."

Rowan plunged into the sensations Clive always seemed to provide. His hands on her skin, lips skating over sensitive flesh. She'd lost her initial suspicion that he'd lose control and bite her. After all, the man had control like she'd rarely seen. He wanted to, she knew that, but he wouldn't.

There was something freeing in that. Knowing she didn't have to hold back. Knowing he would push her limits and she'd love it. It made the sex even better.

And there, on her couch, his now nude body against hers as he divested her of her pants and underwear, she could admit in her head that it only made her crave him more.

Stupid and dangerous as it was, he was right that

they had something. The real question was if it was enough or if she should fuck him and run away.

Just at that moment, as he slid his fingertips against her clit and her body lit up like a pinball machine, she had no plans to run anywhere.

When his mouth replaced his fingers she gave over to him, forgetting, at least momentarily, the darkness outside the room.

His hair sifted through her fingers as she urged him closer, harder, more. *Just more…* Until her climax broke over her system, drowning everything else but that moment.

And then he was sliding inside her, pressing deep. She managed to drag her lids up to look at him, into that brutally handsome face, now softened by sex and pleasure.

She wanted to close them again, wanted to deny what she saw in his features, what she felt in how he touched her. This time was different. Hot on a different level. It left her feeling exposed and unsure.

But soon all there was was sensation. His body covered hers, skin to skin. She fell into the flex and bunch of his muscles. He smelled good. Even if he weren't a Vampire, Rowan doubted he'd have sweated. And still he exuded that masculine something. Pheromones maybe.

Whatever it was, she wanted to lean in and take a bite. But since that might be reciprocated, she managed, barely, to refrain and give him a lick instead.

She shifted, bringing her knees higher, both of them groaning when he slid even deeper. He didn't treat her as if she were fragile. Not rough, but he didn't hold back either, the raw power of him thrilled her as he thrust.

Every once in a while he'd utter a language she'd only rarely heard amongst the oldest Vampires. Their mother tongue, she'd been told once. Back from when they'd lived in keeps like the one Theo had.

The words were smooth, like river stones, exotic. She knew a bit, enough to pick up bits and pieces as he spoke. Words of admiration.

She dug deep for filthy words but came up empty. Same with sarcasm. Which agitated her enough to squirm a little and then delight when the strain marked his features.

His gaze locked on hers, his mouth twisting into a smile.

"You do come in handy, I must say," she sighed as he pressed deep and came. Her body, warm, loose, relaxed and filled with sex chemicals, remained wrapped around his.

"Glad to be of service," he murmured into her hair as he got his breath, and his composure, back.

He could tell she was thinking on how to put distance between them again. She wouldn't succeed of course. She might be the Vessel for a Goddess, but he'd been around for nearly five centuries. He knew a thing or two about women, and this one in particular needed a man like him. Sure she'd have the willpower to resist him if he was a normal man. But he wasn't.

"That smile makes me nervous." She watched him

warily as he got up and headed into the bathroom adjoining the room they'd just used.

He let her stew awhile as he cleaned up. Liked to listen to the way she moved and got back into her clothes.

She was busily dealing with her mass of beautiful hair when he returned. The intimacy of that warmed him. She'd try to hold him back. It was part of her nature to be contrary. He understood her better than she knew. But she'd fail because he rarely did.

"It should make you nervous. Now, what's our next step? If we can assume your cop will work on the things you sent him off to do, I was thinking we should connect with my people."

Her brow furrowed and he resisted the urge to smooth a thumb across it. "Things would be a lot easier if Theo just unleashed his lieutenants on this bastard."

"Except this would be a violation of the treaty you're always quoting." Technically The First shouldn't even be in Vegas, though Clive was sure that mattered not one whit to him. His lieutenants were considered by Hunter Corp. as some sort of weapon of mass destruction. And, he supposed, that was a pretty accurate way to view it.

"Yes, yes, well. My standards appear to be slipping."

"Perhaps it's me who is the bad influence on you." Amused and in a good mood even she couldn't shake, he breezed past her out into the main rooms of the place.

"I've never doubted that. Why don't you go meet

with your people and I'll go meet with mine. If I find him and kill him, I'll let you know."

He took her hand as she passed. "I know what my people have to say. Come on, Ms. Summerwaite, you've got the services of an old and powerful Vampire. You should use them."

"I have a meeting with a source. And that source will not approve if I bring you along."

Must be a Vampire. "Who is it? Oh don't get that look, I'm not going to send anyone over to rough them up. But clearly it's a Vampire and I should know what my people are up to."

"Ha. How about you deal with the one who's up to ripping humans apart and leaving them like garbage in the desert? And then I can deal with my sources who don't need Vampire Central peering in their windows."

It was a good thing he was a patient man.

"When you finish, if you'd come by to update me, I would appreciate that."

She made a sound that he couldn't ascertain agreement from, so he continued to look at her until she responded.

She sighed, clearly agitated. "I'll get you an update when I finish. I'll text it to you."

He realized then it was probably not the best thing for her to go to Die Mitte after that meeting with The First earlier in the evening.

"This isn't over between us, you know that. Any attempt to avoid me is silly. You want me in your bed, I want you in mine. I might even like you a little, though I'd deny that if questioned."

"I need to catch a serial-killing Vampire. That's my focus right now. We are totally wrong for each other anyway."

He took her elbow, firmly but gently, steering her toward the door, handing her the coat she'd hung in the entry.

"This is where you're incorrect. You see, as Alice pointed out to me just this morning, there's no one more perfect for me than you. Which, I must tell you I found myself a tad bit alarmed by, because as you might imagine, I had thought of a nice, calm woman on my arm. You are many things—" he paused while she stabbed the down button to call the elevator "—but none of them is calm. But you're bloodthirsty. Strong. You don't stand for any nonsense and you're quite uninhibited about killing people. Thankfully that lack of inhibition extends to your sexuality. This is a combination that overcomes your personality flaws."

"Careful there, with all those flowery love words I might think you want to pledge your troth and make me your little woman."

Though he wouldn't admit it to her, Clive was relieved to see the resurgence of her bitchy self. The sadness in her eyes was getting to him, damn it.

"I'll be expecting your update. If I don't see you before the sun rises, I'll definitely see you tomorrow after sundown."

"Yeah. Whatever." She paused and then huffed a

sigh. “Thank you. For backing me up with him earlier. And for…well for everything with Jack.”

He slid his fingertip over her surprised little gasp, not giving a single whit if anyone else saw. “Now then, that wasn’t so hard, was it? You’re welcome.”

“You’re going to get me in trouble. I can just tell.” She stomped away to where her car waited. Her waved middle finger in his direction only made him laugh before he headed in the opposite direction and toward home.

TWENTY-TWO

LATE NIGHT AT the Vampyre Theatre didn't make it any more appetizing. Instead, the quality of ladies and gentlemen hanging around only worsened as the pickings thinned out.

Rowan wove her way through the groups, noting how many of them looked tore up. She most sincerely didn't believe Marv would ever shelter or even condone this killer. But he might know something.

"Marv." It was all she said to the chick working the front window.

"In the back. I'll let him know you're coming." The girl licked her lips and looked from side to side nervously.

Rowan leaned in. "Is there something you'd like to tell me?"

The girl looked panicked, but no one else was around just then. Rowan slid a business card across the counter. "If you feel up to talking about it, my contact info is there. I won't expose a source."

"O-okay. Thanks." She took the card and put it in the pocket of her little uniform.

Rowan headed through the now empty club toward the back. The last show ended at two and it was already half-past three. The quiet was restful and she took the small respite as she hailed Marv with a wave and a smirk.

But instead of his usual annoyed face, he looked… relieved.

"Walk with me, Hunter."

She fell into step next to him as they went deeper into the bowels behind the stage.

He opened a door to what must have been his private living space and she went through. Not worrying about him attacking her while her back was to him. He wasn't stupid.

"Now I'll never get the smell of Hunter out of the rugs." He moved past her, rumbling under his breath. "Sit. I gotta tell you a few things. I hear He's in town. You see Him?"

"The First?" She smiled, showing her teeth. "Yes. You know why I'm here, right?"

"Listen, I don't like Hunter Corp. in my beeswax, yanking my chain and in general, causing me issues. But I don't like Vampires who get out of control and bring the heat down on my ass either. So as a general rule I keep my head down and my mouth shut except when things need to be handled. And this needs handling."

"I'll do my best to look stern and disapproving of your coming to me."

He rolled his eyes. "Man's got personal biz and I have no beef with that. Whatever floats your boat, ya know? This may not be as glitzy as Die Mitte, but it's no dump either. We got standards of our own. Sure, we take a sip or two of the audience, no harm no foul.

But, we got rules and the first one is to keep your shit on the down low. No messy situations."

He pushed to stand and began to pace.

"But I got this guy coming around. He's targeting the girls, bringing junk into my place."

"Heroin?"

"Fuck no. We can get high from most opiates, you know that. Meth. And lots of it. Thing is, I used to be under the impression we couldn't crack that barrier. Now, I'm getting the feeling the status quo on this has changed."

Clive would so kick her ass, but this was something the semi-decent Vampires like Marv needed to know and guard against.

"Yes. But it's not good in the long run. The barrier was broken, yeah? But it does massive damage you guys can't heal. Not forever, if you know what I mean."

Marv paused. "That so? Hmm. I'll need to be more watchful with who hangs around my place now, eh? Scion's gonna be hacked you told me that. Appreciate it all the same."

She waved a hand at that. "So what? I'm hacked this was even a possibility and no one bothered to update me when dead tweakers began to show up in the desert."

He laughed, a bit rueful. "I hear rumors about you and him."

"Yeah? I hear Elvis was down at the Bellagio at the breakfast buffet."

"But one of those stories is true I bet."

"Back to the guy hanging around with loads of crystal meth, please."

He grinned at her, shoving his mass of hair away from his face. "He's fucking crazy. Bringing the quality down. Narc cops are gonna get wind of this shit and then I'll have a crapton of blue coming down around my shoulders."

"Is he old?"

"Yeah. That's why I've been thinking on coming your way. Considered calling over to the Scion's office, but I don't like those suit Vampires. Waste of teeth. Worthless, though this one isn't nearly as bad as the dick from before. Still, I got no call to be traveling over there. I'd take care of it myself, but this dude I'm talking about is easily six hundred."

Rowan scrubbed her hands over her face. A six-hundred-year-old Vampire strung out on meth? Fabulous.

"The Scion needs to know this, Marv. This is big. Grudgingly, I can admit he's doing what he can to help. No one wants to be exposed with this stuff. It makes everyone's job harder and I don't like it when other people muck about with my schedule."

"'Spose it helps when your dad is the head honcho. People take you all seriouslike."

She snorted. "Nightly tuck-ins were a total blast. I'm sure you'd be envious." He shuddered and she knew he got the point. "I know you don't want to deal with them, and normally I'd agree with you. But this, well you and I both know this is different."

"He's different, you mean?"

"He's something. But when it comes down to it, he's a Vampire just like you. You all have a certain way of seeing the world and that's fine. This murderous fucker

I'm looking for doesn't and he seems hell-bent on taking you all down with him."

Marv sighed. "Yeah, yeah. Do it."

"When I leave here, I'll go to Die Mitte. I'll do my best to keep you out of it. Tell me the rest."

Marv sat back as he started. "About seven months ago this older Vampire started showing up here on Wednesday nights. He'd sweep in, check everyone out and invariably choose one of the leftovers from out back. Weak willed, with a sweet tooth for substances and flash."

His lip curled. "Anyway, I caught him with meth and told him not to bring any more here. I figured he was using it because he had a shitty thrall, or he just was lazy and wanted his blood partners really dependent on him. It's not unheard of."

He got up and went to a desk on the far side of the room, rifling through a drawer until he found what he'd been searching for. Missing posters. He handed her three of them.

"In the last three months I've had concerned parents, boyfriends and counselors here looking for some lost loved one. Not an unusual thing. You gotta realize that just because we're not eating these humans and leaving their bodies in the sand, it doesn't mean these kids are alive or that they want to be found by anyone. They come to Vegas to be other people. You know that. So I just tack the posters up in the break room and move on."

It was true, she knew it. "He's really chosen the perfect hunting grounds." Except she was there and this would end. She looked over the fliers featuring pictures of the humans who'd gone missing. She'd seen them so often in Paris, in London, Boston, D.C., Seattle, Los Angeles and especially in Vegas.

"I draw the line at serial killing. I know a lot of us don't care one way or another about humans. But I kinda like you guys. You're far more delicious when you're alive and coming to me willingly than carrying torches and pitchforks, which is what would happen if this shit went live."

She looked at the faces in the black-and-white photocopied fliers. "He's totally got a type." Each of the women bore a striking similarity to the three who'd disappeared already.

"Yeah and one of those missing is the roommate of the one who let you in. The girl you gave your card to. Been gone for two days. Last time Honey saw her, it was with this Vamp I been telling you about." He sent Rowan a raised brow as if he'd caught her.

She rolled her eyes. "Do you think I'm surprised that you have camera surveillance at your ticket booth? I'm far from being an amateur, Marv."

"She's one of mine. Not a Servant like you and your line, no, but it means the same to me. This Vampire came onto my turf and he's taken one of my protected."

As a member of Marv's staff, humans and Vampires would fall under his dominion and protection. Of course he'd want to keep his human staff protected.

"Gosh, you're going to make me like you with all this nobility. Stop it."

He flipped her off, but looked a little less angry than he'd been a moment before.

She got a solid description that she sent to Carey's

email with a request to get working on a positive ID. She told him to run it by Clive's people to see if they'd got a hit on the tooth she'd recovered. The sun would be up in two hours so she needed to get moving.

"I've asked her to wait. Honey, the girl from out front. You can talk to her in the break room. It's private enough. Most of my people are gone, anyway."

She paused at his door. "Did you know she was using? What's her name? The one who's missing?"

"I can't keep day-to-day track of everyone. I wish I could." She could see from his face that he did indeed feel that way. She understood it. "She'd been missing work, but her friends had been covering for her." He shrugged. "I'd have fired her for it. But I sure as fuck wouldn't have killed her and dumped her body."

She sighed. "I like that about you, Marv."

HALF AN HOUR later, as the very late-night Vampires were all streaming home, she hit the lobby of Die Mitte.

She'd apparently reached visitor status as no one tried to stop her when she got into the elevator up to where Clive's offices were.

"Ms. Summerwaite, I was told you were on the way up." Once the doors had opened, Alice glided to her, taking Rowan's hands for a moment. "Come through. He's waiting in his office."

Rowan may have been mistaken, but she was pretty sure he looked more smug than usual when she entered the room. Her office at work had one window that looked out over a parking lot. This place was giant with views looking to the east. Dawn was somewhere out there, just on the horizon.

She avoided looking at his desk and wondering what it would be like if they had sex on it. Because that would not be professional. Ha.

"And what is it I can do for you, Ms. Summerwaite?" Clive stood and indicated she sit. Wanting to keep him on the other side of the desk, she plopped into the chair and pulled out her notepad.

"Here's how this has to go. I've just received a great deal of information from one of your Vampires. I'd love to share it and all, but you have to agree, up front, to leave this source alone. No punishment for telling me instead of you."

He frowned and she shrugged. "I can go right now with this. I don't need to be here sharing with you. I am because I agreed to, but I can't in good conscience get this Vampire punished for not wanting to come over here."

"I'm supposed to look away when my own people are allowing this vermin to break our laws so flagrantly?"

"Don't be so dramatic. I'll give you details once you promise and we can move along. Sun's a comin' so let's go." She made a circular motion with her hand, indicating he hurry up.

He may have growled in frustration, which was a cheerful thing.

"Fine, my hands are apparently tied. So tell me what Marv told you."

She should have known he'd anticipate her actions, or even had her watched. She'd have done so in his place.

"Your Vampire is older than we thought. Probably close to six hundred. Hanging around the Vampyre Theatre and he comes to the party with oodles of crystal. I've got a decent description of him from Marv and one of the humans who works for him." She tossed a sheet of paper across the desk before leaning back.

He looked it over before picking his phone up. "China, I've got a description on our killer. Yes, I'm in my office. You can meet the Hunter while you're here."

"Bet she's all aquiver with that one," Rowan mumbled.

He ignored that. "Go on."

"I've got my people working on the description too. If he's that old, there may not be much to find. But if you got a ping on the tooth you'd at least be able to correlate or eliminate him as a suspect." The older Vampires weren't much for complying with Vampire Nation rules about having identification but they still had their own version of DNA so if he was in the database they'd find him.

However, she knew the Nation had resources they didn't share so widely. Her best shot at a positive identification on this killer was through them. If she had to kill him, which hello, she totally did, it needed to be all aboveboard.

"Latest victim is a girl who also worked at the Corsican in the Vampyre Theatre. I mean a girl, she's only twenty-two, for Goddess' sake! She's been gone two days. Roommate says Ellie's, that's the girl who's missing, problems with bitch have gotten worse in a big old hurry. This Vampire, who calls himself Petyr, emphasis on the *Y* apparently, has been giving Ellie wagons of the stuff. Not that his real name will be Petyr, unless he's an idiot.

"Also, he has a type. Long, dark hair. No bangs. Brown eyes. Big knockers, a perennial favorite of the penis I've come to notice. My people are running some cross checks for missing persons with those descriptions. I'm going to take a guess and say this Vampire has to have killed others and we haven't found the bodies."

"I see you're going to blame more on us."

China, Rowan presumed, walked into the room looking very much like an extra from a *Blade* movie. Rowan would totally underestimate this chick as a poser if she didn't already know her history. She'd been taking care of Clive's security problems for a hundred years.

But it seemed that China was underestimating her, which was so very silly. Sloppy even, given her record of service to the Nation. But everyone, she supposed, was capable of letting personal feelings blind them to the truth they'd see otherwise. Only in this case, well, she had a feeling Clive was not going to react favorably to such human behavior.

"Yes, indeed. It's my fondest wish to spend every waking moment finding dead bodies dumped in the middle of nowhere with organs missing and blood drained from every part of their bodies and blame it on Vampires. You're all such sweet innocents I'm sure no one would believe me anyway. Right there in all the mythology books under Vampire it's all entry after entry about you guys walking old ladies across the street and working at soup kitchens every Thanksgiving."

Clive heaved a sigh. "China, this is Rowan Summerwaite, the Hunter. She is also the Liaison, officially sanctioned by The First. So shall we move past your sloppy behavior in displaying such rudeness and do our work? Perhaps you need a reminder of whose name is on the door?"

And he said it with so much beautiful threat wrapped around each word. The power of it rolled through the room, nearly stealing Rowan's breath.

China immediately went to one knee and bowed her head.

Clive didn't acknowledge her show of supplication. Instead he looked to the notes on his desk. "She's been kind enough to share a description of the Vampire killing these human women. I'm sure you can get past your annoyance to do something about getting us a name and location."

"I'll be going. It's hard work, framing you all and I haven't had my daily rest." Rowan stood and Clive joined her, walking around China, who still knelt on one knee, head bowed.

"I'll walk you out. China, I expect this work to be completed by the time I awake at sundown."

Once they'd rounded the corner he paused. "Come up, won't you? You look like you need to eat something. Let me feed you."

He flustered her. It was a completely foreign and not altogether unpleasant sort of feeling. But it nettled her this man caused it, even as she couldn't help but like him. Respected him even.

He leaned close, the thrill of his nearness adding spice to the fear of discovery. "You should know that look of wary curiosity tinged with your natural-born hostility only makes you more alluring."

"I need to go. I'm meeting with some of my staff to go over the description we got. Daylight's a good time to do some searching." She should have stepped away, but she didn't for long moments more as he looked at her like he saw down to her bones.

"Don't go hunting without backup, Rowan. This Vampire isn't to be trifled with."

"I'm the Hunter, Clive, it's sort of in the job description."

"This isn't a run-of-the-mill Vampire. He's not soft and out of shape like Jacques was."

Softened, despite her better judgment, she smiled. Just a very brief upturn of her lips. "Most of my kills have been older Vampires. You have to know this. I know you have a file on me with all that info in it."

"Crystal meth changes that. You can't deny it. Supercharged from age and drug-addled too? Insane and rotting from the inside out. This Vampire is not like any threat you've ever faced. Just—" he paused to issue a long-suffering sigh "—if you do go hunting, don't let your guard down for a moment."

She searched for a snarky retort but found herself tongue-tied. Instead, she stepped back, raised her hand and got into the down elevator. "I am many things. Not all of them good. But I am always careful. Good morning, Scion. Have a good rest."

The doors closed, but she knew there'd still be cameras. She held her head high and marched out to meet the day.

TWENTY-THREE

ROWAN WISHED SHE could talk to Thena, but she and her dashing professor were off on a two-month long trip through Central and South America. Much needed, but it left Rowan with one less friend. One less sounding board. Jack wasn't speaking to her and Susan was busy. And, truth be told, she missed Thena very much. This thing with Clive sent her reeling. Reeling wasn't something she did. Add to it a crazy, cranked-up, serial-killing, six-centuries-old Vampire and what she really wanted to do was eat too much ice cream while taking shots of icy vodka and sleeping it off in Thena's guest room.

She sighed. No use wallowing. She didn't have time for it.

Instead she grabbed some coffee, left a message for David with her whereabouts and headed to her office.

She expected it to be deserted, but clearly Carey had been working most of the night because there was a file folder on her desk with two possible matches.

"Hey, Ro." He sauntered in and sat, tossing his Chucks up on her desk and earning a frown he chose to ignore. "I think we've got it narrowed."

"I think it's this guy." She tapped her fingertip on the piece of paper on the right. "Phineas Bolger. God, doesn't that sound like a character straight out of Hogwarts?"

"Six and some change. You'd have to be fucked up to be alive that long. All those old ones are just creepy and totally random."

"They sort of live in another mental space." She thought of Theo. "Not so much crazy, but they just see things differently. Did you know that their vision improves over the years instead of getting worse like ours does? The old ones, if they make it to five hundred they're considered old." She snorted, making a mental note to poke Clive about that. He was more connected to events and kept contact with people daily, this would help him stave off the worst of the effects until after he hit that six-hundred-year mark. But eventually, he'd be like Theo. The thought made her uncomfortable and slightly sad, mainly because she wouldn't be alive when he still was, wouldn't be there to help keep him anchored. "Anyway, they see colors and textures far more accurately. Amazing, I've always thought."

"Or, you know, random and creepy."

Rowan laughed. "Sometimes, yeah. But this one we're looking for, Phineas here, he's worse. He's been alive for six centuries and he's got to be bored. He's done it all and seen it all so when they finally break the barrier and can get off on meth, what an experience it must be for him. Altogether new and yet, scarily addictive and personality changing."

But he was dying. She'd wager it was slower for the old ones, but it didn't make sense that only those Vampires under a certain age would die and not others. She'd wager it was only that the older the Vampire, the longer it would take for them to finally succumb to the real death.

He shuddered before going back to the file. "What makes you think it's Phineas? Why not Vasily over there? He's four hundred and sixty, that's old, right?"

"Of course. I could be wrong, but I don't think I am. Vasily has a job. He owns a business and has a family. Even though he's got a heavy hand with the ladies, the pig, I don't peg him as our perp.

"Phineas here, well he's got a lot of money and not much else. He hasn't been in Vegas for very long. Six months. Interesting that it was right around the time they broke the barrier and then shortly afterward the first woman from the list of missing women you compiled goes missing. He's got nothing but time and resources. No family. He doesn't nest with anyone. Keeps to himself and many of the ones his age do. Who's going to suspect?" She tapped the paper. "No, it's him. Now, we have to find his bed where I can kill the fuck out of him."

"I so endorse this plan. I'll get some more feelers out on Phineas and his location."

"Great. I'm going to swing by Vasily's place. Better to rule him out totally than get surprised."

"Good idea. But since you're looking like you're going to drop, I suggest you sleep for a few hours and then hunt."

"You're the second person in the last few hours to tell me that. Fine. I'm going to catch a nap and then go back out there. If Jack Elroy calls, give him the list of missing women. I'll handle Phineas myself. Jack is in no shape to take a human out, much less a Vampire."

Instead of heading home, she shooed Carey out of her office and pulled the blinds closed. She had a very comfortable couch along with a nice pillow and blanket she kept around for such occasions.

"ROWAN?"

Someone shook her awake. Cindy, the receptionist. "Wake up."

Rowan sat and glanced at the clock. At least she'd gotten a solid four hours' sleep. Still, she felt a little woozy and slightly sweaty. Great, getting the flu was not on her to do list.

"What's going on? Any news?" Her head spun and it was then she noted the syringe in the other woman's hand.

"Yeah, sorry about that." Cindy cocked her head. "He pays better than you."

"You're working with that Hogwarts asshole? Really? This is about meth? I should have seen the state of your roots before now." At least that's what she thought she said, her tongue was thick as the sedative took hold in her system.

Except what Cindy didn't know and what her master didn't know either apparently, was that the Goddess wouldn't allow the sedative to remain very long. Rowan kept her features slack as the burst of heat clawed through her insides. *Ouch.*

"Why are you doing this?" Rowan allowed Cindy to pull her to her feet, not a bit sorry to make the girl take all her weight.

"He asked me to. He takes care of me. God you're heavy. Don't look it, but you are." Cindy poked her side.

"Need to work out more. Then again it won't matter when he's done with you."

Rowan was *so* going to kill this bitch dead.

"Takes care of you, like how?" Rowan took advantage of the situation to realize her blade was out of reach. But she did have a knife strapped to her ankle and her wrist cuffs had silver wire. She'd take that Vampire's head off with it if she could get close. Not having her blade would suck, but she'd get this Vampire good and killed either way.

"Can't believe everyone thinks you're so scary," Cindy muttered as she tried to maneuver Rowan out of the room. Rowan had no plans to make it any easier to get kidnapped. But she also had no plans to stop it. This dumb bitch was taking her right to Phineas's nest.

She looked around and caught sight of Carey on the floor where Cindy most likely left him after rendering him unconscious.

At the rate this bitch was knocking out points on Rowan's list, Rowan might have to kill her twice.

"Sit here." She tossed Rowan's body onto the couch in the lobby and scurried around, turning the phones off and switching them to voice mail. Why the dumb hooker didn't take care of this shit before she drugged Rowan and brought her out here was a mystery. But Cindy had never been very smart and apparently she was aiding her acceleration to stupid with crystal and hanging with Vampires.

Rowan managed to shove her phone into her underpants. It was on, which meant the GPS would work. That is if Carey wasn't dead and was thinking when and if he came to.

Deep in her belly, Brigid bided her time.

Rowan went with it, keeping boneless and pretending to be unconscious when Cindy returned and had to drag her, those little, nearly useless hands under Rowan's arms, struggling out of the office and to the elevators straight down to the parking lot.

And though she hated it, Rowan allowed the other woman to maneuver her into the trunk. At first Cindy had tried to take Rowan's car, which challenged Rowan's limp state. But even dumb Cindy figured out there wasn't enough space for an overnight bag, much less a six-foot-tall woman in there.

It was a wonder no one saw them, but it was one in the afternoon and in the little lot to the side of the building against a wall. Luck was with Cindy. Or perhaps not—Rowan was going to kill her after all. But the luck could be Rowan's and that's how she chose to look at it.

The dark, cramped space made her memories stir uneasily. This was not a happy-reunion memory. But one of fear and loneliness. Theo had done it enough that she not only managed to survive it, but had been able to execute her escape each time, even at five.

But the fear had always lurked there. The fear that she'd fail and end up locked in a dark hole forever. That he'd change her and she'd be one of them, lost to her own humanity.

In the dark, as the road bumped beneath them, Brigid burned bright within, chasing away the metallic fear she'd been choking on. Filling her with calm. She wriggled a hand down her pants to grab her phone. It took some doing and time to get it out, but she managed to dial only to find out there was no service. Really? She sighed.

Not really being of the glass-half-full mindset, she had to force herself to focus on what she could do. She was strong enough to deal with the situation. Goddess knew people hunted before cell phones and GPS. She had the tools, had the skill and had a triple Goddess currently taking residence in her belly. This would be hard, no lie about that, but she was capable of taking this fucker and his minions down.

She hoped.

So she managed to tap out some text messages to David, Susan at the Motherhouse and Clive, detailing the name of this idiot and also that Carey was injured at the office, and hit Send. Maybe if they did actually hit a spot with service it would go out. Being pretty near full day, the Vampires at Die Mitte would be resting, not that she expected help from that direction. It did disappoint her slightly that Theo wouldn't be around to take this fucker out himself. That would have been awesome to see.

Rowan wasn't sure why they chose now to take her other than the obvious advantage to no one expecting Vampire trouble at this time of day. But Cindy was a dunce and it made Rowan suspicious that she'd missed something. Either that or Phineas Bolger was simply too far gone to realize that someone like this little bag of stupid fake-blond bones was not the girl for the job.

Her muscles were cramped, her head hurt from the drug Cindy had used and the longer she was shut up there in the dark, the angrier and more determined she got.

THEO DIDN'T NEED much sleep. Didn't need much of anything, really. So he sat watching a show on the Discovery Channel about dinosaurs. Peacefully alone as his people rested.

Another several hours before the sun would wane in the wintry Vegas sky and the state of the silly treaty would keep him in the hotel. He needed to think about getting home to Germany.

Maybe.

He liked Las Vegas. So much beautifully exposed human skin everywhere. So many humans who seemed to drink too much, spend too much money and have a good time anyway. The very air was intoxicating. It was easy to understand just why Clive Stewart chose this place rather than any other city he could have held on behalf of the Nation.

Rowan. Pride warmed him when there were days, weeks even where he was sure he'd never feel anything again. She'd made a place for herself in the world. More than that, she owned that place with confidence.

And if he wasn't mistaken there was a blooming relationship between her and his Scion. He chuckled a moment. She'd give Clive something to work for. A Vampire like Clive had it easy for centuries. Power, money, influence and looks had been part of what made Stewart who he was within the Vampire Nation. But Rowan Summerwaite wasn't something to be quantified or prepared for.

And his petal wasn't the kind of woman who'd keep a man around just to avoid being lonely. No, she'd seek out physical interactions when the need came, but a human male couldn't hold her or come close to understanding her path.

Most Vampires would reject Rowan for what she did and who she was. But it was beyond clear to Theo that Clive understood her. And because of that, he'd give her what she needed and Theo wouldn't have to kill anyone over it.

He was sitting there, smiling when unease slithered through his gut.

Standing quickly, he grabbed the nearest phone and summoned his Scion and then dialed Rowan's number directly, only to receive an out-of-area recording. He resisted crushing the tiny phone into dust, but only barely.

Next on his list was her office, where he received another recording that the office would be closed for the next several days.

He snarled as he spun. Enzo stood there, expectant. "How may I serve you?"

"It's Rowan. Something is wrong."

Enzo immediately went into action. He didn't assure Theo Rowan would be fine. He didn't attempt to soothe. He simply did his job in the way he knew it was expected.

It wasn't too very long afterward that Clive showed up, looking like he'd been taking a stroll instead of pulled from daytime rest.

"How may I serve?" Clive echoed the same words Enzo had spoken, and Theo's to his Scion were the same.

"It's Rowan."

TWENTY-FOUR

ROWAN HAD BEEN resting, going inside herself to conserve her power and get herself centered for the battle to come when the car came to a halt.

This time when Cindy opened the trunk, she was pointing a gun at Rowan. It had been a few hours' driving so it was a fair presumption that the sedative would have worn off.

Of course the safety was on. Rowan sincerely hoped Cindy was a rockstar in bed because she was dumb as a pencil eraser, except an eraser had a purpose.

"I hope you enjoyed those last few hours. Get out and don't try anything funny or I'll shoot you."

Rowan got out and took the place in. The place was decent enough for being out in the middle of nowhere. She breathed in deeply, not nowhere at all. This was in Dust Devil ground.

The magick inside her swirled, recognized like energies. Brigid was a blade deep within, waiting. She would burst from Rowan when the time was right. This was simply certain.

"No you won't. He'll kill you if you do. Then again, I'll kill you after I'm done with him, so maybe you should shoot me."

Cindy's eyes widened.

"What? Did you think you could scare me? Bitch, please. You are nothing to me. Even less to him because there's always another junkie whore who'll sell herself and her friends out for another fix. Predictable."

Cindy reached out to grab Rowan, but instead, Rowan reached out and grabbed Cindy. By the hair, which made a satisfying little snatch from the scalp when Rowan yanked her to her knees one-handed while she shoved the gun down the back of her waistband with her free hand.

"Not so fucking big now are you, junkie bitch?" Rowan leaned down into Cindy's face, breathing in her fear like candy. "Shove me in a trunk. Attack my staff and the guy who's saved your job by making excuses for you when you're late? You soulless thundertwat."

"All true. But I'll have to ask you to step away from her, Ms. Summerwaite."

Keeping Cindy exactly where she was, Rowan looked up to the front porch of the house. The voice sent shivers up and down her spine. *Crazy* was a kind word for what this guy was.

She was, she had to admit, a little freaked by the way this Vampire felt. There was no way she'd go into that house. *Nuh uh.* She wasn't alive after all the shit she'd seen because she was stupid or took stupid risks. Still, it wouldn't do to let this pass. Not at all.

"You must be Phineas Bolger. I'm Rowan Summerwaite, the Hunter and I'm here to serve my warrant on you for the deaths of humans. As for Cindy here? I don't think I will be stepping away from her, thanks. You see, I'm out here in the sunshine and you're a Vampire. May as well be raining holy water. Which, come to think of it would be so awesome. Anyhoo, whatcha going to do, come make me?"

"It's winter. Sun will be down enough in an hour or so. I'll come for you." His thrall was intense, dark and sticky, thoroughly creepy. He tried to lure her inside, tried to control that small animal part still deep inside her humanity.

'Course he had no idea Theo had whipped her fight-or-flight reflex into shape by the time she was ten. And yet, there was no denying Phineas was a scary asshole *and* that she was totally pissed off that he tried to manipulate her.

Rowan stood, straightening, and snapped Cindy's neck before she could stab Rowan's thigh with another syringe she'd produced from her pocket. If she wasn't mistaken the syringe looked as if it had been reused. If that bitch had given her Hep C or something else when she stuck Rowan back at the office, she'd be so pissed. But she couldn't kill Cindy twice so she bent and carefully felt pockets, never taking her eyes from the shadowed doorway. "Yeah?" Ah, keys. Rowan jingled them. "Come the fuck on then. But come at me like a man instead of a little punk sending his errand boys. Pussy."

She turned her back and got into the car. Pausing long enough to grab her phone and mark just exactly where this place was before fishtailing off and getting the hell away.

ROWAN DROVE SO fast she should have been pulled over multiple times. Clearly the car was not Cindy's. It had old-school Vamp written all over it. Smoked windows, luxurious and spacious interior—great ride if you weren't in the trunk. The kind of car you could push past ninety and not feel even a tiny shimmy.

She managed to get reception enough to call David, who informed her the entire world had been looking for her, with Theo heading the search.

She didn't quite know what to say or how to process that so she didn't.

"He's going to come at me. I'd rather it be out here where there aren't a lot of people. But I want my blade."

"I'm already on my way." David's response was clipped, indicating he was already driving. "We had a GPS ping so I'm close. About twenty minutes away."

She hung up and called Susan to check in. Susan congratulated her on the liaison appointment, laughed about how upset some were and urged her to "kill the murderous Vampire bastard."

Rowan got out of the car when David arrived. She took her blade and felt the connection to her toes. Every single cell woke up.

"Go. Let the Scion know where I am." She toed her shoes off, not feeling the rocks or thorny bits. Only the singing of the earth beneath her. Only the heat of energy as it surged through her.

"*Déesse…*"

"No. You can't help and I don't want to be worried about you. I got this. I promise you that."

And she headed out, walking along the ley line drawing sinuous around the rocks and strata for miles beneath her. She'd stay right on this path, able to draw huge reserves of power when she needed to. Out here, six-hundred-year-old Vampire or not, they were far better matched then they'd be anywhere else.

THERE WAS NO need to invoke Her. Brigid shone through, surging through her veins, filling her cells, wrapping around her bones, enhancing her strength and perception.

The sun was setting, the sky pink as the light changed from day to night. She stood tall and waited, feeling his approach on the wind.

And Theo was out there somewhere. Rules be damned, he'd do what he wanted and she couldn't complain in this situation.

But flying wasn't like driving with a GPS and as she wagered, Phineas found her first.

His descent was clumsy and she saw immediately just how close to death he was. The drugs had eaten him up and yet he stank of blood and a recent ingestion of the drug that way.

"I never thought I'd see the day when a Vampire as old and powerful as you was so lowered." She sneered and backed up, circling as he did. Dying and drug-addled or not, he was a dangerous creature and she'd be dead if he got behind her.

"Blood bags have no place talking to me."

"Seriously?" She pulled the blade from its sheath and paused to appreciate the deathly beauty of the whisper of steel clearing leather. "Love that sound. Don't you? Well maybe not since I'm going to end you with it. Anyway, it seems to me that six hundred years ago you all had so much more scary stuff to say. Theo says scary stuff when he brushes his teeth." She shrugged. "Guess that's why he's The First and you're not."

He lunged, faster than she'd imagined and she nearly stumbled dodging him.

"Not bad for an old junkie. What's your deal anyway? Six hundred years of relative silence from you so you decide to go out like Jeffrey Dahmer or something? Worried the history books will forget you?"

"You dare compare me to some human?" He lunged again, with some fancy moves and she managed to get a nice slice across his chest even as the sting of his nails on her neck told her he'd gotten his own shot in.

"Gross. I bet meth skank venom is even worse than your normal stuff. Don't you people ever wash your hands? And if you don't want to be compared to a serial killer, don't act like one. Didn't your mother ever tell you you'd be judged by your actions?"

He punched her and she spit a mouthful of blood out. She needed to get in closer. The gun would be useless without silver bullets so she'd left it in her pants.

"You ate a Goddess."

"Um, okay. Is this news? Yeah, I am Brigid's Vessel and she's pissed off." Rowan stepped in, slammed her knee into his junk and when he went to his knees, hit the back of his head with the hilt of her sword before dancing out of reach.

"No matter. I'll kill you both."

"Yeah, nice try. Except I'm not a desperate, dope-sick dumbass like your previous victims."

"They gave themselves to me. Their marrow was sweet and laden with the drug."

It was impossible not to curl her lip at that. "Gross."

He laughed and her skin crawled. "You're all specks of dirt. At least in being the deliverer of the drug, their lives had some meaning. What would they have been otherwise?"

"Oh novel. A Vampire with a god complex."

"Better than a sheep with a coward Goddess in her belly."

The heat of Brigid's full ascendancy burned through Rowan with so much intensity, Rowan nearly dropped her blade. Rowan heard herself speak as her blade sliced out, making a long, ruby line of destruction along Phineas's belly.

"Vampire, you are an abomination and we will end you."

Rowan was there, but not there as her normal speed doubled. But she felt it when he broke her left arm and then pulled it from the socket at her shoulder.

"You fucking piece of shit," she ground out, kicking his stomach and baring her teeth when he howled in pain. "You come here to *my* city and you think you can kill humans and just dump them like garbage? You think you can do that and not face any punishment?" She paused slicing his right ear off, the display of his pain and the beginnings of his real fear spicing the air.

"I am six hundred years old!" He bellowed this as he charged her, knocking her off her feet and to the ground with a whoosh of air from her lips. Her blade fell from her fingers, which she then used to gouge one of his eyes out with.

"Yeah? Big." She punched his temple, her fist slippery with blood, her vision graying with his weight on her broken left arm. "Fucking." She yanked on his hair so hard she ripped a handful out. "Deal." Finally with enough leverage she cast him off and managed to get to her feet, bending to grab her blade again. That's when the blinding pain let her know he'd broken a few ribs.

"You didn't even kill them for a reason!" Somehow this knowledge that he'd just sort of viewed the women he'd murdered as appetizers whose job it was to serve him and his addiction only made her angrier. "You didn't do it for some whackadoodle serial-killer crazy reason like communicating with the sun god or trying to make sex zombies. You are just an old, shot-out waste of power."

"What do you know of it?" He looked her up and down, dismissing her.

"I know. I'm just a girl, how can I know what it means to be some batshit-crazy-ass-tweaker-drug-dealer-serial-killer Vampire? Gosh, I'm confused." She cocked her head and smiled, knowing her mouth was bloody and her arm hung useless at her side. And still, she knew she was just as scary as he.

He blinked his one good eye, first slowly and then he got it and she laughed. "Don't feel bad, many of you guys totally underestimate me due to my penis-deprived state." She laughed again. "Well, um, the not having one of my own that is."

"A human female won't ever best me."

Enough was enough. She closed her eyes, gathered her focus and, one-handed, spun and moved in, slicing him open from balls to the top of his head.

"Yeah?" She stepped back as he sizzled and began to implode. "Good thing I'm not human, huh?" She spit on him. "Die, you piece of shit. This is for all the women you killed."

Turning her back on the smoldering pile, she didn't bother with her usual blessing. Instead she put her blade back in the sheath and used her good arm to give his corpse three snaps as she managed to stumble away.

Clive landed at the car and looked around. He began to call her name until he caught sight of her limping toward where he stood.

Within moments he had her in his arms as she managed to tell him she'd killed Phineas Bolger and that her arm was broken and her shoulder dislocated.

"Let me put you out. I'll drive us home and we'll get it seen to."

She was just about to assent when Theo shot from the sky to the ground with a sound so feral and scary it woke her up enough to get her adrenaline pumping again.

He spoke in their mother tongue and everything around them stopped, even the light breeze. He moved like death and she couldn't seem to tear her gaze from him as he glided toward the spot Phineas used to be.

She didn't know what all he said, but Clive stood there, pale, holding her in his arms while she rested her head against his chest and tried not to pass out.

Theo turned his back and the last bits of Phineas simply burned up and were gone. She knew enough that he'd withheld the words Vampires needed to cross over. Their legend stated that their master could deny that access to final rest.

Theo looked at her, emotion a riot all over his face. He leaned in, kissed her forehead and used his words to put her into a softer, pain-free place. "Take my blood, petal," he whispered, his lips against her temple. "You'll heal much faster."

"I need to deal with the house. His house. There might be people there."

"Nadir has taken care of that. There is nothing there now. Nothing but ashes."

And he put his wrist to her mouth and all was warm and quiet and she knew only dreams.

TWENTY-FIVE

"THERE YOU are."

Rowan opened her eyes to find Thena bending over her bed. When she saw Rowan was fully aware, she bent down and kissed her smack-dab on the mouth. "I go out of town for a minute and you go and nearly get yourself killed. I thought we discussed this."

"Yeah well, I'll try. You didn't have to come back to town, dumbass. This isn't my first go around with stitches and broken bones. Anyway, how'd you get home so fast?"

"Girl, I swear." She sat on the edge of the bed. "Where else would I be?"

"Um, on an exotic getaway with your hot professor husband playing *Give Me a Better Grade*."

Thena laughed. "We play that one a lot. Plenty of time to play it more. I was already on my way back. I had a scary dream. Three of them as it happens. All about you. You needed me and I wasn't here."

Rowan managed to sit up as David materialized to fluff the pillows and help. "I'll return with something to drink. The doctor said you'd need rest, fluids and that if you required the pain medication to take it or he'd be very unhappy with you."

"My arm isn't broken." She wriggled her fingers.

"His blood…" Clive strolled in looking effortless and handsome, the arrogant smile on his face sending her pulse racing. "We got your shoulder taken care of first. The doctor put a temporary cast on it and he gave you more blood a few hours later and it healed."

She knew she blushed, she couldn't help it and she was too tired to stop it anyway.

"That's some magickal shit right there. He was worried about you. Theo," Thena added when Rowan must have looked confused.

"Where is he? How long was I out? What happened to the house? Did anyone tell Jack?"

Clive wished most fervently that Rowan's friend would just leave so he could pull her into his arms and know she was all right.

"The police are still looking for the killer, but Jack knows." Thena looked to Clive quickly before looking away. Clive hated that the other man was such an asshole and would cause Rowan pain though she'd gone out of her way on his behalf.

Rowan waited but when they said nothing else, she got the idea. He hated the sadness on her features.

Thena stood. "I need to go home for a while. I'm glad I was here when you woke up. Glad you woke up, period. Damn it. Rowan, girl, how about an easier line of work?"

Rowan snorted a laugh, but also knew Thena would be on her demanding details about Clive after she'd given her a little time to recover. "Yeah, well luckily most of the Vampires I deal with aren't crazy, drugged-up, six-centuries-old serial killers."

Clive sat on her bed after Thena had gone and

gave in to his need to touch her. She melted against him. "Hi."

"Yes, yes, hello yourself, you damnable, infuriating woman. Why didn't you come back to town where we could have dealt with him together?" He wanted to shake her, but instead held her tight.

"Bringing him into town would have endangered humans. It's my job to protect them, remember? Also that far out I could slice him in half and no one would see."

"Are you actually proud of that?" He couldn't help a smile. She couldn't see it anyway.

"With a broken arm and a dislocated shoulder? Hell yeah I'm proud of it. Piece of shit. I wish I could kill him again."

"I wish I could kill him too. Damn it." He drew her away enough to look into her face. She was soft this way, in her bed with her pajamas on. Pajamas with little white sheep all over them and one black one over her heart. Whimsical.

"The First knew something was wrong. Summoned me and we contacted David. We got the texts shortly after that. Good thinking. I guess I can see why they keep you around at Hunter Corp." After the texts had come, they'd worked on finding her phone with the GPS but when they went out of service, it wasn't working well enough to give them more than a sixty-mile radius and it was still daylight.

He had never in his entire lifetime felt as helpless as he had after her call had come and they'd had to wait until it was dark enough to move.

The First's lieutenants had put them all in a van with

darkened windows and they headed out to where she'd given her last location as.

Every minute had felt like an eternity as they waited in the dark, until dark settled in outside and they could break free and take flight. It was as if his breath had been held until he'd landed and seen her, limping, covered in blood, on the verge of passing out with a pile of smoldering Vampire in her wake.

"You came for me." She grinned and it was lopsided, like she was, and he didn't quite know where to put all the ways she made him feel about her.

"Yes, well. I may have hit my head or something."

She laughed and he made her rest against the pillows. David came in with some juice and crackers along with some pain pills. "Take them. No arguments or I'll have Thena come back over."

Rowan's eyes widened and she held a palm out and took the pills as ordered.

"I'm supposed to be healed with super Vampire blood goodness. Why do I feel like I was hit by a truck?"

"Phineas's venom was particularly nasty. He was dying, his bodily fluids were toxic. You got a big dose of it. He also broke a few ribs. The First healed most of it, but the rest your body will have to heal from incrementally."

He told her the remainder of the story. About the lab they'd found at Phineas's house. About the data that'd been collected about the ways the drug worked on Vampires. Phineas had to have known he was dying and yet there was no doubt he was as addicted as the women he'd been using to feed on.

"We know a great deal more now. At least that much was helpful. It's going to be a problem." He shrugged. "But we all die with this drug. He probably only had maybe a week left. Most of us aren't six hundred."

"Is this a glass-half-full moment? Because I need to tell you I'm going to be billing the Nation triple time if I have to eradicate another Vampire that old and strong who is strung out on super drugs. Got me? Despite my easygoing ways I truly hate having my ass handed to me. It hurts."

He cringed. "It's these moments, dear Hunter, where a man asks himself just what he's doing with a woman who courts danger the way you do."

Her glib look faded. "Yeah? I think it's my sparkling wit and my pelvic floor muscles."

He laughed and hugged her to him gently. "The latter more than the former."

"That's good. I really have to practice the last one. The wit part comes naturally."

"Don't panic, but I think we just had a regular, utterly nonhostile conversation."

"Duh, we're talking about how awesome I am. Who can argue with that?"

Because he didn't want to resist, not after all the panic and worry, he kissed the corner of her mouth, right where it curved up into her smile.

David tapped on the door, but to Clive's surprise, she didn't recoil from his embrace as the other man entered her room.

"You have a visitor. Your foster father."

She started to get out of bed but David put his hands

out to stay her. "No. He said quite clearly that you were to stay resting. He'll come in once you're ready."

"He walked in on me once when I was thirteen. Changing my clothes. I don't think he actually even saw anything, not that I had anything to see then, but I think I scarred him forever."

"I heard that, petal," Theo called out before he entered the room and she laughed.

David's back was pressed so hard to the wall, Rowan worried he'd leave an impression. "You can go. I know you've probably been up taking care of things for hours. Thank you, for all you do for me."

He got over his fear enough to come to her bedside. The Vampires moved, though Clive stuck very close and Rowan told herself she was too weak to stop him.

"You do good in the world, *Déesse*. I'm honored to help you achieve that."

"You're going to make me sniffly in front of the guests."

He smiled briefly as he squeezed her hand. "We wouldn't want that. I'll just be in my room. You'll call if you need anything."

"Did you just boss me around? Damn, David, what a bad influence I am."

He barked a quick laugh and left the room, skirting the Vampires as much as he could while not being disrespectful.

"Sit, please." Rowan indicated a nearby chair and Theo gracefully folded himself into it. He reached out, squeezed her ankle and sat back.

And then he lectured her for five minutes in German about going out there alone and then not coming back to town to get help and how he'd have sent his lieutenants anyway, treaty be damned and if she'd gotten killed he'd have been very, very angry.

She nodded and listened, knowing he needed to say it all and admitting, deep down inside anyway, that it was nice to hear.

They'd never have a traditional or close relationship. It wasn't what he was capable of and she couldn't totally let go of what he'd done, even if she did understand it. But he was hers and she was his in their own unique way and it was enough.

When he was done, he sat back and sighed.

"It's a good thing you're known for your patience," he muttered to Clive, who looked surprised briefly and then nodded. She regretted that she'd fallen off her neck tic plan and committed herself to it anew.

"I'm in the room. Also, this is not 1567 or something and I'm not chattel. Moving along. I'm going to be speaking with the Motherhouse shortly and filling them in on the whole episode. It'll be my recommendation that we create a task force to monitor the situation. Vampires supercharged on crystal meth is a threat and one we cannot ignore."

"We will not accept any new restrictions without a full renegotiation of the treaty." Clive spoke this time, as Scion.

She shrugged. "Yeah well, we all want things. You lose any moral authority when six-hundred-year-old Vampires eat humans and leave their bodies for all to see."

Theo heaved a sigh. "So quickly back to a thorn, my little rose."

"You wanted me in this position, if you recall."

He sent her a single raised brow and she remembered her place quickly enough. But still she took one last chance and grinned, rewarded by an amused shake of his head.

Theo stood. "My time here in Las Vegas is up. I must go home again. You will come to me next time. In just three months, as it happens for the next meeting of the Joint Tribunal. You will take dinner with me."

Oh yeah, she'd have to do all that now that she'd been made the Liaison. She nodded. "I'll see you then. Thank you for your assistance." She hesitated, reaching for…something. "Your help was invaluable."

He paused on his way out. "I am, as always, your father, Rowan. Even when we serve different masters and goals. You are mine, even though I have made mistakes."

He left and she said nothing and Clive, Goddess bless him, didn't press, only straightened her coverlet and let her get herself together again.

It was at that moment she realized she might just have some room in her life for a Vampire boyfriend and a lot of sneaky meetings and probably a fuckton of politics too.

* * * * *

***New York Times* Bestselling Author**

CARLA NEGGERS

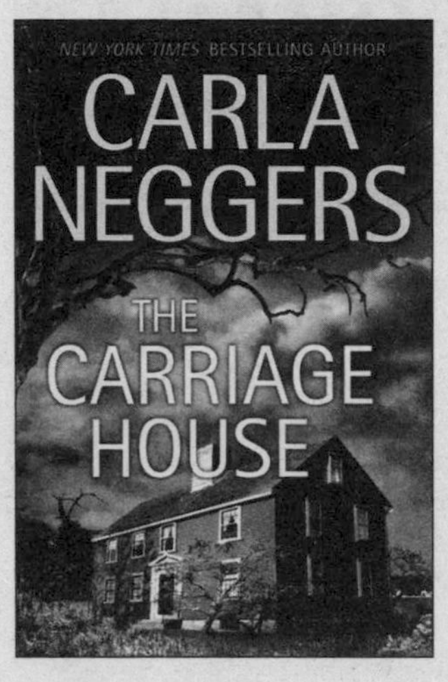

When Ike Grantham pays her for her graphic design work on a run-down nineteenth-century carriage house, Tess Haviland is looking forward to a little fun and hard work.

Then Ike disappears and Tess finds herself with much more than a simple weekend project. There are rumors that the carriage house is haunted, and her neighbor, Andrew Thorne, has his own ideas about why Tess has turned up next door.

But when Tess discovers a human skeleton in her dirt cellar, she begins to ask questions about the history of the carriage house, the untimely death of Andrew's wife…and Ike's disappearance. Questions a desperate killer wants to silence before the truth reveals that someone got away with murder.

Available wherever books are sold.

Be sure to connect with us at:

Harlequin.com/Newsletters

Facebook.com/HarlequinBooks

Twitter.com/HarlequinBooks

MCN1518